SON OF A GUN

Ted Sutton

WingSpan Press

Published in the United States
by WingSpan Press, Livermore, CA

The WingSpan name, logo and colophon are the trademarks
of WingSpan Publishing.
www.wingspanpress.com

ISBN 978-1-63683-069-8 (pbk.)
ISBN 978-1-63683-943-1 (ebk.)

First edition 2024

Printed in the United States of America

We cannot but pity the boy who had never fired a gun. He is no more humane, while his education had been sadly neglected.

—Henry David Thoreau

This book is based on the historical record.

For Joan

1/ KETZEL

So I'm working this dive in Coney Island. A girl walks in and I tell her honey you got a nice ass. Frankie Galluci jumps me, screams you talking like that to my sister? Just speaking the truth I say, meant her no disrespect but as a compliment. Never knew she's your sister.

He slugs me. I pin em to the ground but he's packing a shiv. Cuts up my face and I'm bleeding like a pig. Swear I'm gonna kill him. I don't. That's another thing they got all wrong. I ain't homicidal.

They sew me up—seventeen stitches—hurts like a son-of-a-bitch. I'm stuck with these scars and that nickname I can't live down just cause I'm saying somethin nice.

Move to Chicago. During the day I work at the stockyards. At night meet-cha at Moe's. A bottle of beer, a game of pool, take every eight-ball tournament. Better yet, start to get laid and why not? On Canal Street, a house run by Johnny Torrio. Sure they're whores but treat em right, show em a bit of class, treat em sweet and smooth. So how ya doin? Cold as bejesus outside. Sure they'd know it was just a line but if you could get em to laugh then they'll take their time, smile, play along, soap you up. So what's your name sugar, they'll ask. For fifty cents we could have some real fun.

2 / Pearl

Spotted it right away first time I spent the night, on the bathroom sink, a jar of talcum powder. He must've used it to hide his scars. Couldn't help myself from fiddling with it when he opened the door, knocking first. Always the perfect gentleman.

He seemed such a sweetie, but he did have a reputation for being unpredictable, you might say, and after all, I had been sneaking a peek at his toiletries. There was this expression on his face, startled, unsure, one I had never seen before, but then he regained his composure and asked, Hey doll, what ya doin?

I was embarrassed, but Ketzel—that was my pet name for him—was smiling and I knew there was nothing to fear. He patted my cheek. So smooth, he said. Then he took my hand, laid it on his cheek, the unblemished one.

Whiskers, I whispered.

I'll send for the barber, he replied with a grin, like a boy. Then urgently, no baby we don't want no one spoiling our fun, do we?

Suddenly shy, I nodded and he took out a shaving brush, held it under hot water and lathered his face, his eyes never leaving mine even as he picked up a gold razor and shaved his right cheek, then his left, a little more carefully around the scars, under his nose, his chin, finally his neck, but when he was done, I caught a drop of blood on his chin and just couldn't help myself from reaching out, dabbing it, touching him. You cut yourself, I whispered and licked it, licked the blood off the tip of my finger.

There were mirrors on the wall, opposite each other, reflecting their images, me licking the blood off my finger, him with that smile. A chorus line of Ketzels and Pearls. He took out a tiny white pencil, held it under the faucet, blotted up the blood with his towel, then touched the pencil to his chin and like magic the bleeding stopped. He splashed water on his face and patted it dry with a towel, picked up a bottle, sprinkled cologne on his hand then daubed it behind his ears. Daintily. It was touching he would do such a thing. Go to the trouble. Now he smelled like that, what you call it, bay rum, from bay leaves, the stuff the goyim cook ham with.

He took out the pad he caught me with, brushed it in the jar of talcum and like a burlesque comic, patted his cheek, dramatically, so you could see what he was doing—he could be such a silly boy—then he patted talcum on his neck and all of a sudden the scars weren't so scary—just part of him, who he was. I reached out and touched the one with the tip of my index finger, lightly, cautiously— maybe it was still sensitive—but no, he was smiling, smiling, that million-dollar smile.

He called the next day and asked me out to dinner, all polite and formal, like a regular date. So many questions. Where you from? How long you dancing? When I tell him my father has cancer, he asks, you got a Jewish doc? Then he reaches over and touches me, first time, nothing inappropriate, just a pat, an innocent little pat on the knee, and he took out his card and handed it to me.

Second-Hand Furniture Dealer, 2220 South Wabash Avenue. And I said, What you know, just like Dad before he lost the store. It was a strange feeling, the two of them doing the same thing, Ketzel didn't do rummage, that was for sure. He asked if my parents' apartment had a basement and that seemed a strange question. But it did, and he smiled and said, I got an idea.

The next morning, a guy knocked at their door, tells her father he owns a used furniture business, asks could he rent the basement for storage? Seventy a month. A fortune!

Too much money, really, for a basement, but you don't kick a gift horse in the mouth, and the first of every month, a fifty and a twenty, just like that. Her father can't believe it, breaks down and cries, right at the kitchen table. She can still see him sitting there, with a cup of coffee and a slice of rye toast, a twenty and a fifty in his hand. And only she knows where the money really comes from, from Ketzel, though she doesn't call him that yet.

She asks him the next time they're together, why'd you do this?

He smiled and took her hand in his and she noticed how strong his hands were, he had hairy knuckles and the back of his hands too, big hands, the kind you never forget and he said, Don't you fret, doll, don't you fret.

And she didn't, at least not after that. Sure, she used to worry, because of who he was and what people said about him, but after that morning, when his associate showed up to talk to her about the basement, she never read any more newspaper stories about him. It was just that simple. Here was this man they made all this fuss about, the same man who treated her with respect, like a real lady. Here was this man they claimed was vicious and here was this man who was sweet, who never ever made her do anything she didn't want to. Here was this man, the most powerful in Chicago, who could have anything he wanted, and he wanted her. Oh, how Ketzel was so full of surprises. Stuff everybody else cared about, he couldn't care less. And stuff you never would've suspected he cared about, he cared about.

They developed their own routine. Ketzel would call and she'd pick up the phone and no hellos, he'd jump right in. So what ya up to, sweetheart? he'd ask. She tried to keep it light, sometimes even tease him, something you'd never know, he liked to be teased. And then he'd laugh and, oh, to hear that laugh, deep and rich, husky, nothing held back. It made her feel powerful, knowing she could make this man laugh, that she could make him want her.

She surprised herself. The phone would ring, she'd hear his voice, his question, and she could be bold. And sometimes, make things up, out of thin air.

Hey sweetheart, what ya doin?

She might have been peeling a potato, but she'd say, Just taking a bath.

Hope you're not catchin a cold.

I'm wearing robe now

Was it a nice bath?

That's for me to know and you to find out.

Were there bubbles?

He'd talk like that, like they were playing a little game. How'd ya know?

I know, baby. I know.

And then she'd forget the game, but be straight with him. I miss you.

I miss you too, sugar. Pause. That's why I called.

She was no fool and knew he was married, knew there were other girls, plenty of other girls, but when he talked to her, she forgot all that. He made her feel like she was the only one in the world, not one more ditz falling for one more line, and she knew she should have been smarter, but to be with a man like that, so powerful he could have anyone he wants, and he picks you. Nothing so exciting as talking to him on the phone, knowing it was going to happen. He'd just have to say the word. And

5

in the meantime, she could say whatever she wanted, and no matter how strong, how big, how much a macher he was, he'd lap it up. That's probably why she called him Ketzel, Yiddish for kitten.

The bath wasn't just bubbles.

So what else, sugar?

Oh, I don't know—

Come on, baby.

There was some of that perfume in it.

That French stuff I got you. That smelled like whatchacallit?

Lavender.

Why'd ya do that, doll?

Cause I was thinking of you. While I lay there, in the hot water and the bubbles and the perfume was thinking of you.

And his voice could get so low, so low but so sweet, but still you never forgot just who it was, even then. What you thinking of now?

Oh, I don't know.

Tell me baby. I want to know.

So I'd tell him.

3 / KETZEL

You wanna feel good, real good, get your wallet, take out a fiver, better yet a ten, hey, why not a twenty, big spender. Go downtown, pick yourself out a kid or some poor shmuguzzie sellin apples—I'm a sucker for one with a dog—give em the dough and make sure to look em in the eye. Don't be fraid. Take his hand, shake it. Look em in the eye. Once you get your own ass covered, it's how much you give away that counts. It's how much you give away. Take my soup kitchen. Corner 9th and State. Betcha didn't know bout that. Three times a day, breakfast, lunch and dinner, hundreds of hungry men get to eat. Cause of me. Thanksgiving Day, 1930, we fed five thousand! Wanted to give em turkey, turkey and all the trimmins, but the cook talked me out of it cause turkey takes too much time to carve. So we went for beef stew instead. Bet you didn't know that.

Now, I never found out who gave me the syph. Shoulda used a rubber—no use crying over spilt milk—just put on the ointment and the burnin goes away, the sores too. Doc Gold says they can come back when you're least suspecting it. No way predictin. Outta the blue.

So when Rosa gets pregnant, I gave her some dough, enough to take care of it, but she disappears on me. Decides to have the kid and something went wrong and the next thing I hear she's dead. So my ma takes me to the kid, he's there with Rosa's mother. Ma takes me to him, puts the kid in my arms, shows me how to hold him so I don't drop him on his head.

All of a sudden he looks at me like he can tell I'm his father. Holdin my kid for the first time, couldn't help myself, broke down cryin, cryin like a big baby. A week later Ma introduces me to Mae. She can't have kids, says she'll take Sonny as her own. Two days later, we're married. That night I kneel down by Sonny's crib, whisper into his ear, littlest ears in the whole wide world, whisper Sonny, my little Sonny, and Sonny it was to be, no matter if Albert Francis's name is on the birth certificate. All of a sudden I'm a married man with a kid, the draft board can't touch me.

There's this song— me and Jolson would sing it when we ran into each other: When there are grey skies I don't mind the grey skies You make them blue, Sonny Boy. Friends may forsake me, let them all forsake me. You pull me through, Sonny Boy. Sonny would survive me, gimme heirs, immortality. I'd lift him from the crib, sing songs, operas, show tunes I heard the night before at Colosimo's. I had a good ear.

But somethin's wrong, like he can tell my mouth is movin and my face is changin expression—I could get pretty emotional when I sang—but somethin's missin. No smile, no cooin. A man wants his son to hear him, to hear just what he has to say.

We take him to this doctor, tell him I'd write a check for a hundred grand if he could cure my son. The doc shook his head, promised to give it his best, that's what he said. Then he put that thing, that tuning fork up to Sonny's ear and nothing. They tell me there's nothing to do.

When your hearing's shot, you can't hear who's behind you, gotta watch your step. When your hearing's shot, the world ain't exactly your oyster.

So he learns to read lips. When he's seventeen, we send him to Notre Dame. Used my own alias, Al Brown—like father, like son. Didn't work out. All the whisperin behind his back bout who he really was. Even if he couldn't hear em, he knew.

I never forget what Doc Gold told me deafness can come from the syph. And I had the syph. So maybe I gave it to Rosa, then she gave it to Sonny. It's my fuckin fault. After that I watch myself. Don't want to give no one nothin. There's a string of regulars—bimbos and skanks, floozies—and they do just fine.

A couple years go by, I meet Pearl. She's on stage with Blackstone the Magician

What a knockout, standin there in this little yellow sparkly number. Blackstone waves his wand in the air and there's a puff of smoke. Then he locks Pearl up in a trunk—looked just like a coffin. Saws her in half. Son of a bitch couldn't figure out how he did it but there she is, legs kickin, scared look on her face and he saws and saws right through the box. Waves his hand in the air and Pearl's cut in two! Audience goes nuts. She makes a face. A goofy face. With a smile so you know she's not hurt or nothin. And that's when I fell for her. Big time.

But it all wasn't peaches and cream. I'd get these headaches and son-of-a-bitch there was nothing he could do to get rid of them. Doc Gold said it was the syph. Didn't know what he'd do when they'd come on. Sometimes it was scary. Very scary. I'd pass out and then when I came to, I had thrown a lamp through a window. Couldn't be around the kid. Didn't have no patience. Couldn't think straight.

The second time we're together, one of my fits jumped me so bad all I could do was lie there like I'm dying, so bad I'd puke. Pearl gets me in the bathtub and I'm soaking there and it's a little better and she tells me to close my eyes. Trust me, she says. Trust me. She pours warm water over my head, lathers me up with shampoo, smells like flowers, I feel my headache meltin away. She massages me, my neck, my shoulders. Oh, that's so good, I tell her. Never stop. And she keeps it up. You're so good, she tells me, you're so good. And that gets a chuckle from me and then I feel her hand, all soapy, on my chest, sliding down lower and I know what she's up to, I know what she's up to. And then she starts to sing, It's only a paper moon, floatin over a cardboard sea. And I've been around, I've had my share of women comin onto me, every which way, but none like my Pearlie. So not long after that I want to do something special. We're drivin down Michigan Avenue, she points to this buildin, tells me she went there when she was a kid—called the Art Institute. What's an Art Institute?

A museum, she says.

Then why don't they call it a museum? I ask. She shrugs, tells me she loved the place, still remembers the pictures on the wall. A week later I surprise her. Take her there after it closes. Have the whole place to ourselves. The boss is waitin at the front door. Skinny twerp, kind of snooty, with a bow tie. Wasn't used to our likes.

How do you do, how do you do, he squawks like a parrot. Pearl made me toss out my cigar in the cuspidor. I shake the twerp's hand nice and hard. Now he's no parrot but a mouse. A scared little mouse.

Our collection covers five thousand years, he says like he's makin some kind of speech. A pasty little smile like he dug up all this loot hisself.

So impressive, says Pearl.

Anything you're specially interested in? he asks.

Couldn't really blame the guy for ass-licking. Sent him a grand that afternoon. He knew he had to deliver.

Italy, I say. Got anything from Italy?

He gives a goofy smile. The next thing you know we're walkin down a hallway full of mummies and vases, golden knick-knackery, trinkets, a room full of statues and chunks of buildings. Columns, doors. Cases of gold coins jewelry knives and shields pots and pans. You-name-it. What gets to me though— this thing what they call it— a frieze. Runs down the wall. Can't take my eyes off it. Makes me feel drunk. Roman soldiers, a line of them decked out in armor and helmets—some with swords others grabbin for women tryin to get away. The director catches me starin. This frieze, he says—as if I ever knew what the fuck a frieze was—is The Rape of the Sabine Women.

Don't look to me like much of a rape, I said. Or maybe they couldn't show that kind of stuff. If you catch my drift.

He says this is a legend. From the foundin of Rome. Roman men kidnapped wives from Sabine families. The English word rape means abduction in Latin. Lah-di-dah. This guy's got an answer for everything. Starts to annoy me. But then nothin he says matters no more. Cause all I can think about is this frieze. Maybe it's called that cause they look frozen. Women throwin their arms up in the air soldiers carryin them off babies cryin. Time stuck in stone.

The twerp leads me over to a statue but keeps his trap shut, just points out a plaque on it and fuck it if it isn't from the same story. Only this one's bigger than life this guy butt naked except for some kind of helmet—-his pecker smaller than you'd think, he's lifting this naked girl up in the air. Her arm's raised she's screaming but he's takin her off takin her to be his wife.

Then I notice Pearlie. She's in front of some kind of coffin, a great slab of stone coffin. And it is! That's what Mr. Twirp-face is tellin her. This is a sarcophagi, he says and Pearl says it out loud slowly in a whisper like a kid. Sar-coph-a-gi, she repeats.

And now he's off and runnin. Sarcophagi were above ground and carved and decorated. Used by Romans. Then when the Christians came along they buried em in the ground.

Like it makes a fuckin difference. Whether you're below

the ground or above it. Still this sarcophagi gets to me too. The one that got Pearl's attention has this couple on it turns out they were married and somehow here they end up in Chicago staring off into the future like anything makes sense. Next to them I spot it. That a dog? I ask.

And the twerp gives me one of his fussy little smiles and nods. Yes, indeed. Family pets were often buried with their owners, talking to me like he's a teacher or something.

This gets to Pearl and she starts to blubber and that makes me smile. I put my arm round her. She's embarrassed. It's just everything she says. These statues this place the dog. It gets to me. That's what I loved about my Pearlie. How she could say things she was feeling. How she could put them into words. No bullshit. I put my arm round her waist, pull her to me. That embarrassed her too like the twerp might think we're misbehavin.

We walk through the museum through hallways of armor, cases of clocks, paintings of Jesus and Mary and saints, so many saints. Then we stop by some Chinese vase big enough I could hide in it I ask the twerp how much one of those sarcophagi costs. He shrugged. Oh my, oh my, he says. Priceless but if I had to guess maybe five, ten thousand dollars.

And how do I get my hands on one? I asked.

That stopped him. For a second I think he was scared I wanted his.

I think about it. It would be pretty classy. Pearl heard our little discussion asks me What you up to now? I laughed out loud. She knew me. She knew if I get a bee in my bonnet ain't nothin gonna stop me.

Then I see this statue—a naked guy big grin on his face holding up a bunch of grapes. You wouldn't believe it, twerp tells us he's Bacchus god of wine! Swear to God. I walk up to this Bacchus, reach my arm up in the air just like him, and freeze, freeze like a statue. Pearl's starin at me, starin at Bacchus, a dizzy smile on her face.

That's when really fall for her, hook, line and sinker. Got Mae at home and Sonny too. Got plenty of girls stashed all round town. But there was something about Pearlie. Always a smile, right from the heart. So I'm lookin at her standin next to that Bacchus and I wink at her and I can tell knows what I'm hungry for.

Oh Ketzel, she said. She called me Ketzel. That's Jewish for kitten. Oh Ketzel, let's— and I can tell she wants it too.

* * *

Now, when I caught the clap, way before Pearl, Dr. Gold tells me what to do and what not to do. And he warns me to watch it. That's when I start using rubbers. But that afternoon with Pearl don't care anymore. That's when it could've happened.

4 / PEARL

You miss the curse, a day or two goes by, you figure no big deal, it'll come, you'll bleed and feel like crap and you'll be glad because what's the alternative, but then a week goes by, two, you can't play that game no more, you know, you just know, and you don't need some rabbit to tell you what's up. Accidents happen. And then when a third week went by and I knew I wasn't just whistling Dixie, but pregnant, I was scared, really scared. There was no way it would work out. Ketzel would never leave Mae and Sonny, on that you could rely, and soon I'd show and be out of a job, and we'd be out in the cold. Dad's cancer eating him up. What to do? The only way out tell Ketzel and he would fix things, set it all up with a doctor. But it hadn't been so easy.

Got something to tell you, but it's kind of complicated, I told him. That was how I introduced the subject.

There's nothing complicated, sugar, he reassured me. Ain't nothing complicated I can't fix. And he pulled me to him, crushing my body close to his and despite everything I was struggling to put into words, I felt desire for him, but I knew I had to say it, I had been practicing all week to say it, short and sweet, and when I started to speak, I was scared of what he'd do, so I said it fast, trying not to think about what would follow. I'm pregnant.

I never imagined him reacting like he did: stepping back,

14

looking me in the eye, a slow grin. Ain't that a fact, he said.
You sure?

I nodded.

Have a doc check you out?

No need for that. I'm late.

How late.

Few weeks. And usually I'm regular, like clockwork.

I thought he'd have it all down: tell me not to worry, that he
had a doctor, a safe doctor, that he'd take care of it all, but it was
more complicated.

You can't be thinking of getting rid of my baby, are you sugar?

Honestly, I didn't know how to answer him. But Ketzel had
another idea. So we got to make you respectable now.

What do you mean?

He whistled Here Comes the Bride, and when he did, I was
frightened. You know, doll, how it is with me. I got a family.

I nod.

But I got pals, pals who work with me. Good providers.

I was terrified, for I had seen these pals, met them and the
thought of spending an hour with them, much less the rest of
my life frightened me and I couldn't talk but I knew I had to
think fast, that Ketzel was a man you didn't argue with, that
you didn't challenge him. Ever. I had to think fast. And then the
idea came to me, only what if he wouldn't buy it? But it was my
only way out. But baby, my parents, I said, throwing my arms
around him.

You think your folks want you walking around like this, he
replied, his hands in front of his stomach, pretending he was
pregnant. Think of what that would do to your dad.

Ketzel, whoever I marry, he's gotta be Jewish.

A week later, Howard enters the picture, like magic. Howard,
made for the role: solid, hardworking, attractive and sweet, and
Jewish to boot.

15

Cause soon as those words, He's gotta be Jewish, came out of my mouth and I caught his Ketzelly expression, I knew I had him and had gained a little time for myself, for Ketzel, as he put it, was a family man and had a thing for the Jews, from a long way back. He told me our first night, the night he learned I was a virgin, the night he found out I was Jewish.

We were lying in bed. After. Sometimes, he liked to talk, and it didn't matter if you answered him back. He would make these little speeches about what's right and wrong, and it didn't matter if you answered him back. He would just go on and on. Your ma make rugelach? he asked, just like that, from out of the blue, lying in bed, smoking a cigar, rubbing his belly, and that was how I learned about the Guziks. Of course I knew who the Guziks were. Every Jew in Chicago knew their name, but they were not exactly the type of people you'd invite home for dinner. Still, if it wasn't for them, Ketzel might have been like so many of the other Italian mugs back them, anti-Semitic. If it wasn't for the Guziks, he might not have had this thing for rugelach, or for me. And, God forbid, there never would have been Gabriel and that thought, that awful thought, I can't even bring myself to think it. How could there be a world without my Gabriel?

5 / KETZEL

I worked for Jake and Harry when I came to Chicago from New York. As a bookkeeper. An Italian bookkeeper working for a Jew. How'd ya like dem apples?

The Guziks taught me all about pickled calf's feet and chicken soup and rugelach and matzah brci. They had a big house in the suburbs, kids, a dog, a maid. The whole meggilah. Yeah that's what they'd say. They lived a respectable life. It was the Guziks taught me to value that.

It was the war to end all wars, the Great War, not my war, no way. The poster of Uncle Sam pointing, I WANT YOU, like I'm some chump, willin to get my brains blown out, just because some old geezer with a beard, some Uncle Sam, tells me he wants me.

What with Sonny, no way anyone would get me. I'm deferred. But the real hoo-hah was when the Jerrys give up, the very same day the church bells were ringin, the day the ships with the guns arrived in Europe. Crates of em. Thousands of em. The latest thing. Machine guns. Trench brooms. But what they gonna do with em now?

So we helped out. Took em offa their hands. Cash up front. All very legit. And a couple years later, the Tommys came out. That's what they were called. Named after this General, John T for Takuaferro, if you, please, Thompson.

And boom boom-boom-boom, everything changes. The

17

old days, you had a gun, one little piece, and you'd fire a shot, then another, then another. And then God help you, you'd hafta reload and in the meantime maybe get a piece of lead yourself. So you'd hafta have a good eye, be quick, keep your guard up, all at the same time. Be what they call a sharpshooter. But then with the Tommy's, who needed sharp shooters, gone, gone with bows and arrows and Robin Hood and the fuckin wind. A new age. The machine!

6 / PEARL

All I could do was think about the baby. I knew it'd be a boy, a mother knows these things. And my own mother, what'd I do about her? Couldn't pull the wool over her eyes. So I concocted this story, about this guy Ketzel would find for me, this nice guy, this Jewish guy. I'd have an apartment and stay home and take care of the baby. And, maybe, just maybe Ketzel could come visit. I could imagine him singing to the baby and the baby would hear him too. And even though he wouldn't leave Mae or Sonny—Sonny was deaf—I'd be able to give him that: a boy who would know his father's voice. I had to admit my scheme seemed far-fetched. Like I wouldn't be able to pull it off. But then Ketzel told me about this old pal of his, named Lordly. It was Lordly who introduced me to Howard and, suddenly, I had a way out. My Gabe would have a father, a proper Jewish father.

7 / Lordly Max

Yes, Lordly's the name. Inherited the moniker as a little pisher and it stuck. A step up from Moishe Freigelman; a whole different ring. Once a year I took my nephew, Howard, out for a show and supper, so when Al invited us to dinner, it killed two birds with one stone. When Al made you an offer, you didn't decline. Of course, at the time I didn't know what he was up to, that my nephew was going to be his patsy.

My younger brother, Asher Freeman, had dropped dead of a heart attack at the post office. And a couple years earlier. Least I could do was keep an eye on his son. Tried to give him a job, but he insisted on working at the post office, schlepping packages. Why anyone would do that was beyond me, but even though I hold a grudge with the best of them, I couldn't manage to do so with my own flesh and blood, the only one to carry on the name, though by then we changed our last name to Freeman.

Howard was a good kid, bringing his paycheck home to his mother, going to college part-time, a bit of a shmow, no particular fire in his loins, but what do you expect when you consider his old man?

Me, however, an entirely different kettle of fish. Larger, if you will, than life. Like that night we show up at Colosimo's. I was wearing pinstripes. From Saville Row in London—Howie, the Duke of Windsor shops there. I had gone to England for my business, which you may have heard of, Cavalier Publishing, which I was bringing Howard up to date on as we dined on our first course, Fishermen's Soup. White wine with fish and fowl, I told him, trying to educate him in the ways of the world. Plus, I figured a glass or two might loosen him up. I was educating him on the fine art of the publishing business, pointing out my own spectacular success.

After pouring the wine, I told him the story of Cavalier, throwing in a bit of manifest destiny, the Diaspora, Darwin's Theory of Evolution, with a bissel Freud mixed in on the side; how due to a combination of daring, disregard and devotion— My 3D Credo as I called it, I was able to leap heads and heels above the status quo and land on my feet now planted squarely on terra firma.

Black Friday, screw it, I told him. Let em jump from their buildings and pedal their apples, listen to me for just a minute. Like the soup? Good, isn't it? It needs a bit of salt. Take my advice, this is the time for fortunes to be made! When did I start Cavalier? During the war of all things. Others, off in the trenches, getting their shpilkes blown to kingdom come, the only mustard gas I ever knew was a fart after eating a pastrami sandwich.

I poured myself another glass of wine. Howard had barely touched his.

Oh, I may have made mistakes, I did, only human, but a few things I learned, never be afraid to make em otherwise you end up nowhere. I think it was Shakespeare who said a man is judged by his name, and so I came up with Cavalier. Classy, a bissell British. Leave the Acme and the Consolidated and the Federated and Uniteds to the Palookas, they're a dime a dozen, but believe you me, if you want to make a name for yourself, you gotta stand out.

Now when I began, we had just one newsstand, on the corner of Wabash and Spring. Brought it from a hunch-backed for three hundred bucks I didn't have and now we've got a dozen, but I'll tell you something—waiter, can we have some more rolls, and don't forget the seeded ones—you can't rest on your laurels. With this Depression you gotta be three steps ahead, you following me kid? Good, because you've always been a good kid, why you're still killing yourself at the post office after what it did to your old man is beyond me, I know, I know, you won't be there forever, and, yeah, it's paying your rent, by the way I never graduated from Boy's High, but be that as it may, I got plans now, a few surprises up my sleeve. Your John Q. Public's taste ain't gonna be what it was. Ya see boychik, you never go broke underestimating the taste of the American public, think it was Barnum or Bailey who said that, and because the news today is so lousy, people don't want to read about it, they can see it all around them, it ain't so fresh anymore if you catch my drift, so they want to be diverted.

And then the waiter arrived, bearing our appetizers on a silver tray, and I picked up a shrimp from its bed of shaved ice, lifting it into the air as if it were a sacred offering. Take this shrimp kid, it's trayf, and trayf by any other name is still trayf, but we love it, we covet it, we do everything short of jerk off to it. Just can't get enough of you little mumzer, I whispered, holding the shrimp up to my lips, as if confiding in it. But truthfully now, Howard, answer me this question, if we were living like schvartzes in some hick Louisiana bayou, would we really give such a shit about a dozen shrimp? If we had to go out from dusk to dawn and traipse around in the mud with nets and eat crusty-alacian for breakfast, lunch and dinner, twenty-four hours a day, would it be such a big deal?

It's all because it's forbidden, kid, and what's forbidden is irresistible. Sure, sometimes when life throws us the bummest of steers, we want what's familiar, but usually after all the sorrus, day-in, day-out, in the midst of all the mundanity, we're looking for something different, something with a little spice to it. Spice, don't you know it, is the variety of life, and that's what we're providing.

But I could tell Howard was feeling a little squeamish. He always was whenever I detoured the conversation like this, to topics of human nature, as I like to think of it. Human nature, so much less silly a term than the birds and the bees. And more to the point. I had read my Freud with the best of them!

But it wasn't till four years later, after my dabblings in human nature journalism, that Cavalier really took off. It wasn't my bold strategy but Admiral Hujito's, who after Pearl Harbor, wrote Our force was superior because we were carried by the winds of surprise, who was responsible for my decision to march into a market that was crying, screaming, begging for a little pussy, and it couldn't get that, why then the next best thing.

OVER THERE! the first in my empire, had its inaugural issue in April of 1942 and for three and a half glorious years, until Hiroshima, ended its run, my humble rag, played privy, often in the privy, to the passions of millions of American men. The motto of the magazine, a clever pun on the song—which Irving Berlin was more than happy to lend the copyright to for the war effort—SEND THE WORD OVER THERE, THAT THE YANKS ARE COMING, THE YANKS ARE COMING! The magazine itself was a not terribly revolutionary rag-tag of a rag: of soft poontang, patriotic pabulum, bathing-suited starlets, advertising, and the occasional contest, the first one, the I'm Waiting For You Contest. The rules were simple. All very professional. Howard came up with them himself.

8 / HOWARD

Entries are limited to female United States citizens over the age of eighteen. In 250 words or less, write a letter to your soldier overseas. Include specific details of how you're waiting: I pace back and forth, wearing down the linoleum in the kitchen, desperate to have you back home. Most importantly, include just exactly what you're waiting for: The way you whistle Smoke Gets In Your Eyes, how you look stepping out of the shower with a towel wrapped around you, how you can lift me right up into the air. How your arms crush me.

Essays will be judged according to originality and sincerity. Winners will be published in Over There! and receive a $50 War Bond.

The judges for the contest consisted of me, myself and I. The first entries were ho-hum, lackluster, tepid. Pouring through hundreds of pieces, oh so concrete and literal, most from women such as the winner I chose for July 1943, waiting in her warm kitchen, waiting for that ring at the door, waiting for, democracy to prevail, was not the kind of waiting, however, that my uncle, Lordly, imagined millions of horny GIs had in mind. And when he had read the submission of the woman I declared the winner, he took her entry, written in emerald green ink in, perhaps, the most beautiful cursive penmanship I had ever seen, tore it into small pieces and threw them in the air.

What a ditz, he proclaimed. Lesson one, hubby-boy's not

going to bother ringing to get in. He'll throw that door open. He's hungry, and not just for meat loaf. Ditto with that democracy to prevail crap. Sure we want to win, but everyone knows that. Cut to the chase. You can do better than this, Howard my boy. From now on, write em yourself.

My last writing assignment had been a paper on Henry James, a portrait of an entirely different lady than the one Lordly had in mind. At first I was not sure I was up to the task, but surprisingly, the words flowed:

I'm waiting, waiting, for my Bill, to come home to me. I'll be in the kitchen ironing and it will be hot out, so I'll have done what we gals do at such a time, I'll have taken off my blouse, standing there just in my shorts and brassiere, ironing, listening to the radio, to the latest war news and there'll be Benny Goodman playing. Bill always liked In the Mood. Then I'll hear a car pull up outside and the dog barking from next door and the door's pushed open. At first I'm scared but then I see him just standing there at the front of the kitchen. And I can't believe it.

For three years I've waited for this moment. At night, trying to sleep, I've shut my eyes and seen him there, but funny, now it's happened and we're both so excited, we can't move, we're just frozen. Then he brings his hands into the air, spreads them out and I know any second he'll run up to me and throw them around me and it's so funny, me in my bra, who would've known? And I start to cry, standing there waiting, because I see his hands again and remember how big they are more than anything in the world I want those hands around me, I want to touch them, kiss them, have them hold me tight. In all the right places.

Fifteen minutes after pulling the paper from my Underwood Typewriter and counting 248 words; fifteen minutes after completing my entry; fifteen minutes after sheepishly dropping it in the IN box on the desk of Lordly's secretary, I jumped from my seat, startled to find my own office door thrown open and the commanding figure of my uncle standing there, his beefy arms outstretched. You're a natural, my boy. A natural! boomed Lordly, overcome by warmth, affection and pride, as I surrendered to his crushing embrace, forced to steady myself, feeling as if I might swoon, for at that moment I first experienced the adulation and joy known from the adoration of a literary audience. Lordy grabbed my hand, caressed it and crooned, 'I want to touch them, kiss them, have them hold me tight.' Boychik, this is just the beginning!

Lordly, of course, was a man who had difficulty waiting for anything, and back at Colosimo's , the night I first met Pearl, waiting, even ten minutes after dispatching his last shrimp, was not his cup of tea, but finally the waiter arrived with the prime rib, the baked potato and the creamed spinach—This will put hair on your chest, Lordly laughed, punching me in the forearm—and finally the famous Colosimo's dance floor was transformed into a stage, a stage that rose slowly, magically, majestically into the air and chorus girls appeared, kicking their heels up to the sky as the Stuart Skylar Orchestra played I Want To Be Happy.

They were the Colosimo's Cuties, an even dozen, dressed in skimpy, red-sequenced costumes and matching feathered beanies, each with the shapeliest of legs, the longest and most desirable of legs; legs that could bowl you over, calves curvaceous, knees that could make you quake, kicking, skipping, tapping and bounding about the stage, singing:

I want to be happy
But I won't be happy
Till I make you happy too
Life's really worth living
When you are mirth giving
Why can't I give some to you?

A historic night: not the flaming crepes, nor the cigars or champagne, not the lyrics mirth giving, but that Lordly actually knew one of the Cuties. She's a Yid, kid, can ya believe it? he asked me.

When Pearl took a seat, I was on fire.

Who knows if it was the excitement, the wine, the thrill of eating shrimp, but for an instant I could feel my old life slipping away. How could the post office compare to this? FRAGILE, THIS SIDE UP, CANCELLED, RETURN TO SENDER. A miracle was occurring: my life was beginning and with an actual Colosimo Cutie, Pearl Katz and she was talking and laughing and it was all so very easy and the possibilities endless. I offered her a drink.

No, thank you very much. Can't accept drinks while we're working. We get a half-hour break before the midnight show and you're it!

And you're it! I had never considered myself a break before and sure, she may have used it with someone else, but if she had, who cared, it was a good line, a worthy line, a witty line, and so I asked her if she wanted a cigarette and she nodded and I tapped out a Lucky Strike for her, one for myself and turned to Lordly but the package was empty. With impeccable timing, she said, third strike and you're out! and we burst into laughter. Fell in love with her on the spot. Somehow I knew, as preposterous as it might have sounded, that I was not about to strike out. Here was my chance, unlike any I had ever known, and I wasn't going to let it go.

The next day, for the first time in my life, I walked into a florist shop. A whole new world: moist, fragrant, intoxicating. I had never encountered a peony before. Smelling one, I thought of Pearl, get a hard on, right there, surrounded by pink peonies. Sent her a dozen. I couldn't decide what to write on the little white card. Tore up a few, not wanting to sound like a fool.

Then, someone came in, the florist excused himself, left me alone and I imagined Pearl and me together in a room, a hotel room. She was dressed like she was at Colosimo's, in that skimpy red number with the sparkles and the feathered beanie. She was sitting on my lap and singing that song, I Want to Be Happy.

There was so much I wanted to say. How could I begin? Finally, I just signed my name.

9 / PEARL

They never tell you what a big heart Ketzel had. Once he took me to his soup kitchen. Hundreds of men, all lined up, stretching down the block. He shook their hands, patted them on the back, looked them straight in the eye. Hang in there pal, he'd say. Hang in there.

10 / AL

It was the syph, the syph from outta the blue. Made me violent. And when I came to, I'd be in a cold sweat maybe or burnin up with fever. Couldn't think straight. I'd call them the spells and when I'd wake up I'd hafta deal with the repercussions. Dead men tell no tales. Heard that once in a movin picture. And it's true let me tell you take a look at a dead man and you know it's over. All over.

Do you feel remorse? a reporter asked me once. And I looked him in the eye locked him right in the eye. Him and me starin at each other. I wanted to take him by the neck—the Adam's apple is the place to go for— and then I'd ask him hey buddy you feelin any remorse now? But I didn't. Because there were photographers and they'd take picture and it'd be in the next paper and it wouldn't be good for my image and my image, case you didn't know, it was important to me.

11 / PEARL

When Howard showed up at Colosimo's, he was still boyish, twenty-two, skinny, right out of some Jewish five-and-dime, and cute and crazy. About me, I knew it right from the start, and unlike so many of the others, the stage door Johnnies and the droolers, the Lotharios and the lover-boys, there was more to him than met the eye. Sure, he was hot for me but it wasn't just that. Maybe because he was so smart and even though I didn't know all about politics and literature like he did, he asked me questions, as if he respected just what I had to say. He lent me books, Tender Is The Night and Babbit and Walt Whitman, and I could tell, he knew I had brains, though, to tell you the truth, I always had trouble with Whitman.

I did flirt a little with Ketzel at the start, but what kept it all very interesting was the expression on his face, startled, and with this sweet smile. I was, you might say, a little interested. And the letters he wrote me, and the poems. And that night, especially that first night, when I sat down and had a cigarette with him and Lordly, my heart didn't exactly go pitter-patter, but I thought, here's a guy, a real straight shooter who's nuts about me, and maybe this is the solution to my little predicament, this is my ticket out of Palookaville.

Howard was sweet on me, right from the start, and that made it easier though I always felt a little guilty, that we tricked him the way we did. So easy, though, like feeding milk to a baby, a Jewish baby, and that was a big deal for Ketzel, that Howard was Jewish. He was a big believer in mixing with your own kind when it came to matrimonial matters.

Two weeks later, Howard quits the post office and school and goes to work for Lordly Then, we elope. Lordly, who loved playing Cupid, took all the credit, doubling Howard's salary. He sent us a silver bowl resting on a silver tray, inscribed, Pleased as punch!

When I told Howard I was pregnant, I thought I owed it to him, to confess if he wanted me to, but before I could, he shushed me, he put his hand over my mouth and then took my own hand and broke down crying. Says he loves me. He's crazy about me. That we were destined for each other. Destined.

After Gabe was born, and he's holding him the first time, the first two words out of his mouth, My boy. I was sure then, that that was that. Gabe was his boy and would be his boy forever.

If only you could have known him back then, what he could do with words.

12 / Howard

Hemingway, Fitzgerald, Dos Passos: I worshiped at their altars, longed to stand by their side, dreamed of reviewers hanging onto my every word, but in the end I sold out. A baby, colic, up all night, you try writing the great American novel, see where it gets you. But I still had dreams. Lordly wouldn't be around forever. Then, Cavalier Publishing would be mine, all mine. It might take time, but I didn't care. I would be a publisher. No more porn, no more phony contests, no more salacious covers or leering or pandering. No more heeding Smeilson, our lawyer, or playing up to distributors, taking them to dinner, listening to them talk about their sons, the hotshot dentist with three offices in Long Island.

I had plans, big ones. We would publish books, maybe a literary journal, paperbacks, books for students, books for those who couldn't afford some imitation 19th Century leather-bound behemoth, books for the masses——yes, I had my fling, I was a Red. But after the pact, I walked out—books you could hold onto while commuting to work in the subway. But meanwhile, I'd have to put up with Lordly. And why not? If it wasn't for him, I wouldn't have met Pearl, we wouldn't have had Gabe, I'd be some public-school teacher in the Bronx or still at the post office, waiting for my pension.

Of course, Lordly did take a toll. For one thing, he'd never shut up. That's why, after the war, I encouraged him to travel.

Just to get him away. A little peace and quiet. While he was gone, I stopped writing The Yanks Are Coming, turned over the stories to writers. The streets were full of vets wanting to get their two cents in. I tried to class our act up a little. If I had had my druthers we would have had Henry Miller, D.H. Lawrence, an article on the Death of Vaudeville. Still, Cavalier Publishing got rid of the floss. Then Lordly returned, had his stroke, couldn't climb the stairs to the office. I'm in charge now. Sold off Yank, that's what we shortened the name down to, and Glee and Spree and He & She. No more pictures. No more, as Lordly used to put it, poontang, and I contracted with a new printer. I try to change the name of our enterprise, how I want to change the name, but Lordly won't budge, like it's sacred, like we're the New York Fucking Times, for Christ's sake, so we keep it.

Even though we didn't know it, we were harbingers, new age voyagers on the S.S. Pulp. We started with quarter paperback detectives, then for women, historical fiction. Always, female. You wouldn't know them, they're long gone. But the characters—we're not exactly talking Willa Cather or Virginia Wolfe-types— they're solid and honest and strong. A little quirky too, that's our trademark. Joan of Arc with a thing for the archer. I Married Madame DuBarry. I Sailed With the Vikings. Curie-look-a-likes, French resistance fighters, artists, heroines. That was our trademark. And always, we'd publish two, three a year that I was proud of, ones we'd take a chance on, ones from some hot-shot kid with a literary axe to grind. I always had my aspirations.

We did okay, ten books a year, sometimes a dozen. Never rich but made enough to move to Skokie. Gabe was happy, Pearl too. She took to housekeeping, to cooking and sewing and her charity work. She was always busy.

Her only disappointment, Gabe was no dancer. When he

was four, she bought him tap shoes, tried her best to get him interested, he'd have nothing to do with it. Thought she'd have better luck with a girl, but we couldn't have any more kids. And Pearl never seemed to regret it—she wasn't one to look back. I got my two boys, she reassured me. It's all I could dream of. I kind of wanted another, but it wasn't in the cards, just wasn't in the cards.

13 / KETZEL

Saw this movie. After the Civil War, all these plantations up in smoke, so they take it out on the ignorant schvartzes. Dress up in sheets and hoods, like ghosts—spooks scarin the spooks—ride all over the place, lynchin, burnin, raping. Wilson shows the movie at the White House. A big party. What a country. At least I never rode around gettin my jollies lordin it over ignorant schvartzes. I actually liked schvartzes. Betcha didn't know that.

We sold our hooch to anyone with the bucks to buy it. Didn't matter what color. And when we were rollin in money, I started my first soup kitchen. Betcha didn't know that. They didn't write about that in no history books. Fed twenty-five hundred men one day in the dead of winter. Fed 'em hot soup and a hunk of bread. Newspapers called me Robin Hood. People knew. They showed me respect.

Sonny and me, it's his eighth birthday, we go to Comiskey Park. Greatest day in my life. All over the stands people pointin at us, screamin There's Al, there's Al. They stand up and cheer and clap. They're cheerin me. Louder and louder. Hootin and hollerin. Top of their lungs. Everyone in the fuckin park cheerin for me.

Sonny looking up at me. Deaf as he is, he can hear the yelling. Looks up at me like he never looked before.

Gabbey Harnett, the Cubby's catcher shows up, signs a ball

for Sonny. Like I'm the fuckin king of England. I buy us hot dogs. The kid sellin em can't talk he's so excited. Tip him a hundred bucks. He about shits in his pants. Late that night fallin asleep, I remember the cheering. Louder and louder.

14 / PEARL

I put Ketzel out of my head. After he died, figured I had nothing to worry about. But then, the week of my fortieth birthday and Howard, who never turned on the television, maybe to watch Ed Sullivan once in a blue moon, Howard wants us to watch this new show, The Untouchables, and it's about Ketzel. A lot of water over the mill, still all these years later I didn't want to be in the same room with Howard and Ketzel. Didn't exactly seem kosher.

Like a fool, I agree to watch. Howard, who hated to even use a mousetrap, lapped it up. Maybe it was because it was set in Chicago. Maybe because we met at Colosimo's. Who knows? Ketzel looked nothing like the Ketzel I knew. He was ugly and had this smirk and did terrible things, things he never actually would have done in a million years. He gets his henchman to attack Elliot Ness's fiancé. At her home! And hires gunmen to try to kill Ness. So I decide, never again, and during the commercial, I beat a hasty retreat and never, never for the remaining three seasons do I give in. Always the same, every Thursday, then it moves to Sunday. At nine I go to the bedroom and Howard watches alone.

I always make sure our dog, Shmow, is with me, and I keep myself busy, rearranging drawers, going through clothes for Hadassah, reading the paper, sewing, with the radio on WBNS, they played jazz and show-tunes, I didn't hear the gunshots and

sirens from downstairs. Still, sometimes, it would be loud—
explosions and machine guns and yelling all over the place—
and I'd have to shout down the stairs to Howard, Would you
mind turning it a little lower? and then I'd close the door and
return to letting out the waist of his pants or maybe writing a
letter to Gabe:

Dear Gabe,
    It was so nice to hear your voice tonight! Sundays
just wouldn't be the same without your call! Your
dad and I are so proud you are supporting Governor
Stevenson. Of course, you mustn't neglect your
homework, but it would be such a good thing for the
country and he'd be so much better than that mumser,
Eisenhower.
    I ran into Artie's mother yesterday at the
supermarket. He likes Penn and has joined a fraternity,
but not a Jewish one.
    Aunt Ethel is coming up for a visit next weekend and
will spend the night.
    Shmowie is with me now fast asleep. He is yapping.
You used to call it talking in his sleep!
    I am including a little check, consider it early
Chanukah gelt. It will be odd not having you this year
for potato latkes. We will have them when you come
back for vacation. Take this check for pizza or a book or
record or something special.
    Well, I must go now. All my love, my sweetheart,
Mom

Sometimes I'd wonder why years later, should I be hiding in
my bedroom? Why should it all come to this? It was all because
of what they had done to him, how they tried to make him a

monster, a murderer, a thug. That wasn't the Ketzel I knew, the man who took care of my family, who started soup kitchens for the hungry, who was always up for a laugh and a song

Why did they even call it The Untouchables in the first place? There was nothing un in his touch. Un made something the opposite of what it was supposed to be. And what we had done together: who could ever want the opposite of that?

The night Howard and I had eloped, I had been so careful to play it like a number on the stage, an unfamiliar one, something new, even though he knew I was pregnant. I had allowed myself to show enthusiasm, of course, no need to play the cold fish—what kind of man looked forward to that—but I had also, the first time he touched me down there, to hesitate, as if I felt shy, a little bashful about what he was doing, and when—surprise, my Howie was bigger than Ketzel, who'd of guessed it?—and it felt good, I was careful not to let on, especially as Howard, oh so carefully, slipped the candle in the holder, I knew I couldn't let myself go, not this time anyway, but that I had to watch it, play it according to the script even if the way he was going on, he'd be the last to know. Still, sweet, so sweet, checking on me along the way—Is it all right? Can I keep going? as I whisper don't stop, don't stop, and my, he certainly didn't. After, my arms around him, I cuddle. Are you okay? he asks. Okay? I replied. I could get used to this, I could get used to this.

And he laughed and held me tight, and oh, it was so simple, none of the games and of course the fun that went with them, that I had known with Ketzel, but it was simple and good because Howard was a good man, a sweet man, the kind of man a nice Jewish girl should feel lucky to find. Maybe it hadn't been as wild, but there is a limit to what passion gets you in life.

So twenty years later, here I am, finishing a letter to our son, Gabe, and putting a stamp on it and thinking of Ketzel and of Howard. Then I picked up the paper, the rotogravure and there were recipes, one in particular, which Howard would like. The following week, at dinner, I served it to him: rice pudding. He loved it. Delicious, he declared. Is this a new one, Pearlie? Don't remember it.

Got it from the paper.

Delicious!

You won't believe it, but it's made with skimmed milk. No cream, perfect for your diet

You're kidding me.

 The whole truth and nuthin' but the truth. You heard what Dr. Marcus said, you got to watch cholesterol!

This is wonderful!

A pinch of cinnamon. Like in Greece.

Aha!

And a touch of nutmeg.

Delicious!

Later, in my room, Howard in the den, watching the latest episode, I knew I had made the right decision, to skip the show. Good old Irwin Johnson was on right at nine, right on the dot, leading in with the Song of India. It was Tommy Dorsey, Dorsey who choked to death on a chicken bone, how he could play the trombone, once he had winked at me, as if that would get him anything. Winking. And then in the rotogravure, another recipe, Lemon Poppy Seed Bundt Cake. Howard was just crazy about Bundt cake.

Now some may consider baking a Lemon Poppy Seed Bundt Cake a little tame when you consider my previous career but being on the stage ain't all it's cracked up to be. Three performances a day, closing at midnight, stage door Johnnie's hitting on you, you get tired after a while. Surprised me how much I loved keeping house. Our first place, a two-bedroom in West Rogers Park. Learned to iron—liked it too—and to cook.

Took to it like a cat to milk. When Gabe was napping—he was a really good napper—I would take a nap too or read one of the books Howard had suggested. I had time for myself.

I was surprised just how nuts I was for Gabe right from the very start. The way he would coo, how he'd try to imitate me and then I'd imitate him back and he'd gurgle and break out into a smile, a smile that I was such a sucker for, a smile that could make you swoon. I wouldn't have traded being a mother for all the tea in China. Won't pretend that it was a hundred per cent peaches and cream. There were those moments, those occasional moments, when I wondered what I had gotten us into. I'd be splashing bubbles on him in the tub and he would be babbling and all of a sudden, his cheeks, his nose, even his little tush would remind me of Ketzel, and I worried that when he grew up, he would be the spitting image. It didn't seem a fair thing to do to a child.

Probably that was why, right before he hit puberty and got a little chubby, I stopped baking and put him on those diets none of which really worked. Wasn't till college that he finally trimmed down. Ketzel was a large man. Not fat. Large. Solid, too. And, oy, how he could carry his weight. There was nothing I could do about Gabe's features, but if he was slim, the resemblance might not be as obvious. And his acne, to tell you the truth, it never bothered me. It made him different than Ketzel

15 / HOWARD

After the war, everything changed. With millions of American servicemen overseas, morale was the first order of the day, and while publishers of pornography were themselves hungry for new audiences deprived of poontang, their rags would never cross the Atlantic or Pacific or even be allowed the paper itself for printing, if they didn't play to the patriotic winds blowing.

No naked woman pinned up in the bunkhouse in the Marshall Islands or taped to the walls of a submarine churning through the North Atlantic. That kind of thing would never pass inspection. No more breasts, no more crotches, no more nookie, only the suggestion, the merest of hints that the apple-cheeked babe staring out was interested in a roll in the hay, unless, of course, it was for the war effort.

An example: the stocking shot. A cartoon vixen or a real-life Betty Grable un-peeling her nylons to be recycled as parachutes. Another, photo features showing babes trying their darndest to tackle those jobs the men had left them with: welding at the factory, changing a tire, shoveling snow, delivering the mail. These were wholesome lasses, even virginal—the boys didn't need to worry that Mary or Betty or Edna were out on the town looking for some 4-F flunky to pal around with—Rosie the Riveter but without biceps, thinner and in lingerie, bathing suits, pajamas. Casting calls went out for brunettes—blondes were a tad too vixen—and we'd position her in front of a clothesline, her arms out-stretched, pinning lingerie up, a brassiere or two while she's at it, or reading a book or writing a letter to her sailor overseas. G-Eyefuls, The Soldier's Guide to Arms and Legs, a Babeful Manual, For Our Fighting Men—Women Who Won't Fight Back. Pictures of American women at home, waiting, dusting, doing their part, staying in shape for that great day when their Johnnies come marching home to get theirs. I got the picture. My I'm Waiting column which launched my career as a writer was just what the doctor ordered.

In 1943, I started an advice column for soldiers that lasted for 20 editions. January 1944, for instance:

Tips for Letters That Will Have Her Begging for More!!!

1/ Skip the Dear. Start out with her name. Laura, Anita, Betty. It doesn't matter. Or else use a pet name. Or invent one. Precious, Love of My Life, Doll-Baby, Angel. Snukie-pie. Cut to the chase and she'll be swept away.

2/ Refer to a shared memory. It can be intimate, but nothing that will attract the censor's pen! Keep it discrete and romantic: I remember that night in August at the beach, that polka-dotted bathing suit, how you dried me off... At the dance at the club last Christmas, how swell you looked in that blue number. What a knockout!

3/ Let her know some details of what you're going through, but no need for the grisly. In a foxhole now, waiting to move on, thinking of you. Gosh, it's hot. Back home, there must be snow on the ground.

4/Refer to the future. Give her something to look forward to. I'm thinking of a hot shower and a shave and coming back to you. Can almost smell your perfume as I put my arms around you.

5/ Don't think you have to write her a book. Keep them short and sweet. After all, you're not exactly on vacation. One page is sometimes all it takes to stop her in her tracks and get her heart all aflutter.

Oh, so different than my college papers where the closest I came to the carnal was Hester Prynn and Sister Carrie. But what fun. And given my flattest of feet precluded me from serving overseas, here was my opportunity for serving my country!

After VJ-Day, Lordly knew I was feeling antsy, wanted a change. He was always beseeching me to stay with him. Claimed he hadn't the cash for a buy-out, but promised, stick with me until I get my feet more on the ground, bubbalah, and you want a magazine a little more fancy-shmanz you can create it yourself! I dreamed of such a journal: a cross between Esquire and Partisan Review; elegantly printed, ironic and pithy, and while with, perhaps, a sensual edge, not a nipple in sight, and this was the carrot on Lordly's stick, the carrot which never, came to pass, not until it was too late, for the industry, as Lordly would always refer to it, had gone through its revolution and we were parked on the wrong side of it.

Until the late 1940's, Cavalier puttered along, but then things changed: GIs overseas had their taste of oh-la-la poontang, those cheap sepia French magazines that threw in vintage shots from the 20's and 30's and Scandinavian nudist magazines. In the late 40's, with the paper shortage over, there was a flurry of a higher-class French product: black and white, film-noirish, stylized, and finally the Great Leap forward: off with the stockings and lingerie, a hint of pubic hair, then spread those legs and give us a dry hump. Playboy finished off Lordly's empire. Slick, colorful, available at the drug store, tasteful in its own air-brushed way. Sex had grown up. No need to stoop under the counter. Now it could even be talked about at the water cooler. Hey, did you catch Miss April in the last edition?

In '47, at home recuperating after a burst appendix and I had this brainstorm. I was too weak to hold a newspaper in my hands, too weak to even read one of the new Penguin paperback editions I had been all gaga over, so Pearl would read to me, instead and she read like a pro. Never lost her touch; always the vaudevillian; the entertainer, the show must go on, even if she wasn't dancing anymore. You could hear this in her voice. At night, even Gabe would sneak open his door, just a crack, and listen to the sound of his mother's voice, and just what she could do with it.

What tricks she was capable of. When she read Gone With the Wind, as if Scarlett O'Hara had entered the room, honeyed and husky, all antebellum, flirting outrageously with Rhett, manipulating Melody. She even read Chekhov —it was a family legend that she was distantly related—all the roles in the Cherry Orchard and, indeed, suddenly she had a Russian accent. No matter how weak I, appendix-less felt, how incapable of taking solace in her looks, her legs, her legendary beauty, her voice still enticed me, allowed me to escape the confines of my bed, to prickle up and listen, each word riveting, each word alive.

Who knows, if it wasn't for Pearl, just what she could do with her voice, I might have never come up with the Spoken Word series. I, of course, had listened to radio since I was little, but hearing my wife transform herself and offering such delight, such escape, such consolation to me made me realize, more than ever, the power of the human voice. And on that day it hit me: the impetus for the Spoken Word series. There were tapes available for the blind, of course, but my plan was grander. After all, the blind were a small market. I wanted a bigger one, records with stories in them, stories that anyone could have read to them, whenever they wanted. The Grimm Brothers, Sister

Carrie, Crime and Punishment, take your pick. And there was no reason why there couldn't be a radio program, a national radio show to highlight the records, sort of a medley. Each week a guest star, one renowned for his voice: Orson Welles, Bette Davis, Lawrence Olivier. And every week just some regular Joe, someone who'd audition. Have a kid read too. That would add a little charm, and all the better if they'd occasionally trip over a word; the audience would eat it up.

Lordly, however, had other ideas. "Too high-brow, kid," he declared. "Too far outta our league. What do we know from Victrolas and vinyl? We're strictly a print business. People want to see what they're going to get. May not be Dostoyevsky, and I'll admit there have been bumps in the road, but it's got us where we are.

But that's exactly my point, I insisted. Maybe it's time to shift away, to diversify. To do something we're proud of.

Last month Cavalier Enterprises printed 62,000 copies of our magazines and if you figure, each one isn't just glanced at once, but over and over again, and in the most agreeable of circumstances, and even passed around, that's hundreds of thousands of men grabbing their dreams and their pricks in the bargain. And all because of us. And that makes me proud, my boy, that fills me with pride.

You're proud to be a pornographer?

Lordly swatted his hand in the air, as if to brush off a fly. Never liked that word, son, never used it. We're giving the people what they want. Pure and simple. A picture is worth a thousand words.

And that was that. During the next several years, as television moved into America's living rooms, Lordly was even more inflexible. See, I was right. The tube would've taken the wind out of our sales, boychik. No one wants to hear a scratchy old record when they can see the story played out in front of their very own eyes. Less work. Don't have to use the old noggin' to imagine it. It's all out there, right in front of you! He finally turned control of Cavalier to me, on the provision that our three remaining magazines, Babe, Hot Shots, and Gals, continue publication. Fortunately, we had bought a building on 14th Street in NYC, Publisher's Row, and it had been paid for. Without bothering to inform Lordly, I mortgaged it and had $32,000 to invest. I knew I should be careful. Gabe would be needing tuition for college, and God forbid, something should happen to me, Pearl's social security would need supplementing, but this was a chance, the chance I had been waiting for and I didn't intend to let it slip away.

I brought the copyrights for recording a dozen novels, then had another idea, one far more exciting: recording poets and playwrights reading their own work. There was some of this kind of thing out there: old Edison tapes of Tennyson and Yeats and some newer recordings of Elliot and Wallace Stephens, but they only found in dusty drawers in libraries. No one had cornered the market. And a market there had to be. An academic one, as well a limited public. A few well-placed advertisements in the Saturday Review, others sent to the three thousand college libraries over the US. Thousands of more to high school librarians. For too many people, poetry was relegated to books, and really, it should be read aloud, and who better to read it than the author who wrote it!

And so I composed a letter, and had Connie, our secretary, type out one hundred copies. In July of 1962, English-speaking poets around the world, from Auden to Marianne Moore, from Ezra Pound to Robert Lowell, all received the following message, with their name typed in after the Dear.

Forgive me for intruding, but I have a proposal, one
that I hope might be of some interest. My family has been

48

in the publishing business for two generations and now we are expanding to media.

Beginning in October, we will be recording and producing 78 LPRs of our greatest poets reading their own work. They will be offered to the public as well to schools and universities around the country. Of course, no such series would be complete without selections by you.

There are two reasons for our undertaking. We believe there is an audience clamoring for the chance to hear poetry read aloud. Also, we feel that the author of a poem, knowing it best, should have the opportunity to read it himself, as he intends it to be heard for posterity.

We have no desire to intrude on you anymore than is necessary. One of our technicians would arrive at your home or we would hire a near-by studio. At most, this would take two hours of your time, and you would have the chance to re-record if you are not satisfied with the first recording.

Our lawyers are preparing formal contracts that will spell out the details of such an undertaking. We would provide an honorarium of $150 and a yet-to-be-yet determined amount for each record sold. We would also ask that you allow us to include a photograph of you as well as a short biographical sketch, including the title of your books, in the hopes that those listening to you, might then be inspired to go out and purchase them.

Enclosed is a stamped self-addressed postal card. We hope this will make it easier for you to contact us.

Sincerely yours,
Howard Freeman
President, Cavalier Press & Spoken Word Media Inc.

Of course there was no Spoken Word Media Inc. It was merely a phrase that I came up with, a dream, one that would materialize only if enough poets answered. I, however, was hopeful, but cautious: letters like mine had a good chance of never being forwarded properly and landing up in the trash. That is why I invested in expensive stationary, of the heaviest weight, with the watermark showing, and obsessed over fonts, finally settling on Times New Roman—it implied tradition, dignity and correctness—signing my name with a flourish, with3 a fountain pen, a Tribute to Lordly.

Two months later, we had an astonishingly thirty-six replies, and twenty-one of them bit the bait, among them some of the big fish. I was beside myself. There was a flurry of meetings with lawyers and recording studios and printers, the brilliant decision to hire Stuart Spencer, a Harvard graduate student in English, floundering with his thesis and a new baby, strapped for cash, and surprisingly savvy to the business world. I purchased the most sophisticated of tape recorders, the German-produced Gruening 150-S and mastered the art of using it. Finally on a sunny October morning in 1955, I hailed a cab and set off for my first recording session. The Chelsea Hotel, I instructed the driver. And once there, sweating profusely, but feeling young again, and just a little like that first night when I met Pearl, strode into the lobby, informing the clerk at the desk, Mr. Thomas' room. Mr. Dylan Thomas. He's expecting me.

16 / PEARL

Ketzel had this thing for fingers. He liked to suck on them, seemed especially fond of my thumb, taking it into his mouth, biting down on it, not so it would hurt—Ketzel would never want to hurt me—but just so that I could feel him, his teeth, and, sometimes, I screamed out loud, not in pain, never in pain. I screamed because it made me feel so goddamn alive. We called it the Biting Game. And he liked it. It made him laugh and he wouldn't let go. He was so strong—such big hands—made me feel like I couldn't get away. And I'd do the same to him. I sucked and I bit. We just couldn't help ourselves.

So different than the way it came to be with Howard. Not in the beginning, mind you, but after a while how it ended up. On Saturday nights we'd do it, or sometimes, just for a little variety on Sunday morning before he read the News of the Week in Review. So gentle, so sweet, and patient. Always making sure I was ready, those were his words, his words I'll take with me to the grave, are you ready, are you sure you're ready? And when I was, and to tell you the truth, half the time I really wasn't, it didn't matter, I just wanted to get it over with, he'd come inside me, and then so much the same old thing.

Mind you, I'm not complaining. It was pleasant enough, but there were no surprises. Always the same. I'd make noises, moan a little because it got him going. And it didn't seem like it was asking so much. And then he'd roll off of me. He could be very sweet then uncharacteristically cuddly and huggy, but to tell you the truth I was usually glad it was all over with.

Never that way with Ketzel. With Ketzel, I wanted it so bad, I never wanted it to end. With Ketzel. I'd cry out loud. He would too. Sometimes, right in the middle, he'd laugh this crazy Ketzelly laugh that would really get me going and I'd laugh all wild-like right along with him. I couldn't help myself. I really couldn't.

Sometimes, going down the aisle at the grocery store, in the middle of a manicure,

waiting for the attendant to fill up the car with gas, I'd think of Ketzel. I'd remember something—his laugh, his gold cufflinks with the pearl, his smile—and wonder where I'd be if I had ended up with him. It would make me shudder. How lucky I was, to have my Howard and my Gabe. Life may not be as thrilling as it had been, but it was comfortable and for that I was grateful.

17 / GABE

2001

One last look in the visor mirror, preening and pining, wondering will she even notice, then, finally, time to face the music. I get out of the car, walk into Kensington Heritage Village—they called it that even though it's a nursing home—and tell the receptionist," I'm here to see Pearl Freeman."

She glanced at a list and shook her head. "Hasn't come to dinner yet," she replied. "Was she expecting you?"

Was she expecting me? "She's my mother," I sigh.

I walked through the solarium, yes, they called it a solarium. Who has a sunroom any more, and why did all these places have to have this prim look of down-on-their-heels country clubs, colonial upholstery in a sea of pale chintz, wing chairs, dried silk flowers, a piano gathering dust and the grandfather clock—can't forget the grandfather clock, so obvious a symbol you'd think they'd ditch it and get a nice digital, be easier to read.

There, in front of the flat screen television was Pearl, fast asleep, slumped in an armchair, wrinkled, jaw descending into her neck, brown moles, balding but still blond, hair teased, and her trademark pink harlequin glasses. She was dressed sedately: purple slacks, a mauve sweater with a falling leaf pattern—Pearl was big on narrative designs in her sweaters—and gold lame ballet slippers. Who could blame her for anything? Her short-term memory was hanging on by the thinnest of threads. Even her longest wasn't anything to write home about. The last time I had visited, a couple of months ago, she even seemed fuzzy about dad. He had died almost forty years ago, when I was in college, but it seemed at the time she couldn't remember him.

I stood there, watching her and then, the television interrupted my reverie: news about a school shooting, this time in Utah, a twelve-year old, the culprit. What a crazy country, children set loose with guns, politicians afraid to ban them, the Supreme Court giving their blessing. What was it all coming to?

Suddenly, Pearl opened her eyes, spotted me and craned her face for a second look. Her features tightened. "Gabe," she demanded, then her eyes narrowed as I approached her." What's happened to your face?"

"What do you mean?" I asked, her coy little boy.

That, she said, touching my cheek. Your zits, she said pronouncing the word with a dismissive nasal Yiddish inflection, as if they were unworthy of a moment's attention. They've disappeared! A smile crept over her face. Finally, finally you stopped the picking.

But I never picked, I reminded her, even though I knew she didn't believe me. You pick a guitar, you pick a lock, you pick your spouse, but not, for God's sake, pimples you don't, even though no matter how hard I tried as a teenager, I couldn't help touching them, patting them, smoothing them away, as she would do her best to divert my attention, juggling with lemons, asking me to find a pie tin from the highest shelf in the pantry, telling me stories, it didn't matter if they were made up, when she told a story or delivered a line, it seemed to have authority behind it. Like right before my Bar Mitzvah, I'm trying on a pair of pants when Pearl barges into the changing room to check up on me. Can't you give a guy a little privacy? I ask.

I used to wipe your tush, she informed me. Believe me, you got nothing to hide.

But as a kid, I tried to hide. The state of my face tormented me, even though Pearl told me I was being melodramatic, that I shouldn't be preoccupied with my complexion. Now, half a century later, I wanted my mother to see it, my new face, the one that thanks to the judicious aim of my dermatologist's laser gun, had rid me of the acne scars that had plagued me all my life. Time to reveal her sonny-boy in all his glory. You can't judge a book by its cover, she liked to say, but I knew she did, even if she could never see any imperfection in me, her only child, as if I could be anything less than perfect.

I sat down by Pearl's side before we went in to dinner and told her the story, the one I hadn't wanted to tell on the phone, and her blue eyes opened wide in disbelief, then wonder, and she asked, Are you sure of this derma-dermatologist, god forbid he's not some shyster, some gonif, some thief, then they'll grow back and all of this will be a big disappointment?

Mom, he's the big man.

Big man, the name she'd use for the doctor you'd have to wait months to see, the chief of the department, the one who went to Harvard Medical School, the very best.

You were so beautiful as a baby, she began, Of course when you turned twelve, they sprouted and I thought they would go away if only you wouldn't pick, and it just broke my heart to see what it did to you, and she was off and running now, back to my tortured adolescence, but, surprisingly, it was interesting to hear her go on like this, even though many of her memories these days had the air of revisionist history about them, and so I lapsed in and out, half-listening to her. Finally, she stopped talking, reached out, caressed my cheek and whispered, if only your father could have had this fancy treatment.

What was she talking about? What need could there possibly be for my father, smooth of cheek, with the clearest of complexions, for laser therapy? Ma, what are you talking about?'

She looked at me as if I was the village idiot. His scars. The ones right there. She touched my cheek, my neck.

What scars?

She appeared irritated, like I was challenging her. The ones from Coney Island. When he was a waiter. When he stood up for that girl, for her reputation. Then, as if a light was flickering, she seemed confused.

Ma, what is it? What's wrong?

She was fumbling in her purse and finally found what she was looking for, a wadded-up piece of Kleenex. She blew her nose, rather violently. It's just, she said, twisting the Kleenex with both hands, That I've always been so proud.

Proud of what?

That I did such a good job. No one ever knew.

Knew what?

What I just told you.

Sometimes when she got confused like this, she would go back on herself, deny something I needed to know, something she might have let leak out: that she had stopped taking her diuretic, that she had misplaced her VISA card again, that she was still accepting car rides from Frieda Katz, her ninety-seven year old neighbor, and then I had to be stealthy, to try to get the truth out of her. The important thing was not to challenge her. It would only get her hackles up.

You did do a good job, I said.

Really? she asked.

And now I felt a tiny bit guilty. She had taught me well: a boy never lies to his mother.

She smiled, took my hand and kissed my fingertips. Always such a sweetie, she said. He would have been so proud of you.

Carefully, cautiously, don't make a big deal of it, just ask the question matter-of-factly. Who?

Your father.

Oh, I knew behind the bluster and the—

Not him, she said dismissively. I mean your real father.

What could she possibly be talking about? Dementia, Alzheimer's? But this wasn't so simple: her memory was slipping and sliding away these last few years, but she didn't make stories up out of thin air; that wasn't her style. I struggled to remain calm. Oh him, I managed to say.

She nodded like a schoolteacher, praising a student. Most people didn't know, she said matter-of-factly, but he was a very nice-looking man. The scars, of course, he couldn't help. And after all, they were only skin deep.

Then she took off again. Scars: they seemed to be triggering something. And they weren't that bad, once you got used to them, I said.

Exactly, she replied.

I took a deep breath, started to speak, then decided to remain silent. Mom had a story, a new one. But it was precisely at this point that she decided enough was enough and shut down, doing what she was famous for doing whenever she found a conversation unpleasant: change the topic. Now she wanted to talk about the Bar Mitzvah of my grandson, Adam, and whether I had been dating or was it still too soon, even though it had been almost two years now since my wife, Gloria, had died.

Now she wanted to go to dinner and all I could get out of her was that in her opinion, I should stick with the steak medium rare, although some preferred the chicken tenders, and so without any real appetite, I ordered. You made a good choice, she assured me. A good choice, and then she asked me an interesting question. Do you remember when we saw The Wizard of Oz?

I shook my head. Why do you ask?

Oh, just curious, she replied. Just curious.

18 / PEARL

When the conversation was leading to dangerous ground, I knew how to dodge the bullet. Oh, what tricks I had up my sleeve.

That reminds me of a story.

What a beautiful watch!

Have we met before?

Been meaning to tell you.

And when all else failed, I'd steer the conversation to food. Did-you-know questions.

Did you know in China they eat bird's nests?

Did you know ripe cranberries bounce like rubber balls?

Did you know the first recipe for soup is 5,000 years old and is made from rhinoceros and crows?

Did you know chocolate used to be used as money?

Did you know Koreans eat fish sperm?

(Not always to be used in mixed company)

By sticking Did you know in front of an interesting fact, you're not really asking the person you're talking to for an answer of yes or no—you don't really give a shit—you're just trying to shake them up a little, grab their attention, divert them.

Danger may be lurking, at least for me it was. Because of

what I had to hide. Not that I was sneaky or a liar, no, just that I was good at changing the subject.

For instance, once after Gabe just left for college, I was sitting across the table from Howard at dinner and we were eating pizza from Urbino's—we often ordered one on Sunday night—pepperoni and mushroom and garlic—and I was thinking of Ketzel and wondering if we had ever had pizza together and Howard asked, What you thinking about? You look so far away, and he had nailed me, cause I was thinking of Ketzel and I said, Oh, nothing, but I got worried he'd know I was putting him off, so I asked, Did you know pizza was invented in Coney Island? He looked at me, like he still might be kind of suspicious, but then he fell for it, because we were eating pizza, it makes sense that I might be thinking of how it came to be invented. A perfect example of changing the subject, a subject of which I was a master.

Sometimes, though, after I'd change the subject, I'd be sorry. What if, for instance when Howard asked me what I was thinking of, I told him the truth, or what if the truth came tumbling out on its own? What if I said, oh, I was just thinking of Ketzel, he's the guy I was with before you. He's the guy who's Gabe's real father. He's the guy who made me feel alive. Alive and excited like I never felt before. Or will ever feel again.

19 / GABE

When I was a kid, Pearl would seize words right out of the air and magically transform them into expressions on her face. Mirror, mirror on the wall, who's the fairest of them all? I'd ask and suddenly my mother, Pearl Freeman became an Evil Queen, then Snow White, a cockamamie prince, and a dwarf, not just one, but all seven: Sneezy, Doc, Grumpy, Happy Sleepy, Bashful—one after another, faster than I could pronounce their names, she would mimic them, saving my favorite, Dopey, for last, milking her audience, and me, in the process, so excited, I once peed in my pants. How she could gesture, hunching her back, throwing back her shoulders, framing her face with her hands, making language come alive.

The lines she had at her disposal; how she could dispatch them: I'm tickled to death; You can't judge a book by its cover; The sunny side of the street. Cliches, perhaps, but when she delivered them, they might have been spoken for the first time, as if they explained the world, how it worked, what life boiled down to. Often, they were lyrics from the songs she sang in vaudeville: Toot toot tootsie, goodbye…When the red red robin comes bob bob bobbing along….Blue skies shining at me. As I grew older, they would echo back, and mom would suddenly appear beside me, like last month, when I sought deliverance with my esteemed dermatologist, Dr. Donald Dover. As I sat in his chair, I imagined her, patting my hand, calming me down, whispering, A watched pot never boils.

Dover was her kind of guy: dark and charming, sunny, glib, full of bon mots, and looking in his starched white, suspiciously tailored-looking doctor's coat, the spitting image of a Hollywood heartthrob. When he first stepped into the room with a stunning Eurasian assistant trailing behind, he was oh so consoling as he wielded his laser gun. It will feel like mosquito bites but be over within a couple of minutes, and then we all donned plastic sunglasses.

I shut my eyes, then a tingling sensation and my skepticism melted, all doubt disappeared, as I became a true believer, swept up by a fervor brought on by the tiny needles shot into my face. I imagined crazed monks flagellating themselves and understood the promise of redemption: that pain ultimately vanishes and then the chance to be the man you were meant to be.

Not so quick. It would take a month or so for the full effects of the procedure to reveal themselves, and there would be some scabbing, a word not particularly endearing, but even now, just a month later, gazing at myself in my rental car's rear view mirror, the scabs seemed to be fading.

Then a wave of melancholy. If only the laser had been invented when I was the gawkiest of adolescents. How different it might have been, for as a teenager I was certain that every girl who looked my way was blinded by my complexion. If they smiled, it was out of pity; if they spoke, it was due to embarrassment at having been caught staring; if they befriended me, it was out of compassion. While there had been a few girls whose faces were as blighted as my own, and I could have, perhaps, attached myself to one of them, but I wasn't attracted to them. And if that wasn't bad enough, everyone would have known what I was up to; even if they possessed other attractive qualities: wit, intelligence, passion, everyone would realize that the only reason I was dating them was that no one else would have me. Misery loves company, Pearl would have put it.

But my life wasn't exactly miserable. Depressing, maybe. Miserable? Not by a long shot. Still, Pearl's pronouncement about my real father had taken some of the wind out of my sails. It wasn't even wind or a breeze, more the ground rumbling, the tiniest little hike in the Richter Scale, a sense of disquiet.

20 / PEARL

After we bid our fond adieus, I waited for the elevator doors close. Then back to #402, be it ever so humble, where it dawns on me, for the first time, you see, we have these little shelves next to our front doors, for nick-nacks and tchotchkes. And I have a little ballerina that used to sit on the buffet at home and a Chinese vase Gabe sent me from when they went to the Orient but what hits me is this. If for some reason you should forget your apartment number then all you have to do is find your shelf and you're home and home free. They must have done this on purpose.

Now, inside. Safe inside. Looking at the pictures in front of the icebox. Gabe in front of a birthday cake. But who's that smiling? What's her name? His wife. Gloria. Of course, Gloria. Gone now. Look at Gabie, his Bar Mitzvah picture. If you squinted, the scars, the scars were still there. And now they were gone. And he looked better, nicer. Maybe this would be good for his self-confidence, he would get out more now. He was still young. Could have his pick of women, Just like that. They'd all be after him. Now he was on his way to the airport.

Suddenly, I wanted the box, the box on the top shelf of the hall closet. The perfectly ordinary shoe box that would be the last place anyone would look for anything. Down the hall, in the bedroom, in the closet. Just reach for it, but then I feel a little light-headed, a little dizzy, tell myself don't worry, it will go away. It's nothing. Really nothing. And here it is, the old shoe box, Florsheims, size 9 and a half, the number printed on the side.

Who'd think to look in a shoe box? It was all safe there. Just like my good jewelry in the Cheerios box on the top shelf of the kitchen cabinet

Inside: my shoe box, no diamonds or rubies, but very previous stuff. Birthday cards pale and fading, a white yarmulke, a little colored paper doll, flattened, one of the grandchildren had made who knows when, my letters from Howard, held together by a red rubber band. There was more too, precious objects, believe you me. This was the box, everything held together in Howard's Florsheim box, size 9 and a half. And then, there it was, way below, hidden sort of, the blue silk scarf wrapped around, where was it, here, the brush, the sterling silver brush, all tarnished now. Such a shame.

It was time, it was probably time, some things you shouldn't put off, and it was time the brush went down the chute, the garbage chute, down at the end of the hall, you just open it up and everything goes down to the basement and you don't even have to think of it anymore. It's all done for you. No more shlepping the can out on Tuesday morning. They take care of everything here.

It wouldn't be nice to leave the brush for after, when Gabe had to go through everything, to decide who gets what. It might attract attention. If it wasn't for the initials, he'd never be the wiser, but what would he think, a brush with the letters A and C on them? A, you're adorable, B you are beautiful, C, you're a cutie full of charms. D, you're a darling and E, you're exciting and F, you're a…feather in my arms.

Holding the brush now like a microphone. Singing into it. A and C. No one would ever know. So what's the harm to hang onto it? For old time's sake. Who could it hurt? They'd think it belonged to some uncle, some cousin, had been passed down, and then they'd never give it a glance again. It would be forgotten.

What if, just what if I told Gabe? Never. Never in a million years. It would destroy him. The way he goes on about things, he'd never stop thinking about it, never stop wondering about it, never live it down. But, funny, now that the cat's out of the bag, sort of, a little, I would, oh, so love to tell the whole story to somebody, anybody at all. Not just to tell the story, but to hear myself tell, and hear what they would say. It is, after all, quite a story, you got to admit.

21/ PEARL

The years go by, I hear nothing, nothing at all, then the phone call: "Be on the corner State and Wabash. With the kid. Tomorrow at noon. Mr. Brown wants to see you." Brown was one of the names Ketzel used when he didn't want to draw attention to himself.

It had been raining cats and dogs when his car pulled up beside us, but what's a little rain, and Gabe didn't seem to mind. He was a kid and kids loved puddles, always had, ever since he was a little pisher and, every puddle was an invitation, a chance to splash, play, kick, to hear the sound of water. But when he saw the car, the LaSalle, his expression was anything but playful, and when it pulled in beside us, he looked in, even as the passenger window was being rolled down, and for a second everything---rain, water, puddles--everything stopped.

Then from inside the car, I saw Ketzel's face, a shadow of his former self, a pale gray shadow; haggard, weary, all used up; his eyes sunk and dark, no sparkle, no twinkle; his lips twitching, but then that smile, that million dollar smile and I was beside myself and knew there was no pretending I hadn't recognized him, seen him, known him, fucked him, had his child, the boy whose hand I held, the boy whose hand clutched mine, more tightly now, and it was the boy he was looking at, staring at; he knew, oh yes, he knew that he belonged to him, they belonged to each other, even though it had been years since they last saw each other.

66

"How ya doin', buddy?" he asked him, then he turned to me. "How's Tricks, Pearlie?"

I answer "Okay," just like that, just as plain as the nose on your face, I answer okay, and then I asked, "How about you?"

He seemed to consider the question. "Can't complain," he said. Then we were both silent. Finally, he asked, "Want a lift?"

I stood there frozen. Couldn't talk.

"Want a lift?" he repeated, like it was still a question, a request, all up to me. That's what did it. That's what did it the first time, too, he never demanded, but always asked, nice and polite, always left it up to me.

So I shrugged and told the boy, we're going for a ride, and the door opened and he climbed right in, so innocent and trusting. "We're going for a ride."

"Want to go to the movin' pictures?" Ketzel asked. Still, I can't talk. Finally I just nod my head. "Hey kid," he said, looking down at the boy, "You like the movies?"

But Gabe seemed scared now. I could see it in his eyes: Who is this strange man, the man in the big car, the man who keeps staring, the man who suddenly sticks his hand in his coat pocket and shows him a thick wad of money and peels off one bill, then another and another and asks him, "You like popcorn, kid?"

Gabe nodded.

"Tell me," Ketzel said.

"I like it," Gabe said.

"Buttered or plain?"

"Buttered."

And that made Ketzel laugh, a hearty laugh, a laugh to tear your heart out, and he pressed the money in Gabe's hand.

And then we were all at the movies and he handed the usher a twenty and the usher looked up at him and suddenly recognized him---it goes with the territory, he had once told me---and it was like the old days when everyone knew who he was and everybody looked at me differently because I was with him.

Then there was a drum roll, the beating of a drum: The March of Time, and Hitler was marching around with his arm up in the air---Sieg heil! sieg heil!--- and a cartoon, a Popeye cartoon. He was new then. First time Gabey ever saw him. I yam what I yam cause I yam what I yam.

The movie bowled me over---that song, the rainbow song and suddenly a tornado and everything in color and this crazy land called Oz! On one side of me, my son, on the other this man, this man who changed my life, this man I could never return to. I didn't know what to expect and wondered if Ketzel would be up to his old tricks, coming onto me. He liked to play around, and just after Dorothy landed at Oz and there's color everywhere and the little munchkins are all singing and dancing, Ketzel makes his move. Casual-like at first, his hand just brushes over my thigh, then pressing down harder, spreading his fingers, grabbing ahold of me, grabbing as much of me as possible. It hurt a little, but how could I want him to stop? I could feel myself losing it, getting wet, can you believe it? Glanced over at Gabe, but his eyes were glued to the screen.

I turned my face to the moving picture. Ketzel's hand doesn't move an inch. He just presses harder, eases up, presses harder, eases up. He's waiting for me. I try to talk myself out of encouraging him. But I can't, or I don't want to. I take my raincoat---it's draped across the back of the seat—and, nonchalantly, placed it over my lap. Then, with my left hand, moved it over to Ketzel's.

I look over at Gabey---he doesn't suspect a thing---then at Ketzel. He's got a smirk on his face. Then, before I could talk myself out it, I strike, put my hand on his crotch, press down on his cock, feel it growing hard in my hand. I want to milk him, that's what we used to call it in the old days, and I do, too. Nothing like it, in all the world, to have this man, the most powerful man, to have him in the palm of my hand.

I knew I'd have to put the brakes on---he could get noisy when he was feeling his oats---and after a couple minutes, I did, but he seemed to understand. I took my hand away and as I did, brought it to my mouth---I really couldn't help myself--- took a deep breath, and he got a kick out of that.

At the end of the movie, when Dorothy and the Scarecrow and Lion and Tin Man

discover the Wizard's a fake, Gabe broke down crying and Ketzel reached in his pocket for a handkerchief, one of the ones with his initials, AC, monogrammed in the corner, and he said, "Here kid," and Gabe took it and wiped off his tears, then didn't know what to do with it, so I took it from him and don't know why, I put it in my pocketbook. Later, in the LaSalle, on the way home, I was crying softly, softly to myself. I would never see him again. I knew I couldn't trust myself to be with him. Ever again. I took the handkerchief out of my purse and dabbed my eyes with it. "What's wrong, mommy?" Gabe asks, "Did the movie scare you?"

"Nothing, sweetie, nothing. It just made me sad."

"But it was happy at the end. She got to go home."

"Hush, shainehla, it is nothing."

Back home, I made him promise not to tell Daddy. "Why," he asked? "Why?" And I said it wasn't important. And I took the money from him. Let's count it up, I said, and there were three hundred and twenty dollars. And he said, "This is a lot of money. Do I have to give it back?"

"No," I said, no. "It's yours to keep. But I'll put it in the bank for you. And it will be our secret. I'll take you to the bank, show you where they'll keep it. It'll be our secret, just you and me."

And then, he really couldn't help himself, he had to ask, "Who was that man, Mommy?"

And I said, "An old friend."

What's his name?

"Mr. Brown, dear," I said, "Mr. Brown."

22 / GABE

When I was a kid, back in the '50's, sneaking around in the basement closet one day, I discovered a carton full of magazines: black and white pictures of naked women. It wasn't just that they were naked—after a while one's pretty much the same as the other   but what they were up to. Cavalier Publishing didn't play the nudist colony card. The rump card, Lordly called it. Didn't dabble in healthy Danish couples romping au natural, tossing a volleyball back and forth. No, Cavalier went more for the story steeped in suggestion: a naked secretary in front of a typewriter; a nurse taking a blood pressure, three blond buxom types playing golf.

Frankly, the women disturbed me. I knew they were supposed to be turning me on. But they didn't. It was the weirdness of them that got to me. Later, when I was a teenager, it all changed and I would return to the carton and hunt for my favorites. It always struck me as odd that this was my father's job.

A week after he died, and Pearl was out, getting her hair done, I went down to the basement, dragged out the carton. She had been going through his things, filling cartons for charity. What would become of these magazines? Somehow I didn't think they'd land up at Hadassah.

But I didn't exactly want to have this discussion with her. So I went through them, quickly, and, oh, how easy it was to decide which ones to take. Five months later, I graduated Kenyon, married Gloria, then Rachel was born, abandoning my thesis, giving Coleridge the old heave-ho, then me deciding to give up teaching and taking the reins of Cavalier. Twenty years. Then, Gloria's diagnosis of breast cancer and she died two years later.

So I sold Cavalier, decided to reinvent myself and moved to Cambridge, revisited, so to speak, my thesis, found myself supremely bored by it all, tried a novel. No dice. Felt in the deepest of ruts, the dreariest of doldrums, took a couple of classes, one in jazz, the other in the Transcendentalists, but realized I wasn't going anywhere.

Maybe that was why I was so excited now, at Starbucks, trying to put together the events of the last few hours and Pearl's startling revelation.

For years my life had been so tepid. Nothing happening. Now, a couple hours after Pearl slipped me the news about Dad, after ordering a double tall decaf non-fat latte It was all I could do to find a package of Splenda for out of the blue, the heady realization that anything can happen: the past can suddenly, dramatically, sweepingly be rewritten, and off I go, floating in space. Then I fell, and, oh, so dismal my descent, as I felt sympathy, for, of all people, the real victim in this: the man whom I had always assumed to be my father, my biological father, Howard M. Freeman. He had done his best, and there were some rather tender memories of him buried here and there, but it wasn't his fault; there were compelling reasons for his constitution, his pathos, his tendency to the lackluster. Why should he be hoisted over the railing, thrown overboard, just because someone else had beaten him to the punch? One itsy-bitsy sperm, swimming downstream in a tablespoon of come. How could it compete with years of paying the mortgage, watching Little League, college tuition.

But even to consider such a thing. Preposterous! Suddenly, I felt ashamed for falling for Pearl's folly. It was senility, that's what it was. Senility, dementia, it didn't matter what you called it, but, ultimately, it was out of the question. Oh, for a comforting sip of latte, but it was too hot and also, tasted suspiciously creamy. Had they forgotten to make it non-fat? I looked at the cup. No one had written N for non-fat which only heightened my suspicion. Should I return to the counter, risk losing my seat, inquire of the barista just whether, perhaps, a mistake had made? No, it wasn't worth it. If it was 100% whole, then it was meant to be, and my cholesterol would just have to suffer the consequences.

What would this mystery man have done in such a situation? After all, he was some big-shot businessman, not just a pasty-faced paper pusher, but a man of action who, in such a situation, might jump up to his feet, demand an explanation, not take no for an answer. And then I thought of my father, the man whom I had always presumed was my father; what would he do? My cholesterol was too important to be left to chance. I would go to the back of the line so I didn't appear to be cutting in, and wait for all the others ordering their mocha espressos and chocolate hazelnut soy-cappuccinos and finally, finally arriving at the head of the line, rather than simply stating, I ordered non-fat; this is regular, instead say, Excuse me, I believe there may be a mistake with my coffee.

And really, was it such a big deal in the long and short of it, so monstrous a deed that I should knock Howard off his paternal pedestal? Compared with the Columbine Massacre or the Holocaust or Justice Melita's swing vote striking down the climate change bill, this was definitely the smallest of potatoes. Scalia turning America into some Rome. He was the true monster. How Dad would have hated him.

Howard was a solid guy, a bit of a nebbish, but a good man, decent as the day was long, never voted Republican, read the Saturday Review of Literature every week, claimed Pearl's brisket (which could, upon occasion, simmer in the oven for four, even five hours if she was in a forgetful mood) was the best he ever tasted, treasurer of the United Jewish Fund Appeal, tended a Victory Garden the envy of his neighbors, and don't forget the yearly contribution to the United Negro College Fund.

Why dump on Howard? Howard who would never kill a fly unless Pearl had run handed him the swatter; Howard who was such a proud father, that when I received the draft lottery number, eleven, in 1968 burst into a rage and was inconsolable for days. No, no I won't give that murderer my boy! he had shouted to Nixon's image on Walter Cronkite, and now, his boy was marching off into another man's embrace, a phantom's clutches. I sipped my latte and felt a little better. No need for guilt; Howard would never know. And since he had changed the spelling of their name back in 1938, wouldn't he, somehow, understand this ultimate quest for identity. After all, look at Friedman, hardly an uncommon name, hardly unpronounceable, yet he had taken the I, blithely tossed it away, substituted an e, in effect raking the coals of the fried man, freeing him in the process. Dred Scott, eat your heart out. Yes, there was something Underground Railroad-ish about the transformation —all aboard, Mr. Freeman, all aboard!

I sipped the last of my latte, removed the lid and discretely, with my index finger, scoped up the remaining froth and licked it. It was whole milk, not non-fat. It didn't matter. If anyone thought I was being impolite, they could just screw themselves. Then a girl, probably high school, took a last swig of her coffee, but left her cup on the counter across from me and walked to the front door. I glared at her. Why couldn't she walk five feet and throw it in the recycling wastebasket? I thought of saying, oh, miss, you forgot your coffee, and shaming her into doing the right thing, but didn't want to make a scene.

23 / PEARL

Trazodone. 50 milligrams. Every night before bed. No need to worry about turning into some kind of addict, just have to watch myself when I get up to pee—it can make you dizzy. Take it with a glass of water. Well, you're supposed to, but that was a problem for me because taking fluids at night can make you need to pee more. So, this is what I do, though I don't tell Dr. Goulder because I don't, necessarily, think he'd approve. I put the Trazodone in my mouth and crunch it up and then take, not one glass, but half a glass, just half, of warm water.

I have this theory that the warm water dissolves the Trazodone and gets it working quicker in the part of the brain which makes you sleepy and you don't need to drink as much fluid and, voila, don't end up having to pee as much!

After I'm done crunching up the Trazodone, I turn off the lights and make my way to bed. You have to be careful when you're taking Trazodone because it can make you dizzy and dizzy is the enemy. It can lead to broken hips and half of all the elderly (a word I, frankly, dislike) who break their hips end up in a box or an urn within a month. Oy.

Other things, too, you got to watch out for with Trazodone— nausea, vomiting, and diarrhea, drowsiness, dizziness and blurred vision. The list goes on, but I won't bore you.

Luckily none of that stuff happens to me and if it did, well then you don't always get something for nothing. And a good night's sleep is nothing to be sneezed at, that's for sure.

24 / GABE

Later that night, after visiting my Pearl, after standing up to the asshole at Starbucks, I found myself in front of yet another mirror. I had gotten up to take a piss and when I caught my reflection, I couldn't help but turn to the right, then the left, remembering what Pearl had said, then so dramatically denied, or at least, taken back, and now there was no point returning to my Truman biography. Who could read after such news, even if the chapter I was in the middle of, chronicled August 6th, the day before Hiroshima? I was a child then, living in the most woeful of ignorance, not merely about who was going to be blown to atomic smithereens in the morning, but who was my biological father.

The worst part of Pearl's bombshell was not simply the news itself, but that the truth might never be known; that more than likely, she'd wiggle and play-act her way out of it—No, I never said such a thing. Don't put words in my mouth.

My father had always been and was still Howard Freeman, that benign five- foot seven lump of dough, the daddy who never went through a single yellow light, who read the entire Haggadah at Passover, never omitting a single paragraph, the schlep who wore both suspenders and a belt, who never went to bed without pajamas, Howard Freeman whose only scar was from a burst appendix; Howard Freeman, who never screamed and cried only twice, once when his mother died, and again during the final scene of The Diary of Ann Frank. Howard Freeman was my father, not some scar-faced waiter.

I sat on the bed, turned on the television and surfed through the channels, but they all mocked me. The Tammy Faye Baker look-alike on the Shopping Channel was hawking make-up which she was applying to some poor grandmother. Makeup to cover her complexion! The Food Channel with a sushi chef pirouetting in the air, brandishing a lethal-looking knife. President Shrub hunting a moose.

I always had thought it odd that I resembled not a whit, pop or Pearl, and was ashamed that my acne ravaged my otherwise non-descript features, but Gloria, pooh-poohed this, convincing me, sort of, that none of it really mattered, that what was important was that my face had character and that I should count his blessings, that I had escaped the Oscar Milquetoast countenance that ran in the family. It was Gloria, in fact, back in 1962, on our first trip to Europe, after I had declared my love for the glory of the Tuscan countryside, who suggested that I looked Italian.

Then it hit me and left me reeling, all those stories, memories and vignettes. Mom used to call me bambino; she loved Italian food, particularly veal scaloppini; opera was often playing in the house, and when La Dolce Vita came out, she saw it three times. Could it be that my real father was some stranger, some Italian thug to boot, the boot itself, from the map I innocently colored in, in fourth grade when it seemed I would never be able to spell Mediterranean on the geography test?

If only I had a sibling who might know something I didn't. If only I hadn't been an only child. An only child who then went on to have an only child—my daughter, Rachel, who would then go on to have an only child of her own, my grandson, Adam. Was there, in fact, something a little strange about our whole family, all the ones, only ones.

Suddenly, the whole Italian house of cards came crashing down: the Pinocchio balloon in my own little Macy's Parade floating off to the Isle of Lost Boys, the spumoni turning to vanilla, the Puccini back to Gershwin, the cappuccino dissolving into Sanka. This simply could not be but was some mere figment of dementia. Too much television, too high cholesterol, maybe she wasn't getting out enough. She had even stopped her weekly canasta with the girls and just last month had turned over balancing the checkbook to me. This was some fantasy, that was it, and in ten minutes I was in cyberspace reading about Alzheimer's.

Dementia symptoms may include asking the same questions repeatedly; becoming lost in familiar places; being unable to follow directions; getting disoriented about time, people, and places; and neglecting personal safety, hygiene, and nutrition.

But no, not so easy. She still was a spiffy dresser. Her hygiene, as far as I knew, and, truthfully, I didn't want to go any further, seemed good and her appetite was fine. She was getting places earlier, but that was classic. There were nine different warnings here and in only two did Pearl seem suspect. Still, this could be the beginning. And all the comforting talk about the promise of research wasn't exactly so reassuring. They had to feed you this crap. These websites were probably funded by the drug companies. Then I sighed, remembering there, was, indeed, hope in sight: Level 2. She could go to Level 2. For six years, Level 1 had been just perfect, but now it seemed like it might be time to up the ante, ratchet up the care level, just to make sure.

The next morning, I paused by the front door to Kensington, the widest of front doors, large enough to accommodate wheelchairs, stretchers, coffins, they thought of everything and I ruminated—I am among other things, a prodigious ruminator —why the building looked so bland; why it evoked in me the same feeling as a CVS. I stepped inside and felt calmer. Maybe it was the Muzak, which was low in volume, some blend of easy-listening soft classical. No, it was a movie theme, a just short of peppy ditty, with the faintest bit of life squeezed out of it: Raindrops Keep Falling On My Head.

Flipping through a copy of ARP Journal, waiting for the social worker, I kept reminding myself, Level 2, Level 2, Level 2, and then the door opened and fortunately the social worker was extremely understanding, empathetic as the day is long, with an unfortunate tendency to nod.

So good of you to see me so quickly, Ms. Chu, I said, taking her hand.

Please, call me Marcia, she replied.

And Marcia, who seemed fond of a perfume reeking of carnations and who had a framed picture of what appeared to be an elderly golden retriever on her desk, made it all seem just as easy as pie. She had already checked with the team. None of this had been a figment of my imagination. Pearl had seemed more confused lately.

Then questions, so many questions. How was she with her medication? When I visited, did she always recognize me? She asked, oh, so non-judgmentally, how often I visited. I explained I had wanted Pearl to move to Boston, to an assisted living there, so we could be closer, but that she hadn't wanted to leave Chicago.

Then the little speech about the levels. One: where she was living now, in an independent apartment with kitchen, but breakfast and dinner provided in the dining hall. Pause. Two: a small studio apartment, no kitchen, all meals provided, round the clock nursing service, medications given and charted, more supervision. Pause. Three: a traditional nursing home, double room, with constant care, and provision for any sort of medical intervention. In other words, last stop, end of the line.

And finally, to complicate it even further, these decisions were sometimes delicate ones and Pearl fell in the middle of the range of Level 1. The staff certainly felt very comfortable maintaining her there. She swung into full social worker mode. Is there anything, specifically, that is troubling you? she asked with a little too much eye contact. I thought it over, then decided what the hell. Last night, I visited her and she told me my father is not my father.

She looked perplexed. You mean?

I mean that, well, this is a little embarrassing—

She paused, a trace of a smile, the most understanding of smiles, a little curl at the lips.

That the man who I had always thought was my father, her husband for fifty-two years, was, I don't quite know, not my real—

Biological.

Biological father.

Did she tell you who your biological father was?

No, eventually, she took it all back.

Did anything else seem particularly unusual about her that day?

I shrugged. I had just got in. I hadn't seen her in a couple of months. No, she was pretty with it. At dinner, I showed her a picture of my grandson, her great-grandson, Adam and she was her old adoring self.

And then Marcia Chu, LISCW sprang into action. Often times residents at Kensington experienced all kinds of confusion, she explained. While this seemed a bit, well, unusual, it was nothing, necessarily to be alarmed about, and there was no reason, necessarily, to take it as fact. Then she introduced the topic of fantasies and how we all have them and now she was sounding rather patronizing. I, of course, had spent decades off and on the couch, and was quite conversant with the idea, but there was something charming about her, her aw-shucks enthusiasm and fifteen minutes later, as we stood up, having agreed not to do anything yet, but to monitor the situation, I felt relieved.

And as I waited for the elevator to see my mother, I decided to share none of this news with her, but still was uncertain; something was gnawing within, then the automated voice: Fourth floor, signaling the door was about to open, carrying me up to her embrace, perhaps, to more stories, more details, none of which I, particularly, wanted to hear. Fuck it all. It had merely been confusion, some fantasy, a slip, but then again, perhaps it could just possibly be true.

But never again, during the visit, did Pearl go off as she had that first night. Never was she so out of character. Finally, two days later, at the elevator, after trips to Target for new towels and socks, an appointment with her podiatrist, a visit with her oldest friend, Shirley, and an early bird dinner at the Top, it was time to leave.

In the hallway, she turned to me and said, I'll walk you to the car.

No Ma, it's easier this way.

C'mon.

I shook my head. Why was it so easy at times like now, to just come out and say it? Our dialogue was well-rehearsed, she delivered her lines, me my own, like a play or a poem, a scene you had heard over and over again, one you knew by heart; simple words, none wasted; life distilled, parsed down to its essence; simple words, ripe with implication.

Don't leave me yet.

No Mom, it's easier this way.

C'mon, please, don't know when I'll see you, again, don't want to give you up.

I'll be back soon. A month or soon. I promise. I realized

she was thinking that this could be it, the last time, our final memory of each other. What if, just what if she was right? Then I never would have a chance to know the story, the real story of this man she was claiming to be my father. It all seemed unfair, to be so dependent on her whims, on some figment of an Alzheimer's imagination. I felt a frisson of that Starbucks anger and I wanted to shake her up, to demand she tell me the truth. Instead, I wimped out—I just didn't have it in me to threaten my mother at such a moment, just as we were saying goodbye.

I took the smaller victory: denying her the chance to walk me to the car. I won. I always won, at least when we said goodbye and as I set down my suitcase, she stood there in front of me in the hallway and put her hands to her eyes. Boo-hoo, she cried, playfully—at times like this she could be surprisingly melodramatic, silly, antic, over-the-top, but as I opened my arms, silently, she stepped into them, as if she had no choice, that this was her role. As we hugged, I was surprised how frail she had become, how light, and then kissing her on each cheek, how soft; how soft and now as she returned my embrace, how fresh her kisses; she made little noises now, puckering, smacking, cooing noises, as if she were on stage and wanted the audience in the back of the theater to know what was going on, and it was a little embarrassing, but what could I do, and who cared anymore, really, this was my mother, a little zany and off-the-wall, but sad too, and oh so human, doing her best, delivering her lines, maintaining the dialogue, bestowing her love, not yet ready for the curtain to fall.

25 / ADAM

Ever since they separated, dad picks me up on Wednesdays and Sundays, but something was up this Sunday. Mom and him wanted to have a conference with me. Whenever they say conference I know it's going to be a big deal. They wanted to talk about my Bar Mitzvah. It's time to hire the DJ they tell me and I say I don't want a DJ or a party and they try to talk me into it. And then I cry. I try not to. But can't help it.

That night, after I get back, Grandpa calls, probably because I cried. So what's happening in school? he asks. This is what Grandma told me is called going in the back door. You have something on your mind but don't want to bring it up right away

Not much.

There must be something, he says.

Well, there's this report for history.

What's it on?

Vikings.

I always liked Vikings, he says. That's one of the things about Grandpa. He comes right out and tells you what he thinks, even if it's a little weird. Did you know we published a book about them, long time ago.

Maybe I could use it for a source. We have to have three.

It's not what most teachers would accept as historical, he says. Though it is based on fact. Then he pauses and adds, Sort of.

Maybe I could take it out of the library?

I don't think it's in the library. But it's upstairs in the bookshelf. I'll show it to you next time you visit.

But my paper's due on Friday.

Hang on, I'll get it.

A couple minutes go by, then Grandpa shows up on Facetime holding this book I Sailed With the Vikings. There's this woman on the cover, she's in front of a Viking ship, the kind with oars on the side surrounded by all these Viking guys who look like super-heroes, but they have beards and wear funny kinds of horn hats. Cool, I said.

Grandpa was getting excited. This was a very, very popular book, he said. We sold over sixty thousand of them.

Did they make it into a movie?

No, he said and then he smiled and asked, Want to hear me read a few pages?

Sure, Last time Grandpa read to me was when I was a kid.

Let me see, he said, going through the book, then, No, this isn't so good, then, finally, he settled on a chapter. Chapter Three, Grandpa began, his voice like an announcer at a football game. Ransomed at Sea.

Thorgerd awoke in a small, dark chamber, her hands and feet tautly bound by rope. She struggled to break free, but the knots held tight. Then she remembered the raid on her village. Seized and blindfolded. Marched to the beach. The roar of the waves. A wet cloth pressed to her nostrils and the scent of kelp, of myrtle, of mustard, and finally sleep, the deepest of sleep. Deep sleep, dreamless sleep, darkest of slumber. Now, awakening, she grew nervous. Quickly, she surmised she was aboard a boat. In the distant she could hear a chorus of men chanting, Hogva, hogva, hogva, and after each word, the sound of oars plunging into water.

Grandpa sounded so funny shouting Hogva, hogva, hogva,

that I couldn't help it, I cracked up laughing and that got him going—Grandpa loved joking around—we both shouted, Hogva, hogva, hogva, together. I couldn't stop laughing.

26 / PEARL

Oh, so many memories, the ones that don't go away, not all the way away, still here, buzzing round like bees. Occurs to me, what if, what if after the brush goes down the chute, then the memories go too? Sometimes you touch it, you hold onto it, and then, even if it's been years, what's inside your brain defrosts, like a frozen lamb chop out of the freezer, and the memories thaw back. In you all the time, but you never really knew it and suddenly they disappear again, maybe this time forever. Like the elephants in Africa. To that mysterious place they go to, off to die, all by their lonesome. This brush, better to keep them here in my box, my Florsheims shoe box, size 9 and a half, and then I'll be sure, I'll be sure. To remember.

27 / GABE

When she goes let it be at night, warm and cozy in her
bed. She used to always worry, God forbid I break my
hip! or If I lose my memory, you'll do something, right? The
implication, I could put her out of her misery like we did with
our dog, Shmow. A week after my visit, she did fall. Not a bad
break, the nurse told me over the phone, But her arm. We can
all be grateful it wasn't worse.

They moved her to a room in the Special Care Unit and she
was not happy. They should have left me alone and this would
never have happened, she said. Because I know how to fall. The
first thing they teach you on the line, because you're going to
fall—it happens to everybody—and when you fall, you got to
know how to pick yourself up.

But Mom, they were only doing their job.

Nope, it's all their fault.

There was little point in trying to reason with her.

And when you pick yourself up, you got to smile, to look
out at the audience and flash 'm a smile. Like it never happened.
Y'know, the show must go on and most of the time, they won't
really notice or remember, as long as you keep on kicking. By
the way, how much more do we have to pay for this room?

Don't worry. There's plenty of money. It was true. Howard
had left her enough, more than enough, though she still couldn't

help herself to packages of sugar and sweetener when I took her out to eat. And when I sold Cavalier and retired, so to speak, there was even more in the kitty, if she should ever need it.

She looked around the room. This ain't exactly the Ritz.

I laughed. Oh, how easily this was going, I never thought it would be so simple, if and when it came to this. And it had, and she was being so good, so accepting.

I need my slippers, she said, the flannel ones. It gets cold down here.

Sure, Mom.

They're at the back of the bedroom closet.

I'll pick them up for you. How you feeling, Ma?

The pills help.

She looked exhausted; her face caved in, her color pale and gray. Maybe you should take a nap.

She shook her head. Why? I'm not going anywhere.

Later, up in her apartment, it seemed too quiet. The television was off and it seemed eerie and unsettling. Best to find the slippers, visit a little more, then leave for the night. Opening the closet doors, all of her clothes, staring me in the face, such bright colors, all lined up, no, it wouldn't do to get sentimental now, so I bent down, felt my lower back ache, and there, there they were, her pink flannel slippers. I put them on her bed and turned toward the closet. There, on the top shelf, the shoebox, the shoebox she had shown me years before. After I've gone, make sure not to throw this away.

I reached up and took it, then carried it to the counter in the kitchen, carefully setting it down, as if it were a museum artifact. There, on the side, Florsheim, 9 ½. Under the lid: papers, curling black and white snapshots, an empty package of Lucky Strike cigarettes, a yarmulke, a manila envelope with letters and papers in it, from a child, her great-grandson, my grandson, Adam.

I sat down and read the first one. Dear GreatGrandma, it began. Sweet, the GreatGrandma: how he compressed it into one word.

How did you know I wanted the Lego Hans Solo Star Wars Missile Launcher? It has these really neat launch pads I love. It's so cool. And so are you! Love, your GREATGRANDSON Adam.

It's so cool. And so are you! What possessed Adam, who was only eight or nine at the time, to call his great-grandmother cool. Did he mean it? Or was it mere flattery? And to make special reference to the launch pods. You could see he was trying to keep the letter going. Maybe he would turn out to be a novelist. No, kids didn't want to write novels anymore. They wanted to create Apps or start-ups.

I looked back in the Florsheims box. A locket of hair. My own! Pearl had shown it to me when Adam had been born. From my first haircut. Reddish-brown, still shiny, tied with a strand of blue ribbon. My hair. After I've gone, make sure to keep this, she told me. Pearl, not known for her sentimentality.

What else? One of dad's old business cards, before he retired, HOWARD FREEMAN, PRESIDENT, CAVALIER PUBLICATIONS INTERNATIONAL. His watch, the Bulova, looked like it was from the fifties, before he got the Omega. And some more letters, a child's book report, and then a brush, looked sterling silver, with the initials A.C. and badly tarnished, where had it come from? I touched its bristles. When had she last drawn it through her hair? Why was it here?

28 / PEARL

I had been taking a little nap when Gabe shows up —a regular Lone Ranger—and when he vamooses all I want is to go back to sleep another knock at the door, a knock with real heft behind it, and authority, then, you wouldn't believe it, it was the rabbi, Rabbi Saunders, who didn't even bother for me to say Come in, but just barged right in like he owned the place and moved a chair next to my bed. To tell you the truth, I felt a little trapped. Wasn't exactly in the mood to talk to the rabbi. Never really considered myself a religious woman and only attended high holiday services for Gabe, to give him an example. At least Shapiro, who was the rabbi before Saunders was easier to take. Forty years of hundreds, thousands of people seated in front of him, expecting sermons, advice, condolences, mazel tovs; so doted on his every word, some of whom actually asked him for reprints of his latest sermon—this was before computers—had taught him something, about how to put on a good show.

Sanders, on the other hand, didn't even look like a rabbi. As he marched in all full of himself, like some Grade B actor, short and spry in a navy crew sweater, Ralph Lauren, for Christ's sake, and khakis, like he was on his way to play golf. Two years ago, the last time I had been able to sit through high holiday services, he had delivered a sermon all full of mushagosh—the Dali Llama, the NRA, quality time, self-esteem, the death of his beloved father-in-law, Sol, and the equally shattering demise of his adored Schnauzer, Chutzpah, as well as quotations from Casey Stengel, Henry James and Arthur Miller (at least he was Jewish).

Hello, my friend, says Sanders, placing his hand over mine, all haymish, wearing some silly ring with Hebrew letters, like the pope or something.

It was creepy, but I had to say something. Hello Rabbi, I began, then I sighed. He was silent for a moment, finally he nods and sighs, really a rather splendid sigh, more full-bodied than mine. Didn't know exactly what to say and felt a little as if I were with that therapist, the one Gabe had made me see after Howard died, when they claimed I had been masking a depression, masking, that was the word they used like it was Halloween or something, and they were worried about, what did they call it, mania. Mania shmania. I knew even if they didn't and I certainly wasn't about to tell anybody, I was only feeling relieved, and to be truthful, free, not quite like I was a kid again, but free in a way I hadn't since we had been married. If the shrink had been a little more of a schmoozer, had made it a little more inviting, I might've talked to him, but it had been so damn unpleasant, waiting around, all those damn silences, and then, finally, the shmendrick would look up and start to speak and there would be hope, but only for a second before he'd ask So how are you feeling today? or What's on your mind?

Finally, Rabbi decided to speak. Hello Pearl, he says, not exactly inspirational words, but at least a start.

How are things at the temple? I ask.

We call it a synagogue now. Back to the old traditions, Sanders smiled. Things are better. We have a capital improvements plan that we're gearing up for and attendance at Shabbat services is up almost six per cent over last year.

That's...wonderful.

But tell me, Pearl how are things...with you?

I looked around. This ain't exactly Miami Beach.

Sanders laughed, a little louder than I thought my remark warranted. How wonderful humor is, he began. How wonderful you are.

I'm not feeling exactly wonderful.

Of course not, but here you are, making a joke. You know, I have a theory about humor and the Jewish people—

Then I knew I was really in for it. I rested my head back onto my pillow. This could be five minutes or more and would only necessitate nodding or mumbling interesting, or, perhaps you don't say, every so often.

And people wonder why the Jews are such a humorous people, why us more so than gentiles, And if you reach back further, to Buddhists, Hindus and Confucius, then it seems even more remarkable, that in the whole world—

Why does it always come to this? Not just smarter, more liberal, more philanthropic, more educated (grandpa started in rags, ended up a manufacturer of children's pajamas and grand-daughter Hillary is a dentist!)

That because of our faith, we are certain of our moral position, our authority, if you will, even as we're jumping off Masada or marching to Auschwitz, we have our faith! And because we're so sure, we can afford to let down our vigilance, unlike others more ambivalent, who need more towing in line, and that allows us to take a collective breath, look around and even in the darkest of times feel the freedom to make light of a situation, see what others cannot, the humor in it, for, after all what is humor, anyway, but the ability to put distance, yes, distance between ourselves and—

He was off and running and I was feeling exhausted but nothing would stop him: Last spring, I went with my son, Jonah, to Nepal, a chance to get away just the two of us, for a little bonding. We did some trekking, nothing heroic, mind you, we're not quite ready for Everest yet, ha-ha, but what most impressed me, just as much as the scenery, the grandeur of the Himalayas, was what we learned from the sherpas who guided us along the way. There was one remarkable man, Lanzu, so gentle, so wise, who taught me something that I'll never forget—

I closed my eyes and pretended to be drifting off, smiling at Rabbi Sanders who finally shut the hell up and paused and took my hand in his own, but then he kept on going but speaking slower; The sun was setting, and he pointed out a mountain in the distance and said——

I was conscious of the words, something about mountains and keeping your eyes on the horizon but was unable to make any sense. No rhyme or reason. Ketzel, Ketzel again, his hand, how different than the Rabbi's; Ketzel's, when he took mine and how it felt to press his hand back. It was in the car, in the back seat. The glass was up so the chauffeur couldn't hear and he said, Hungry, Pearly? and I nodded and then he talked into the little funnel, and the car flew off, just because I accepted. Ketzel didn't have to worry about things like speeding tickets like mere mortals and then we were at his place in Cicero, there were black iron gates and men everywhere and in the kitchen, he said, I can cook us spaghetti, or I have a chef, he'll make us anything, anything you want, and no one had ever said that to me before and I tried to think of what I really wanted, some spaghetti would be nice, something to maybe settle my stomach, but I wasn't hungry and so why should he go to all the trouble but it would be impolite not to eat, so I did what I had been finding myself doing with him, just saying what I really was thinking. That was the thing with Ketzel and me, we could talk without all the bullshit, so I told him the truth, I'm not really hungry.

But ya just did your act.

I shook my head. He opened a refrigerator, the biggest I

ever seen: all kinds of cheeses and packages, meat and chicken, it could have been a butcher's shop, and a shelf full of tomatoes and oranges and pineapples. He closed the door, stepped up to me, took my hand. You're different, he said.

Different than what? I knew what he meant but wanted to hear him say it out loud.

You know, he said, almost in a whisper, And I just ain't just giving you a line, baby, I mean it. He moved closer and I could feel his body pushing into mine, I could feel his hard-on, and he kissed me on the lips and there was a scent of his cologne. The bay rum. I could feel the stubble from his whiskers, rough, bristly, I didn't care. I opened my mouth. Then I asked for a drink. Thought it would help. And he laughed, he knew, he always knew, and as he took out the bottle, I looked up, I had never felt as excited in my life. I knew what was going to happen and it never had happened before, but it wasn't going to stop me.

Everybody thinks they know everything, and I was just like that, thought I'd get married first, settle down, but now I knew that was just bullshit. This was what was real, what was happening: me telling myself it's going to be okay, and if Ketzel had been any more, well, forceful, like everybody claimed he was, then I would've been scared, probably never have come here in the first place, but I knew that now I had come this far, there was no turning back. So, he poured us some Scotch. To your health, kid, he said, and I touched my glass to his and it made like a little sound, a ringing sound. I took just a sip. ever drunk scotch before. Then we knew what would happen next, we knew.

Then I sort of came to and, bingo, it's seventy years later and right in front of my very eyes, Rabbi Saunders going on about who knows what and for a second I thought he was Ketzel and I smiled at him and he kept on talking.

29 / RACHEL

Hadn't seen Grandma for so long, felt bad about it, though my shrink labeled it inappropriate guilt. It was perfect timing when the deposition came up in Chicago. Chance to see Grandma and Dad, too. He had been sounding a little weird, lately.

It wasn't till we actually met, though, when I sat down across from him at dinner at the hotel, that I realized just how different he looked. At first, I had thought he had just lost weight or something, but, no, it was his face. Dad, I said. I can't believe it. You had Botox!

He smiled. Then, all of a sudden he was shy. What do you mean?

Your face, your... scars? They're gone! You're not wearing make-up, are you?

That got another smile out of him. He shook his head. Oh, that. I had a laser treatment, the latest thing. And then he told me the whole story. I felt shaken. Underneath it all, all these years, he was handsome. And I had never thought of him as handsome before.

The other thing, that he would do this. I never had thought of him as vain. Is there some woman? I asked. Who's put you up to this?

He shook his head, Mr. Shy Guy, then changed the subject. Asked about how the separation with Brian was going, how Adam was doing, and then, in the middle of it all, the strangest question: Did Grandma ever mention someone with the initials A.C.?

I didn't know what he could be talking about, but try as I might, he wouldn't give any details. Finally, he said, just some initials I saw, on an old document from a bank, wondered if they made any sense to you. He was lying. I could tell. I haven't been a lawyer for twenty years for nothing. And to be looking at his handsome face and know he was lying to me, to know something was up, it really was upsetting as if he wasn't himself. But someone else.

30 / GABE

Finally, back at home in Cambridge, going through notes, folders and index cards, flashes in the pan scribbled at two o'clock in the morning, random thoughts jotted down when I still went to work, articles from the Times and the New York Review of Books, notes written to myself, inspiration from out of the blue—Rumi, Emerson, William James—looking for some connect-the-dot image, one spelling out a thesis, a main idea, where to go.

A book. A grand book to make my life cogent. A thread: boredom and how it plays upon man, especially in post-computer VCR, DVD, iPodsized society. English teachers, with the best of intentions, none-the-less conspiring to bring down the student in a cesspool full of Hester Prynns and Ethan Fromms, endless themes and blather contributing to the decline and fall of the theater, literature, the imagination, and then it hit me just as I was reading a quote from Albert Camus and my eyes caught the initials and I remembered the brush. AC. One name I hadn't quite imagined: Al Capone.

Capone my father? What could be more preposterous? Ridiculous, absurd, this whole confabulation of Pearl's, for that matter. Crazy, demented, senile—it didn't matter what you called it—right this very moment plaque was attacking the cells of her brain, shriveling them all Alzheimer-up and in their place, where there used to be quadrillions of synapses flashing through gray galaxies of matter, now, nothing: the blackest of holes, the vastest of wastelands. But then I remembered her story. And Al Capone had a scar. His nickname, for Christ sakes, was Scarface and that's what Pearl said about this mystery man, that he had a scar running down his cheek.

It was probably that everything was all mixed up in her head now: movies and reality, confusing one with the other, like Reagan those last years at the White House imagining he had been at Auschwitz, when he had only seen films of concentration camps and besides, there was no way of ever knowing the truth. Imagine strapping Pearl down and hooking her up to a lie detector, or truth serum or hypnosis.: twisting her arm a bit, nothing that would hurt, just enough to catch her attention, but none of it would work, and besides, she probably actually believed the story by now.

Making Peace, the book my shrink had given me: that was what must be done; Make peace with the story. In fact, call it just that, a story. I repeated the words over and over and over, as the book had suggested: a story, a story, a story, a story and then added made-up, made-up, made-up, made-up and just for good measure, a maraschino cherry on top: Alzheimer's, Alzheimers, Alzheimers.

It worked, if only for a moment, no bliss, but a diluted measure of peace, and then I found myself running for the phone book, the phone book! The old one from 1930 that Pearl had hung onto and snatched it up, returned to my desk, thumbed to C. It had never dawned on me just how many people had the initials A.C. Anthony Cabot, Austin Cable, Alexander Chadwick: names Henry James might have pulled out of his hat, and plainer American names: Alan Caldwell, Albert Crockett, Mike Cunningham.

Then the odd names, the ones that somehow just couldn't be—too foreign or funny or weird— Chronopoulous and Cash,

Chalk and Casanova; Cherry, Champion, Comfort and Cypher; Crudder & Crutch. Take Courage! Take a Chance! Take some Candy while you're at it. Then a name that particularly charmed me: Ducky Carlisle.

Then Cohens, nothing but Cohens, marching down the pages, not even counting Kohns or Cohns, six hundred of them. And at the very end, at the back of the track, a slew of names singularly unpronounceable: Czyzyk, Caproky, Czajkinsi, Chennomordik and Czajkowski. Then, back again in the middle of the C's, jumping head-first into a sea of C's, and, suddenly, one name jumps out: Arthur Colosimo.

Colosimo: a name I had grown up with, perhaps the first Italian name I had ever known. Colosimo's: the nightclub where destiny struck, where one February night, the 21-year-old postal worker and part-time college student, Howard Freeman had been the guest of his beneficent uncle, Lordly Max; where Pearl caught Howard's eye. Maybe my biological father was Colosimo. But no, his name was Jim, Big Jim, and he had been shot years before the fateful meeting. In fact, it was Al Capone or one of his hench-man who was supposed to have shot him.

Then it hits me: right in the kishkes: those initials, AC, the ones on the brush—they really did belong to Capone. A sucker-punch to the guts, leaving me dizzy, nauseous, reeling, then, the most perfunctory of denial: No, no, nothing could be further from the truth. But the scar. The scarface. So crazy, how could I come up with such a notion, one which made such sense, such perfect sense.

I had to get away, to escape from all this so I drove to Harvard Square. If only Gloria was still alive, she could be in this with me, we could figure it out together. I got out of the car and stumbled like a drunk, afraid someone might spot me, take me for crazy. My reflection in a store window was frightening. I had turned into Dr. Jekyll.

Where to go? Starbucks could be full of cellphones. But what I yearned for now, more than anything else, was quiet. Crimson Books, up on the corner, that was a possibility: a novel, some poetry: escape, consolation, the world that I had constructed for myself, that no one could take away. But once inside, I realized something terrible had happened. The bookstore was different: up in the front, by the cashier, up where there should have been new books hot off the press, were postcards, calendars, audio books, stationery and pen sets, and worst of all, stuffed Harry Potter dolls: so much merchandise, but no books at all. And while I had been around the block, and followed all the disasters befalling the publishing industry, with independents beaching themselves like whales, somehow this struck me in a way it hadn't before. The world was going to hell, even in this bookstore, and there was nothing to be done about it anymore, and, somehow, I felt a terrible complicity. People just wanted to have a good time. Diversion was the name of the game. That's entertainment. They didn't read anymore, but collected DVD libraries, joined book clubs to talk about what they were reading, couldn't even trust themselves to make up their own mind, and then I thought of Al Capone, who, despite it all, seemed just like the rest of them: all those dot com entrepreneurs, megamedia tycoons, pornographic web-wizards; spinning fortune out of pleasure, offering John Q. Public what, when all was said and done, they really wanted: a good time, a good drink, a good lay. And what was so wrong with that? But what about the rest: the killings and the bombs, the beatings and the maiming, the threats and the fear? Yes, this man could well be my father. I couldn't escape the fact, even at a bookstore.

Then, as I turned a corner, all those dark Orwellian clouds lifted and the pitchy dark gloom vanished, as in the children's section I paused, standing in front of a display of books. CLASSICS FOR ALL TIME, it read, somewhat redundantly, but, hey, no need to be the party-pooper when surrounded by hope, no need to play Killjoy with Charlotte in her web, the Little Engine That Could chugging down the track—I think I can I think I can, Ferdinand sniffing the cork tree and Mike Mulligan throwing his steam shovel into third gear. These books, the very ones I read as a child, yes, all right, the very ones I had been read to as a child, been read to by my father, adopted, biological—I really didn't care anymore what I called Howard—whoever it was had read them, for Christ's sake, that was what mattered and these stories stuck, and that I had dreamed of learning to read them myself, vowed to do it, and I had, I had at the age of four, I could still remember that first book, and here it was now, and I picked it up and read those first words: Good night moon, and I couldn't help myself, tears welled up in my eyes, and then The Story of Ping! I turned to the first sentence: Once upon a time there was a beautiful young duck named Ping. Was there ever a more extraordinary first sentence in the English language? Ping lived with his mother and his father and two sisters and three brothers and eleven aunts and seven uncles and forty-two cousins.

I was seven years old again and studying the picture on the first page: ten white ducks and a small yellow one walking down a gangplank from a boat moored on the Yangtze River, walking to the mainland. So many questions. Would the little yellow one turn white when it grew up? And why eleven aunts and only seven uncles? Did some uncles die or get made into Peking Duck? Were some aunts like Aunt Vicky? They never got married.

I wanted to buy a book for my grandson, Adam, and I started to browse, but then decided not to bother. The last time I had visited, alone one day in Adam's room, Adam off at a tennis lesson, I had taken down a book I had given him, The Swiss Family Robinson, one of my favorites, and it had never been read, I could tell about these things, and I knew not to ask Adam about it or, worse, to suggest he give it a try: children his age hated being told what they'd like to read, so I simply re-shelved it and sighed and turned to the boy's computer. Now if it had been a particularly hot video game.

No, no use to go back there. It was enough to see these books, to know they were still being printed, and now I didn't feel as morose as I had before, and so I walked outside and, indeed, it was a beautiful day: the sun was shining, a teenage boy was kicking a soccer ball down the sidewalk and for some reason that seemed to me the most beguiling act in the world and I was swept up, buoyant—this must be what it's like and then, I really couldn't help myself, the word cloud nine popped into my head and I wondered where it originated from and remembered the cloud chart I had taped to the wall of my bedroom when I was little; the pictures of the clouds, their evocative names: Cirrus, Altocummulus and Stratus, Neocummulus and Cumulonimbus, my favorite, low and puffy, cottony, happy, a scrappy guy.

Then, I found myself in, of all places, the CRIME section. Yes, there was a sign. Yes, it read CRIME. No coincidence, I told myself. This, all of this, was meant to be! The books were arranged in alphabetical order and C, the letter C was calling out to me. Maybe, just maybe, there'd be a book here, a book that might explain things and then, I spotted it, grabbed for it and stared, dumbstruck, at the cover for right before my very own face was... my very own face.

Not exactly—Capone was heavier; he wasn't going to the gym three times a week, swimming, cycling and pressing free weights—but the resemblance was unmistakable. I had seen the picture before, it did have a certain familiarity, but it wasn't iconic like the image of all those others: Hitler, Stalin, Charles Manson, and perhaps for this reason, the resemblance seemed less preposterous, more a feeling like, yes, this guy looks like me, we share some of the same characteristics, he could be my father. Father. To even entertain such a notion; to consider it; to whisper it, just too mind-boggling. I tried to consider the situation calmly; studying the shot, Capone looking not exactly Hollywood handsome, nothing to write home about, or for Pearl to bring home to mother: balding, a hefty neck, a certain unjolly jowliness, not that bad- looking a guy, all things considered, and in the shot where he was looking straight at the camera, a certain flat impassive charm. No snarling, fuck-you arrogance for C28169, his mug shot number hand-printed in white ink in the corner, across the shoulder of his pin-striped suit); no disheveled, unkempt Saddam Hussein being poked for lice; just a guy, a regular guy glaring at the camera, keeping it together, doing what he is told. But what was he thinking in that simmering nefarious Caponean brain of his? God only knew. To be humiliated and finger-printed and stuck in a cell; what vengeance was he plotting?

A far more flattering photo was the one on the back cover, a close-up, almost like a Hollywood studio shot, the kind you'd send out to the members of a fan club: Capone wearing a pale fedora and a double-breasted jacket, white shirt, stripped tie—nice knot, perfect dimple—and while he wasn't exactly smiling, he managed, given his reputation, a benign look, placid in its way, impassive, even pleasant. To tell the truth, he looked a little ordinary, like he could have been anyone, any Tom, Dick or Harry, but gazing closer, there was a certain something: a heaviness, those dark eyes, the solidity to the face. And surprise, you couldn't really see the scars, not in the picture, anyway, and since they couldn't digitalize them away back then, they couldn't have been all that noticeable. Still, it had to be hard for him, carrying around that nickname; it could help to explain why he had a certain axe to grind—people can be so cruel—and then I caught on to the biggest surprise of them all and despite the recoil from this shock, despite the knowledge that my world was turning upside down, despite the fear that I knew not where I was headed, right there before my very eyes, were my own eyes, my most very own: dark, deep, intense, and the manner in which they were gazing out at the world carried a certain familiarity, as if here we were, father and son, son and father; here we finally were, together at last, and finally, after all this time, finally now we might begin to piece together a relationship. No trips to the ballgame or rides in the car; no ice cream cones, but still, unfinished business and the chance, at last, for my world to make sense again. I put the book down and clutched my chest, wanting to feel my heart beat, realizing all that held the two of us together: brain, genes, nature, nurture, like-father-like-son, the apple doesn't fall far from the tree; it was all there, all there, and desperate to make sense of it, even as I realized that sense could never really be mine anymore, I took one step then another, frantically trying to escape just whom I had become.

31 / Pearl

So I'm lying there, cause I have to wait till it's time for my pain pills and a nurse comes in. Hello, Mrs. Then she looks at her clipboard to get my name. Mrs. Freeman. How are we doing today?

We are doing fine, just fine, I say even though my arm is killing me.

Could you do me a favor? she asks, all smiley.

My pleasure, I say.

Could you rate your pain on a 1-10 scale for me, one being no pain at all, 10 being intense pain. Then she holds up a chart with 10 happy faces on it, at least the first one is smiling, that's cause it's for VERY MILD PAIN. Nothing to call home about. But, get this, each face gets worse. 2-DISCOMFORTING, 3-TOLERABLE, and it goes downhill fast, ending up with 8 UTTERABLY HORRIBLE, 9 EXCRUCIATING and finally 10 UNIMAGINABLE or UNSPEAKABLE, the happy faces slowly dissolving into blank faces, then their smiles flattening out, turning into frowns, and finally they're crying, tears running down their cheeks.

The pictures were silly, like something a kid would draw and, suddenly, I was sick of it all. I hurt. A lot. They should just give me an OxyContin and then I wouldn't hurt. How should I know if something is discomforting or tolerable? Why should I care? But the nurse is waiting there, looking a little impatient, like she has better things to do than wait for me to decide whether I'm my pain is merely discomforting or unspeakable. But the more I think about it, the harder it gets. What's the difference between excruciating and unspeakable, for God's sake? And doesn't unspeakable mean you can't speak about it? So why should I even try?

This was all so annoying. Probably best to just give her a number and shut her up.

But then I get a little curious. Under 10, it says THROAT CANCER, MASHED HAND and I realize they're giving examples of when 10 would fit the bill and I feel a little guilty because my pain could never be compared to something terrible like that. So I say, Five, maybe a six. Then I worry cause what if that's not high enough for me to get another OxyContin. And that that shuts her up. She writes it down and I repeat the number to myself, to remember it for next time. Six.

32 / GABE

Outside the bookstore, the god-damnest thing: I feel lifted up, up into the air, besotted by the clouds, by the warmth of the breeze, by buckets full of yellow tulips, daffodils and pussy willow in front of the florist, in the display window at the bakery, crusty loaves of fresh bread stacked up in the window. Why not? I walked in and asked What kind of bread is that? pointing to a loaf, a small humble one, resembling a football, its crust sprinkled with seeds, dusted with flour.

The clerk, a young woman in her early twenties with lustrous blond hair the color of applesauce, and a charming gold hoop in her nose, answered, It's a multi-grain peasant bread. Actually, it just came out of the oven.

Multi-grain peasant. What could be better? I'll take it.

Sliced? she asked.

Oh no, I answered. To deliver it up to a stainless-steel machine, whining and whirring as it dispatched the loaf into even uniform slices, mutilating the precious bread in the process, would have been sacrilege. I longed to take the loaf in my hands, to hold it, caress it, feel its warmth, and then and only then to tear a wedge from it, a heel, my favorite part, and devour it, right there on the spot.

Okey-dokey, the apple-saucy hoop-nosed girl replied and she placed the bread in a brown paper bag. I paid $3.99—what would Pearl say—thanked her, deposited a dollar bill in the jar labeled TIPS and walked out of the bakery.

There on the sidewalk, I felt barely able to contain myself—it was all I could do not to rip off a crust— never had I so wanted to break bread as much as this moment and I looked through the window, caught a glance of the girl and she smiled at me. Dare I? Go back in? Buy another loaf? Maybe, this time rye? Schmooze her up a little. Ask her if she'd like to get a coffee after work? The customer is always right.

I walked down the block and crossed the street to a little park and wondered why the world was so intoxicating, this world and all its glories: bread, boys kicking soccer balls, daffodils, the clouds, girls with applesauce hair.

Could it be that my recent discovery, of my possible paternity, far from hurling me into the blackest of holes, instead, was revealing something miraculous to me: that there was more to me than met the eye, that there were currents, strata, spiraling DNA, forces and knowledge I had no inkling of and that finally it had become time to understand them, not damn them or dam them, nor cast them aside or shirk them off. Finally, at last I had hit bottom, rock bottom; finally I had discovered who I came from.

I arrived at the park, and really, it was a lovely little spot: a few oak trees, a bench, a square of cement, and thou, oh multigrain peasant. Off by one of the trees, a middle-aged man walking an elderly beagle. How touching. They appeared, as dogs and owners sometimes do, as if they belonged together and then I noticed chalk marks on the pavement and considered them: faded yellow and blue and red lines, remnants of rectangles, even a number—it looked like three—poking out and then it hit me: this was from some kind of game, a child's game, like hopscotch and as I eased myself down on the bench, I felt warmth toward the children, whoever they were, tenderness toward the world; children still playing hop-scotch, girls selling bread and men walking beagles. I broke off the heel of my bread and took a bite of it and at that moment, as if on cue, the sun peeked out from a cloud. There were no more secrets and there was bread to be had, fresh bread to be had, and finally, I realized who I really was. Not just a creature of my demographics: college graduate, widower, retired and Democrat, a little bored. Now it was as if I had finally been given permission to leave all these labels behind me and to be brand spanking new and full of bliss.

I brushed the crumbs off of my jacket, started humming, What the world needs now is love, pure love, that's the only thing that there's just too little of, wished I was dancing with Diane Warwick, the way she was in the pre-Psychic Hotline days, back in the Sixties, and, indeed, I felt as I did when, back in the 60's, I spent the weekends in Vermont, at Harvey's commune, the one where the children were named Sequoia and Zephyr and love was abundant—as was the mescaline— and I crossed the street, pausing in front of a mom and pop toy store and thought of my grandson, Adam. Maybe I'd get him a present.

Of course he was in the doldrums of adolescence now and he would never be seen in a store like this. Toys were embarrassing, old stuffed bears, Legos, checkers: dusty relics all. Still, I strode in—I couldn't help himself—and walked up one aisle, down another

So many toys evoking so much sentiment, just like at the bookstore, so many memories: my first Slinky looping down the stairs, puppets and how Howdy Doody, though I never admitted it, always freaked me out; and then the dolls, Barbie in her latest e-incarnation; action figures, GI Joes from their mission in the Iraq and, yes, GI Nell's just behind. And then, there it was right next to the rubber tipped bows and arrows and water pistols: a gun, definitely not of the squirt variety.

Or even the more realistic cowboy revolver set in its Wild West holster. No, this gun looked real, it was most definitely a revolver, like a cop would have, or some secret agent. Metal with a black handle, all the better to shoot you with, my dear, and for a second I felt flabbergasted, it was one thing for a child to be eaten by a wolf, or chased by a tiger or Bambi's mother keeling over: those images seemed unfortunate, of course, and scary, but somehow okay, part of the big picture, some grand opera spinning Grimm-like as it had forever, but this gun was a different story.

Sure, kids played with guns before, but that had been before Columbine, before all these horrific fantasy computer games of exploding dismembered bodies. This wasn't cowboys and Indians. Come to think of it, how could you even justify shooting an Indian these days? This was different. This was wrong. I picked the gun up. Unfortunately, it was set into a large piece of cardboard packaging and sealed with a heavy plastic cover, and I couldn't get the feel of it.

Which was disappointing. I wanted to feel it, gauge the heft of it, and the weight. I wanted to see just how it fit in my hand; how the handle would settle in my palm; whether it seemed natural, like it belonged there. And that was that: I had to have the gun, and surprise, it was only $4.69, a bargain! I took it to the cashier, paid in cash, that was pleasant in itself, no need for VISA to have any incriminating records of such a transaction. Paid in cash, a greasy five-dollar bill with a portrait of Lincoln on it, Lincoln who had met up on the wrong end of a revolver, and in a moment I was outside, out in the light of the day, and I took the package out of its bag and start to open it and all of a sudden it hit me, what it would look like, how ridiculous to inform that lovely old lady in the yellow baseball hat shlepping the grocery bag, It's only a toy, only a toy.

So I placed it back in the bag and thirty minutes later,

safe at home, in the front hall by Lorely's punch bowl, I took it out. Reach mister, reach for the stars! Funny, how carefully they enclosed it, in thick plastic packaging, the kind you need scissors to cut through. But I didn't need a pair of scissors. I tried to bite through the cellophane, tried to tear through it with my teeth, but still it resisted me so I got some scissors and went at the package, carefully, it wouldn't do to stab myself while unwrapping a gun, imagine explaining that to the resident at the emergency room—You see, it was a gun, but only a toy. Then those little twisters holding it securely in place, finally, unpacked, untwisted, it lay there. I snatched it up.

It was cold, cold to the touch, and curiously, there was something satisfying about that. It wasn't plastic, but metal, so much more authentic, the genuine article. I picked up the gun with my left hand, then lay it in my right, surprised at how easily it fit in my palm, how naturally my index finger reached for the trigger and right at the knuckle curled around, making a little u, and now I gripped the gun tighter, extended my arm straight out in front of me, and, how thoughtful, there at the tip of the revolver, was a metal tab, a pointer or aimer whatever they called it, a little helper, how convenient, and I jerked my arm up so the gun was pointing at the ceiling.

With the greatest of stealth I stalked. All around the room. As if I was hunting: for a prowler, an intruder, an assassin; someone in the house, someone capable of committing the most heinous of crimes, the most monstrous of harm; someone who now, thanks to this revolver, would have another thing or two coming, someone who would get what they deserved because I would find them and make sure they would never prowl again.

Never had I felt so alive. Nothing, nothing, nothing, I told myself could be taken for granted, and as I walked, I was quiet, tiptoeing, no need to give any warning. I pointed the gun at the closed door of the bedroom closet, then under the bed. Calmly,

I walked into the bathroom. Maybe behind the shower curtains he was hiding.

But no, not a sign. Then back into the kitchen, maybe he was in the pantry, after all, the door was shut. Come on out I ordered, my voice, given the circumstances, remarkably calm, I've got you cornered. Silence. All right. I'll give you to three. Still nothing. And so I counted. I had no other choice. One, and I paused, then Two, another pause and finally, Three. And then for no reason at all, I wasn't thinking what I'd say next, but the words leapt out, on their own, laced with a cold sober tone I did not recognize, and a sarcasm I knew all too well, irony too, and no matter if they were a cliché, out of some Edgar G. Robinson movie, who cared? You asked for it, I growled and fired once right in the center of the door, and then again and again and again, and the gun worked, beautifully, just as I knew it would, and it was all so easy: no need to think about it. Just ready, aim fire.

For a moment, caught up in the act, I felt giddy, passionate, alive, then, the slightest bit ludicrous. I placed the gun on the kitchen table, opened the refrigerator and drank from the Tropicana carton, shut the door and glanced around the kitchen: at the coffeemaker, the microwave, the dishwasher, all the bourgeoisie appliances propping up my most conventional of lives. I glared at them and they seemed to scowl back, mocking me: the coffeemaker with its nozzle that could steam latte, the microwave with its sensors that could determine when a potato was perfectly baked, the dishwasher and its smart button that could decide when a dish was clean; they now seemed somehow sinister, as if for all these years they had been standing in the way of me and all that was real. And it wasn't just the appliances, it was the whole kitchen: my panini maker and Waring blender, the French omelet no-stick pan and the Bose FM radio in the corner. The wine, the cases of 1994 Bordeaux I had so happily stocked for the years ahead, and the counters, the polished gray granite counters. Now the only gray granite I could imagine was rough, gray slabs, cut into stone, gray gravestones. My name and the date of my birth and my death. And what would follow? Beloved Son, Father, Husband, all true, yet all clichés, why not just add, Whatever, and yet how once I had wanted to be more: Poet, Writer. So it hadn't exactly worked out that way, so my name chiseled in granite wouldn't exactly stop the anonymous stroller in the graveyard; it wouldn't ring bells. Just another name.

My life was vapid, a sham. Should I purchase orange marmalade or try something a little adventurous, say the McGriven's Grapefruit-Lemon Blend. Was $4.99 a jar too expensive? Should I gift more to Rachel next year? If interest rates held, the estate could handle it, or should it go to Adam's college fund? Maybe go back to Anguilla in February or try Costa Rica or Belize. Supposed to have great snorkeling. More off the beaten track. And no memories there of Gloria.

In college, I would have scoffed at the Caribbean and dreamed of going to Nepal or Sikkim; I would have wondered if I had the patience to teach in Samoa for two years in the Peace Corps or whether I should head to New York City to write the great American novel. I would spend hours speculating if I could be satisfied with just one woman because there were just so many, ripe for the plucking, because back then I had a beard which covered up my acne scars, lending me a rather dashing air. And I didn't have to be careful and ask so many questions before I even got their tee-shirt off. You'd meet one at party and take a walk, five minutes later find yourself talking about Vietnam and what'd you think of Zen and the Art of Motorcycle Maintenance and if you both loved it, or, maybe, if you both didn't, maybe you'd share a joint and ten minutes later you'd be getting it on and you didn't have to talk about Are you safe?

She'd probably be on the pill, but if she wasn't, no matter, you'd have a rubber in your wallet, and it was all so easy. And now it wasn't. And women had so much baggage and so did I, f or that matter.

Then I entered the study and there was the iMac. I had put it to sleep per chance to dream, but now, impetuously, I touched a key, and there was his picture, Al Capone, standing in shirtsleeves with a wide tie and a big grin, an impetuous grin, his arms outstretched, embracing the world, inviting a hug, a bruising hug, no mere pitty-pat on the back, but a manly hug, a crushing hug, a hug you had no choice but to submit to, a hug from which you could never break away.

33 / ADAM

Mrs. Flannery is my favorite teacher. She makes boring stuff interesting, plus she's not serious all the time even though what she teaches us is sometimes serious like the Doomsday Clock. I wrote a 3-page research paper on it and she gave me an A+, one of only two A+'s in the room and the other one was Linda Batgen and she gets an A+ on everything and smells.

The Doomsday Clock is not a real clock but sort of a pretend one invented by scientists in 1947 when they thought us and Russia were close to a nuclear war which would be the end of life. As we know it. Humanity would become extinct.

So they set the clock at three minutes of midnight to show just how close we were to extinction and things got worse and worse and in 1953, it moved up to two minutes of midnight. Midnight meant pretty basically the end of the world. Then it got better when the Soviet Union ended in 1991 when it went back to 17 minutes of midnight. Everyone was happy until Global Warming and now this year the minute hand is up to three minutes of midnight. This is really, really bad because if it gets to midnight then it's what they call a global event which probably means the end of the world. As we know it.

I really liked the title for my report, Tick-Tick-Tick. Mrs. Flannery must've too. She drew a sad face next to it.

34 / GABE

Sitting at the kitchen table, reading the New York Times, the whole house of cards comes tumbling down: it was the article I had read on A-6, an article about Supreme Court declaring another environmental bill unconstitutional. Another 5-4 decision, spearheaded by Chief Justice Molita. The world was going to hell.

I glanced at my toy gun, laying on the kitchen table, by the pepper grinder, and then something I had noticed when unwrapping it, but had not thought about since, struck my eye: the orange plastic cap, maybe half an inch long, sticking out of the muzzle. It looked like the cap from a tube of toothpaste and now, once I considered it, it was annoying. It didn't look like a real weapon anymore. Why should they put a stupid orange cap on the muzzle, anyway? I remembered an article somewhere, cops shooting children, children who they thought might be pointing a gun at them and the gun being a toy and some law. Minutes later, thanks to Google, I had my answer: a Federal Law, Title 15, Chapter 76, Section 5001, no less, stipulating: each toy, look-alike, or imitation firearm shall have as an integral part, permanently affixed, a blaze orange plug inserted in the barrel of such toy, look-alike, or imitation firearm. Such plug shall be recessed no more than 6 millimeters from the muzzle end of the barrel of such firearm.

Given the state of the world, the law was, no doubt, a sound

117

one, probably saved lots of innocent children in the projects from being blown to smithereens by cops. Why, then, was it so annoying? Picking up the gun, aiming it at the microwave, slowly pressing the trigger, once, twice, and once again, for good measure, I considered the question. The orange plug did its job, only too well. It destroyed any credibility the gun had, like a man dressed in a pin-stripe suit but wearing a clown's nose. It rendered the gun ludicrous, a joke. I gripped the revolver in my left hand and tried with all my might to pull the plug out of the barrel. No dice. It wouldn't budge. I got a screwdriver, a small one, and attempted to wedge it between the plastic and the nickel plate. Nothing. I took a pair of scissors—I knew this could be dangerous—I might really hurt myself but didn't care—and carefully maneuvered the tip of the blade in at a strategic angle, but when I applied pressure, it slipped and caused an ugly white scratch to appear on the plastic, a reminder of my ineptitude. Then, once again, the orange plastic plug, mocking me like a bully in a playground, teasing me for what a complete and utter fool I was: what a pretender, what a wimp, what a wuss.

That grand sensation of invulnerability had vanished and there seemed no hope of recovering it, not as long as Title 15, Chapter 76, Section 5001, was a law of the land, and then I remembered when I had been Googling, there had been a web site—it hadn't seemed to the point, I had only glanced at it—but there was hope, now there was hope and I rushed to the computer, scrolled down History to, there it was, REPROUCTION GUNS, clicked return, and, indeed, in just twenty-six hundredths of a second there were 170,000 sites to choose from! The largest of gun bazaars imaginable—real ones——but if it had just been them, simply a long banquet table of Uzis, Tommy Guns, Colt 45s, Magnum and M16s, of revolvers and machine guns and Berettas, it would have been one thing, and even pretty interesting. It was the people selling these guns who were so threatening. Weird names of sinister companies; horrible verbiage, hideous promises. Sickening, revolting: the whole lot of them. But what was my recourse? The last time I had ever touched a gun, other than this orange-plugged imposter, was back at Pine Crest Ranch when Uncle Al deposited a Daisy bee-bee gun in my hands and truthfully, I had been rather a wash-out, never hitting the bullseye, not even once. Since then, until today, nothing. What could you expect from a member of the ACLU, a devotee of Swami Mathayatha Rush, and can't forget, a member of the Jewish faith. After all, Jews had no particular longing for guns. Leopold and Loeb, maybe, and then there was Jack Ruby, and of course the Rosenbergs, they might have had one stashed away in the closet. And, yes, that rabbi in Buffalo who murdered his wife, but he had hired some hitman to do it for him. No real surprise: back in the shtetl, who had a kopek for a gun? And finally, once there was money, who needed a gun? If there was trouble, you called 911 or a lawyer. If you needed a hobby, for Christ's sake, you would never go hunting. Guns could backfire, just like that. And they were dirty, and you could get lost in the woods where there were mosquitoes and bears. The country club was as far as you'd go: a nice golf game, a buffet, and maybe, just maybe, in the winter, you'd ski.

I remembered, growing up, David Lipitsky, Bar Mitzvah Murderer! That had been the headline, clear as the light of a Saturday in 1957, and only two hundred miles away, David Lipitsky, the little pisher, mounted the bimah, oy, he looked so grown-up in his blue suit, and there before his beaming parents and grandparents, and all his friends and relatives, there on the bimah of Beth Shalom Synagogue (it was coming back now, all the details I had memorized) he grinned, took out a gun and fired twice at his Rabbi. Today I am a man!

The tragedy, spoken in only the most hushed of tones at home, fascinated me: that a boy, a Jewish boy at that, could do such a thing; that someone my own age could violate so many commandments (I had counted them up at the time and chalked up three: Remember the Sabbath day to keep it holy; Honor thy father and thy mother; Thou shalt not kill.) Three of them, in one fell swoop.

The trouble was now, now that I knew the thrill of stalking about the house, aiming this way and that, and had enjoyed it, I didn't want to file it away under Deviant Behavior. Still, I couldn't stop myself from asking why it so excited me. Perhaps it was in my blood, questioning my motives, all those quibbling motives. Enough of questions, of questions and worse, answers: smug, oh so-sure-of-themselves answers: this was for that and that was for this, rebuttals, refutations, rejoinders; the reason for this, the explanation for that; justifications and warrants, reinstatements and pattest of excuses, alibis, extenuating, mitigating circumstances. Was it any surprise why now I felt like I was penned up in some courtroom, my hand thrust on the Bible, just like Al's had been back during the IRS trial? But it wasn't just that, simple identification with the aggressor of aggressors, daddy dearest. It wasn't being hounded and cornered and badgered, why'd you do this? Why didn't you do that? Why a gun? It was all the why's, all the questions, all the replies, all the answers; so many of them, ultimately, hopelessly, painfully unknowable.

Maybe it just felt good holding the gun, and if Rachel or a shrink or one of these gun-banners cornered me and tried to determine why, or worse, if I would engage in what I had spent so much of my life caught up in, the need to get to the bottom of it, I would end up, maybe a little wiser, but oh so much sadder.

And fun it had been, buying the gun, hiding it in my pocket, taking it out at home and pretending, not just in cops and robbers with Adam, where it would be obviously play-acting, but with myself. No thinking, no questions, just falling into desire, lurching into longing, letting go, letting fucking go and seeing where it led me, and not having a goddamn plug, a goddamn orange plastic plug get in the way. Barrels, in Berettas or barrels hurling down Niagara Falls: merest of containers, hiding objects from view, but they must, eventually, be opened so the surprise can come barreling, shooting out. A bullet, or the promise of one; that is what I dreamed of now.

William James would understand, even though you didn't usually think of old Waldo with a gun in his hand, then why was I hunting for him now, but there was his old book from college:

If we stand still, we shall be frozen to death. If we take the wrong road we shall be dashed to pieces. What must we do. Act for the best, hope for the best, and take what comes...If death ends all, we cannot meet death better.

Oh, how easy it had been back then: just underline the words or highlight them in yellow; repeat them over and over again, better yet, get stoned and read them aloud, maybe with a candle burning and the Beetles singing The Long and Winding Road in the background; read them aloud to Lynne and Freddy and Larry and Ellie, all seated in a circle around the candle, listen to their comments: Wow; heavy; what a dude! Never dreaming that it will be over forty years until you read that passage again and then the world would look upon you as a retired gray-haired widower not exactly stuck on any mountainous pass. So why William James? Why now?

Because the decision, once I had returned to the computer, to pop for the gun could always be written off as a whim, not as a true Jamesian moment of will, a clean cold Jamesian choice: to proceed through the instructions, hand over my VISA card number, this was no whim, like walking into the toy store, deciding to blow a few bucks on a tacky toy revolver with an orange plug up its butt. Spending $119.32 for Model M85 was another thing, a choice, a real choice and before even getting to SUBMIT, there had been so many other choices along the way. Oh, the mountain pass was snowy and misty, but I never had been blinded, not once, and even though I wasn't sure what to do or what path was the best, I plunged ahead, carefully and with the greatest of deliberation, made my decision. The M85, for instance, when I could have just have easily chosen the 92F! And why not? The M85 just had so much going for it:

The Model M85, a medium-framed automatic pistol is the standard military sidearm of many Eastern European countries and is also used by many police organizations and many of the world's government agencies where its small size makes it suitable when concealment is called for.

Where its small size makes it suitable when concealment is called for. Oh M85, you little concealer, you little pisher, you hider and seeker, less is more, you. Stashed discretely in an inside pocket, for instance, then suddenly grab it: SURPRISE, PUT YOUR HANDS UP! DONT GIVE ME ANY BACK TALK. THAT'S IT, SPREAD YOUR FEET. UP AGAINST THE WALL. NOW, I'M ASKING YOU FOR THE LAST TIME.... Oh, so suitable. So very suitable, especially since these non-functioning models are molded of solid resin with no moving parts. They are weighted and look just like the originals. This gun was a favorite of Secret Agent 007 James Bond and all international security forces. If it's good enough for James Bond, it's good enough for me. And all those international security forces, why they were the frosting on the cake. How could you go wrong?

It faithfully matches the appearances of its operational counterparts, and is ideal for collecting, theatrical use, starting athletic meets and firearms training and teaching firearms safety.

Whoever wrote the copy for the M85 certainly was the optimist. How many prospective buyers were ever going to use it for theatrical use? Or firearms training? Or starting athletic meets. No, there was more to the M85 than met the eye. But instead of deliberating, investigating, Googling, ogling, I Dead Sea-scrolled to the M85 and fed them my VISA number, my expiration date; anything they desired they could have: my sperm count if they wanted, and when I pressed SUBMIT and just seconds late received my confirmation number, I could all but feel William James patting me on the back; I could all but see my father, my real father in the corner of the room flashing me a smile, whispering, That's my boy, that's my boy. Yes, indeedy, I typed in the Visa's Expiration date and now I felt hopeful. I would not be just an old man, waiting for his own expiration day. I could be anything, I could be anyone, anybody I dared to be, anyone I was meant to be.

Waiting for the package was to prove a heady experience. Having rushed into Caponean judgement, surrendering myself to a premise which only a week ago would have seemed crazy, I now felt an overwhelming sense of relief, as if a weight had been lifted. Somewhere, somehow, some way, I must have always had a hint, a presentiment, an intimation that something was out of whack; out of kilter, or maybe simply askew, and now I knew what it was, and it made sense, perfect sense. Everything was falling into place. Come home to daddy, my little bambino, come home.

Once sparked, dozens of images cascading down: a night in July, a warm breeze of lilacs, snuggled into his shoulder, my real father's shoulder, no matter what he is, who is, and while that might be just the slightest bit scary, he's your father, your real father, forever, and he won't let anything or anyone harm you. Fireworks launched into the night; each one dazzles: crescents, stars, streams and streaks; flowers with petals of magical light arching across the night, shocking, lurid colors: purples, yellows, blues; then they fade, die, puff into smoke, but they were there, he was there, above you, beside you, and suddenly the knowledge, the certainty, that there is no other place you would rather be, no one else who should be sitting there besides you, nowhere else you actually belong. O solo mio, oh star of light; in your eyes is my delight. I had played the song on my trombone, rhapsodically, compellingly at my recital and my teacher, Mrs. Summers, had told me afterwards, Gabe, you were inspired! And was it any surprise? Playing the song, squeezing my eyes shut, I didn't have to try to feel the music, it coursed through me, so much more so than Ayn Kahlahaynu or Dayanu or any of those other limpid lack-luster dirges the choir sang at High Holy Days. Italian songs, strong and passionate, full of love, not promises to God, from God, about God, but Latin lullaby caresses, Milanese marches strutting through my heart, nothing to be ashamed of, and then the ones like the cha-cha, which I mastered at dance class—one, two, cha-cha-cha—and Louie Prima, Tony Bennet, Hey Mambo, Mabo Italiano; oh, Dean Martin, When the moon hits your eye like a big pizza pie, that's amore.

But the next morning, as I waited for my package, why was I thinking of Popeye the Sailor Man? He wasn't Italian. Bluto might have been (he sort of looked Italian.) Growing up, I had been mesmerized by Popeye, intrigued by his lust for the lowliest of homeliest Olive Oyl (another Italian reference) and that even though they weren't married, there was this baby, Swee'pea, in the picture. But what most intrigued me was the phrase Popeye repeated over and over again, I yam who I yam cause I yam who I yam: the purest line of poetry I had ever known: lyrical, repetitive, in its own way I-yam-bic, pithy, profound; a phrase that you couldn't get out of your head, that once hearing, you couldn't escape, a phrase you had to repeat, to hear it come out of your own mouth, spring from your own lips, setting me, the prepubescent poet to wondering about Popeye: what would move him to repeat what was so patently obvious, and then to try to put it together and to wonder about it himself? Why did I not feel the same way? What kept me from throwing myself into the world the way Popeye did, full of piss and vinegar and blimey, with the utterest of self-confidence, and if anything more should be called for, well then, a can of spinach would do the trick.

Had to get out of the house, couldn't take the waiting anymore. Ended up at the library and there in the stacks, in the biography section, tracked down six books on Capone, six books to lug to the chair by the corner, six books to peruse, then the great discovery: the truth; the truth that set me free: the heart-breaking tragedy of the son of hard-working immigrants, the ambitious young man who started out straight, oh-so-straight; a gutsy giant full of dreams, pie-in-the-sky American dreams. Sure, there were the incidents back at P.S. 7 in Brooklyn, but teachers used physical force, especially against immigrants, some whom they'd refer to as spics and wops and dagos; students who couldn't always understand what they were being ordered to do. ESL wasn't exactly around yet, so he didn't have a prayer after the problem with the bitch, Miss Angyllis, his sixth-grade teacher; and they expelled him, when now he'd be spent to a Special Ed program, maybe a resource room, given tutoring, classes in Anger Management. What might Ritalin have done?

Other boys his age, thrown out on the streets, might have fraternized with delinquents. Al worked hard. The only street corner he hung out on was at 26th Street and Avenue R, where he had his shoeshine stand, a fixture there, the scrawny Italian kid yelling, shinola, shinola, get your shinola! Later, setting up pins at the bowling alley, eight, ten hours a day, the sound of the ball barreling down the lane, and always, always home by 10:30, Friday's salary handed over to mama, who gives him a kiss, calls him, Mio piccolo uomo. Months working the counter at Irving's Candy, making change for a nickel, his only crime nabbing a string of licorice when old man Weiss was in the can. When the Titanic sinks, Al had been at the paper factory, for three years,

And the syphilis? Well, penicillin wouldn't be around for almost a quarter of a century, and all that time, unbeknownst to Al, to Mr. C., to Snorky (as he liked to be called) but don't say Scarface, never call him Scarface, it wouldn't be in your best self-interests—all that, time he'd never know, cause the deed was done and there's no turning back. The real story of Al: Lawrence Bergren's 1994, 701-page biography, Capone, The Man and the Era. A masterful work, meticulously researched, beautifully written, beginning with the lines from Julius Caesar: The evil that men do lives after them/The good is oft interred with their bones.

700 pages, it could have used some editing. I skimmed it, best I could. Before the syphilis had spread; the handsome, roguish adolescent: slim, well-built, charming as the day is long; full of dash and bravado; nobody's patsy, nobody's fool. Oh, what did they know, what did anybody know, anybody but me and perhaps a few scholars and historians? Everyone thought they were so fucking smart: watch a movie, read a textbook, surf the History Channel, think it's for real, but all of it, malarkey, hokum cooked up for the masses: photos of the Saint Valentine's Day Massacre—Al was in Florida at the time—and DeNiro wielding a baseball bat, finishing off a stoolie at a conference table. All of it lies, or if not lies, not quite the whole unvarnished either, for there were reasons for Al's occasional violent episodes, clear, justifiable, legitimate reasons. I shut my eyes, imagining myself in court, defending him:

Exhibit A, indeed, the only exhibit the defense intends to offer to the court. Bailiff, if you please, yes, this test-tube, this vial of blood, as red as that of any red-blooded American's, redder for that matter, more full of life and color! But alas, this blood is tainted. Befouled. A test, developed by August Von Wasserman in 1906 when my client was but a child of seven, a test performed upon Al Capone's blood one decade later first detects the spirochete, that dreaded spiral-shaped microorganism, Treponema pallidum.

I beseech you! Al Capone was a victim, an innocent victim, of a merciless affliction. A wonderful son, a devoted family man, a true benefactor and friend to the poor. He was not perfect. But who of us is? And who of us has had syphilis?

Do not turn your heads away; do not shirk at the mention of the word, forget Dr. Carl Nazi-lover Jung, that great know-it-all, who spoke of syphilis as the poison of the darkness. Let us, instead, look at the glass as half-full. Let us acknowledge all those syphilitics who came before Al, bequeathing him such a rich and creative legacy: Beethoven, Schubert and Schumann, Baudelaire, Flaubert, and Joyce, Nietzsche and Van Gogh! The list is endless. And of course, like Capone, their end was no picnic, but consider how their art was transformed in the process.

And then the end as his biographer, Bergren pointed out, the end which could never justify the means: Under the influence of the spirochetes gnawing at his nervous system, he became ever more temperamental—by turns gloomy, ebullient, and violent—without apparent cause. He suffered from a dimly perceived but keenly felt need for greatness or grandeur luring just beyond his reach, tantalizing him, driving him on, tripping him up. He was a Caliban driven mad by syphilitic voices and visions he could scarcely comprehend.

And finally, as Pearl would put it, the frosting on the cake, in Deborah Hayden's Pox: Genius, Madness, and the Mysteries of Syphilis. Before insanity set in, brief episodes of uninhibited, uncharacteristic behavior presaged the madness to come. Right before madness, the syphilitic was often rewarded in a kind of Faustian bargain for enduring the pain and despair, by episodes of creative euphoria, electrified, joyous energy when grandiosity led to new vision. The heightened perception, dazzling insight and almost mystical knowledge experienced during this time were expressed while precision of form of expression was still possible.

So as the illness spreads and attacks the brain, something happens, some fabulous burst of synaptic electrical activity, a grand neural lightning storm and then a great hallucinatory light, a let-there-be-light light, a ferocious glowering fireball before night finally descends. Now I have become death, the destroyer of world. Uh, Houston, we have a problem. This passage explains it all: those unfortunate lapses, the unpleasant allegations regarding the baseball bat incidents with Scalise, Anselmi and Giunta (one, two, three strikes, you're out!) The whole nature of Al's rather mercurial temper. But it also provides insight into how a nineteen-year-old factory worker could rise to such heights in so short a time. So no one ever gave him piano lessons, he would never have an SAT coach or compose a Ninth or paint a sunflower; still, he could take in all that surrounded him and become a master, a genius, an artist; creative, powerful, supreme above all others. If it wasn't for the syphilis, Al would probably have been just one more guy, slaving away in some slaughterhouse, one more common criminal. The syph was what inspired him to rise above it all. The syph was what fired up his brain, his brilliance, and lent him such bravado. It transformed him.

Slumped in my chair now, exhausted, incapable of digesting another word. Suddenly, I had to get out and so I stumbled to the door, not even bothering to reshelve the books. Fuck it. That's what a librarian's for. Finally, outside, blinking in the glare of sunlight and, surprise, it is a beautiful day: the sun shining, a teenage boy kicking a soccer ball down the street, a warm breeze, fresh air.

35 / PEARL

How do they expect me to do my puzzles with my hand in a cast? I have always done them. And I miss them so. The occasional funny question: for the front hall and the bald head: rug, and the ones that aren't giveaways, but you get right away because you've been around, like garlic-basil sauce: pesto. Something clicks, you write in the word, you feel smart, just that simple, and you're sharpening your mental faculties in the process. And by the way, I always use pencil, and with an eraser.

Other questions, frankly, more annoying, I mean, who really knows who the 1996 Oscar Best Actress was so you skip ahead, and, hopefully, recognize some other words and then the name will come to you, eventually, but I wouldn't hold my breath. And then there are the ones that maybe my great grandson, Adam, could answer but they shouldn't expect people like me to know. 12 down, Matrix of computer networks —it just ain't fair for us alder cockers, but at least on Monday and Tuesday, lots of easy ones: a three-lettered word for skillet beginning with p? Give me a break? It's pan. The Thinker sculptor? Rodin, of course. Monk title? Friar. Forty winks. Couldn't be simpler: sleep

Of course, if they were all that easy, it wouldn't be so interesting, and if you want to stay sharp you gotta use some of the old brainpower, but if you're patient—a watched pot never boils— a lot of them will pop out when you're least expecting it. Mariner's concern, for instance. At first, I think albatross, but that's eight letters and won't fit in the five boxes, so I put on the old thinking cap and like that, it comes to me: storm. It makes perfect sense; it fits into the boxes and the s that it starts with it also starts the word for 11 Down. (Clue: twinkle, twinkle. Answer: star.) Oh, my puzzles: How would I start my day without them? Like now: 22 Across: Songstress Vicki. And then I remember her, Carr, Vicki Carr, it's been so long. But here she is right in front of me. Vicki Carr singing Tenderly. Vicki Carr right in front of me even though I can't remember what I had for dinner last night.

36 / GABE

Finally, three days after my great discovery at the library, I glance out the window, spot the truck and my heart is leaping as I race down the stairs to the front door. What if they think no one is home and leave a slip for next day service? No, another buzz and there is a moment to wait at the front door, to catch my breath, to open it, to feign innocence: Oh hello? A package? For me?

Back in the kitchen, armed with a pair of scissors and a steak knife, trying to open the package but the gun is encased, just like the other one, in cardboard and bubble wrap and is a pain-in-the-ass to get to, but finally there it is, in a little nest of Styrofoam and a goddamn staple I have to yank off with pliers. I caress the shiny nickel barrel, and then, gingerly, lift it out of its bubble wrap and place it in my palm, stroking its muzzle and bring it to my mouth; it is cool, cool to my lips and I wonder what the fuck I'm doing—it does seem a little weird. This may not exactly be for real; it actually couldn't shoot anyone—but it is the next best thing in the world, a 100% actual reproduction, and anyone seeing it, seeing me holding it, would never know it was incapable of inflicting damage: a mild graze to the arm, a shot to the leg, or, now we're talking, or more to the point, a slug to the head.

No orange plug, just a barrel, like a real gun. For several minutes I sit, stroking my reproduction M-85: Getting to know you, getting to know all about you—Getting to hope you, getting to hope you like me,—and then, impulsively, I put on a jacket, a loose-fitting rust-colored Gore Tex jogging jacket, one I bought after Gloria died, one I think of as rather snappy, and place the gun in the front pocket. No one will ever suspect a thing.

I step up to the mirror in the hall, the one above Lordly's silver bowl and ponder my reflection. The scars are gone, all of them. My cheeks are clear. There is nothing to be ashamed of. And I rather like what I see: my cheeks, smooth unblemished. Now, I have never considered himself a handsome man—nothing like a parade of acne scars to scotch that kind of notion—and I still don't for that manner, but it's amazing what a little laser resurfacing will do: how it can suggest possibilities, possibilities you never thought might exist. I take off my glasses. True, they are chic glasses: Italian, titanium, elegant but somewhat sporty, and I consider one of my dermatologists' remarks, the one about the lasectomy, the procedure the colleague of his down the hall was such a hot shot with. Nothing to do but make an appointment and in three minutes, the same laser that performed such miracles on my face could do the same with my eyes. Ever since I was ten, I have worn glasses, contacts never really worked, no matter how hard I tried. What would it be like to be free of glasses? I pat my jacket pocket and feel the gun. For the first time I realize the beauty of the phrase concealed weapon and I open the door to an absolutely spectacular day, sunny, not a cloud in the sky, the loveliest breeze, in the distance birds singing, chirping away. I pick up my car keys, lock the door to the house and drive to therapy.

Fifteen minutes later, I take a deep breath and deliver the news, the idea I had been playing with, of my paternity. Got to give him credit. Doesn't even break a sweat. Then I as if there's some pathology this might all fit into. Eventually, he asks, Why presuppose, why classify, why relegate whatever it

133

is you are experiencing to some DSM-5 sea of symptomology, some ocean of hypothesis? after I had begged him for a name, a classification, anything that would make whatever was going on in my head seem more ordinary, more mundane, more commonplace, like a cold, a nosebleed, dandruff; some routine disorder I could share with millions of others of hapless victims.

When did it start? Nahal asked.

Two days ago, I told him.

What did you feel was different?

It was like a flood, a dam breaking. Suddenly all this, this stuff washing over me and I couldn't stop it.

What kind of stuff?

Awful things. That my grandson, Adam, would drown. They have a swimming pool, you know, and live in Miami. I could see him in that pool. Floating. Or that there would be an explosion of some kind. Terrorists, what have you. And I had impulses, ones I never had before.

Like?

Like when I was driving my car, I 'd think of flooring the accelerator, smashing into a pole or driving off the road.

Are you afraid you actually will hurt yourself?

I thought about it for a while. No, not actually. If push comes to shove, I wouldn't do anything self-destructive. But it's the thought that gets to me.

Yet, when our session was over—I couldn't bring myself to show him my gun—and I returned to my car, I felt anything but anxious, in fact, I felt uncharacteristically sanguine: I didn't exactly know where I was headed, but I felt vigorous, free, alive. If Al Capone was my father, well then, Al Capone was my father, and the funny thing, it felt now like he was, but there would be no real way of ever knowing. So be it.

Then it struck me, that the pure bliss of ignorance, of not knowing, never knowing, could be the greatest gift of them all:

so much of my nature, or the nature I assumed was my genetic legacy, was the pursuit of knowledge, but now I seemed to be gently falling down into a new world, holding onto an umbrella all the way—you don't want to fall too fast—floating down to a terra more firma if less familiar. The fact that Howard Freeman's chromosomes had nothing to do with my own, that his unique hopscotch of DNA was not spiraling and helixing inside of me and that the Freeman genes had nothing to do with my own, all seemed beside the point. Who gave a flying fuck? Spilled milk, water over the damn, let sleeping dogs lay. Granted, my world had been toppled, and it had been an earthquake at first, but really, this wasn't so high on the Richter scale, a few moments of moral foundations quaking and shaking before landing on Caponean bedrock, or not, and now a certain giddiness. Maybe it was true: da-da was one of the 20th Century's most infamous of men. But maybe not. There was no way to really know.

The silliness with the gun—I patted my pocket now to make sure it was still safe—was understandable. Allying myself with who might have been, might be, my father: acknowledging that maybe, just maybe, that the winding helixing chains spelled out C-A-P-O-N-E and that the silver mezuzah I had once worn around my neck on a chain of its own, should have been a simple cross, but not one to merely bear, because, after all, who of us gets to choose our genes? We're stuck with them and make the best we can out of what's there, and besides, really, when you get down to it, to the most DNA-y nitty-gritty, it's all out of our hands.

What was different now, and, perhaps, accounting for the giddiness I was experiencing, was the knowledge that, while sure, the guy I had spent so many hours duking it out with in therapy, Howard Freeman, had really played a prominent role in my life as a step-father, and had influenced me greatly, but that somehow, now, I was finally home free. There was another part

135

of me I never had known existed, one that had been lurking—
no, lurking was too negative—a part that had been patiently
waiting there for all these decades—and that now finally it had
revealed itself to me and I could do with it whatever I wanted.
Al Capone was safely buried in the ground. While I wouldn't be
pushing to follow in his footsteps, to preserve the family name,
to become the new Godfather, still, suddenly, I was there beside
him waving hello, making myself known, and in the process,
feeling a certainty I had never known before, a certainty of just
exactly who I was.

37 / ADAM

If the world is going to end, it would be helpful to know exactly when that end is going to be. Obviously, I would like it better if it was 5000 AD or even 2121 because then I wouldn't be around to notice. But say the Doomsday Clock went off in 2019 when I'm in college when I don't exactly want to experience Doomsday, there'd be all kinds of problems like what should we do with our dog, Jasper? Would he get loose and roam with packs of wild dogs? I don't think Jasper would be so good at being wild.

Who invented the Doomsday Clock in the first place? Maybe I should ask Grandpa. He was alive during World War II. There wasn't a Doomsday Clock then, but if there was, I bet it would have been awfully close to midnight. Maybe I should ask him. He seems to be wise.

38 / GABE

Driving down Beacon Street, not knowing or caring where I was headed, but growing more and more peeved at the SUV which seemed to be tailgating me even though I was driving at the posted 35 miles per hour. Up ahead, at the corner of Walnut Street, the traffic light turned yellow. It would have been easy to drive through, but I decided to stop. What's the big hurry? So I braked, somewhat abruptly, and from behind, heard the squeal of brakes from the SUV. Then it honked. Not just a mild tap of the horn, but a pounding rat-a-tat, three in a row, the sound persistent, shrill, accusing, as if I had committed some monstrous sin merely by pausing before a yellow light, exhibiting a little caution.

I glanced in the mirror to catch a glimpse of just whoever was inside. It was hard to tell, though, and then the SUV pulled over to the left lane, just beside me. It was a black Mercedes, grotesque in its own way, but worse was the driver who was frowning in my direction, and since the SUV was so much taller than my own Toyota, looking down at me, glaring with disdain, shaking his head from side to side as if I were some pathetic vermin. And if this wasn't bad enough, he was talking on a cell phone.

What was so important to talk about that he could have plowed into me, rear-ended me, mutilated, maybe even killed me? And now, the driver was shaking his head and I wasn't merely peeved but pissed off. I lowered the passenger window, casually, as if I was simply wanting some fresh air and then it happened: The driver, a man in his thirties, glared at me, removed the cellphone from his ear and bellowed, You gotta problem, Buddy?

You should watch how you drive, I said. You almost caused an accident.

He didn't seem grateful for the advice. Go fuck yourself.

I was considering how to best reply when I remembered what was resting in my pocket and smiled.

What's so funny, asshole? he asked.

This, I replied, removing the gun from my pocket, positioning the M85 in my hand, casually, as if it were a cigarette or a can of Coke. This was going to be fun, more fun than anything I had ever done before. I didn't want to show it to him yet, however, but to squeeze every bit of anticipatory pleasure from the moment, contemplating what was about to happen, and I knew it would happen, in just a moment, nothing could stop it from happening, but, oh, what bliss, holding back, like before you're coming, when you fuck.

I stuck the gun out of my window and tapped the barrel on the rear-view mirror.

The man in the Mercedes dropped his cellphone and actually put his hands in the air in classic I-give-up manner, then stammered, Listen, I'm, I'm s-s-sorry. He was stuttering and this pleased me.

Freeze, I ordered.

Indeed, he did. Never, in fact, had I seen a man more frozen in all my life.

And don't move a fucking finger.

A feeling unlike any I had ever known: of confidence in myself and what I could pull off; a delirium of sorts; of the giddiest, wildest, most breath-taking pleasure imaginable.

For once, I could do whatever I wanted to, and no one could stop me.

His hands remained held up in the air—I could see them shaking—and this made him seem all the more pathetic. Now, what was it, exactly, you told me to do? I asked. Still want me to fuck myself? Then, I couldn't stop myself. I aimed the M-85 directly at his head.

He was silent for a moment and then he managed to whisper, I'm sorry, as if that should serve as an excuse for his reprehensible behavior.

Suddenly, the light turned green, and I saw a car in my rear-view mirror approaching. Go, I demanded. Get the fuck out of here. He dropped his hands to the steering wheel, floored the accelerator and burned pungent Mercedes rubber, racing down the street as fast as his Mercedes SUV could take him.

Slipping the gun back in my pocket, I felt elated. I drove through the green light. Mr. Mercedes was nowhere to be seen. Then I remembered. The shmuck had a cellphone. Maybe he was calling the police at this very moment. But he took off without a chance to catch my license plate.

Still, it could be embarrassing. Off in the distance, a cruiser with a red blinking light, then a siren…You have the right to remain silent…frisked, spread-eagled and handcuffed right here on Beacon Street, and then the gun. Oh, but officer, it's merely a toy, a present for my grandson. No, that must have been an entirely different man you're looking for. I would never do such a thing! Then the line-up. You, number four, step up to the glass, turn to the right, to the left. But all of this was ridiculous. Paranoid. There were no laws against replicas of guns. Still, it could be awkward.

Down the block, I turned into the parking lot for Stop & Shop. In the back seat of my car was a roll of paper towels, for emergencies. I took several sheets, wiped the gun free of incriminating fingerprints, then wrapped it in the paper. I glanced around, got out of the car, walked to a trashcan and dropped the gun in, then returned to my car, but still I felt nervous. What if they were looking for me? Perhaps an all-points bulletin. Well, why not stay here for a while? Matter of fact, do a little shopping? Paper towels, a quart of non-fat milk, Oat Squares. Ten minutes later, standing in the 12 Items and Under Line at Stop & Shop, I opened the box of no-fat chocolate cookies, took one out and began to eat it, even before I had paid for it.

Later, at home, slouching on the couch, sliding into the most profound of funks, sipping a glass of Burgundy, lamenting the gun which was now gone forever: the beautiful, nickel-plated reproduction revolver, the M85, deposited ignobly in the green plastic trash can at Stop & Shop. Maybe there was still time to drive back, to retrieve it, but the police could still be on the prowl, and it would look odd if a cruiser came by and they discovered me thrashing about in the trashcan.

I felt bereft. Suddenly something was missing, something that I had come to rely on. No use trying to shrug it off, and while of course it was all related to Capone and I could analyze it to death, still it wouldn't go away, this feeling, not exactly emptiness, but a sense that something was lost, that life no longer was as much fun as it used to be; that there were fewer possibilities. Maybe it was simpler than that. Maybe it was that these were the first two guns I had ever owned, and this was some kind of boy thing I had missed out on and had been mourning.

Pearl had never allowed me a toy gun. In fact, she had seemed quite adamant about it. Usually her theories of child-raising seemed laissez-faire, but I could still remember coming back from Gene Landy's eighth birthday party with a cowboy pistol—I had won it legitimately; it had come out of a piñata—but Pearl wouldn't have it in the house. Why all the fuss? Then it struck me. She was afraid: the bad seed; the apple doesn't fall far from the tree. She must have been fearful that somehow I had more of Al in me than met the eye; that despite the Hebrew and the trombone lessons, the weekly ballroom dance classes at the Jewish Community Center, that despite my stamp collection and aquarium, that despite the fact I had read all 126 Hardy Boy books by the time I was eleven, that there would be a time when my true genes would win out, and she would have to remain vigilant and nip any Caponean vines in the buddino.

Of course, it would be simple to order another M85. But I didn't want to. It wasn't the cost or the embarrassment, more that I had done it already, that I had shown I had it in me and to go back and return, so to speak, to the scene of the crime, to return to the exact same web site, seemed depressing and yes, infantile, like a baby crawling towards a rattle that he had grown bored with, just to have something to play with; a rattle, a stupid little rattle that had been laying under the couch for weeks and no longer meant as much to him. Ah, no use to berate myself. At the time, it was the right thing to do, and it had been an important step, allowing me to leave behind the ludicrous orange plug in the process, but to order another reproduction, no matter how much it looked like a real gun was many things, among them, a waste of my precious time. I felt cold and somber and sober, now, as if I had landed at a destination I hadn't intended to arrive at, but that I couldn't turn away from, not to a toy gun or the reproduction M85, and it was then that I made a decision, one I had been waiting for, and once having made it, there was, as they say, no turning back.

39 / PEARL

I was lying in bed, watching America's Most Wanted, wondering how it all could have come to this: Thank God, Ketzel was different. He had style, he had class. And he would never have done any of this stuff. Then it came back to me, the brush, back in the apartment, the brush. If anything happened, Gabe would find it, and since he had been in such a lather lately, it could lead him, who knows where? But there was no getting out of here. The door to the elevator was locked. Still, somehow, there must be a way to get the brush and finally get rid of it, somewhere where no one could ever find it. There must be a way.

Later that night, I remembered, Ruthie, the nice black aide, the spunky, funny one with the wig. Why not give Ruthie the key? And a five-dollar bill. No, a ten. And tell her where to look. Ruthie would bring it. Gabe would never need to know, and he'd never suspect a thing.

40 / GABE

Couldn't sleep, but rather than counting sheep or taking an Ambien, my thoughts kept drifting back to that asshole in the Mercedes SUV. I was still angry. At myself. For throwing away my precious M-85. Why had I overreacted and in such an ignoble manner, in the garbage can of the Stop&Shop? How silly to think that the cops would want it for evidence, some Exhibit A, for my trial. It's hardly against the law to brandish a toy gun.

Then it hit me, safe in bed, the real reason I was angry with myself. The reason I had ditched the gun: I was afraid of how good it felt. To wave the gun, to threaten the asshole, to have him so under my thumb, my thumb on the gun, my finger on the trigger. If only it had been a real trigger, I would have had the chance for even more fun. To carefully aim, all the better to draw out the pleasure, to aim at, maybe, the tire or the Mercedes SUV hood ornament—that could be tricky, but it would be elegant—and then have a minute or two of even more exquisite pleasure as the asshole pisses in his pants begging me for mercy, as I raise the gun up and carefully aim at his head. Then, there in the safety of my bed, a sudden, spontaneous, erection.

I grew frightened, for now I couldn't be really sure of anything anymore. I was hard. I didn't have the gun. I was dreaming of the gun, imagining, just for a moment, but an undeniable moment, killing another human being with it. What was happening to me?

Something, indeed, was. Something prompting me, after finally falling asleep to awaken bright and early at 7:00 AM in order to arrive right at 10:00 AM when Russell's Sporting Gear opened its door, but as soon as I opened that door, I realized I didn't belong, but, still, I stood frozen in place, unable to extricate myself from this den of death, or, maybe, just for sport, if you please, as if that made it any better, or, if not sport, then for that intruder, jimmying your window, climbing through, stealing your silver and flat screen, raping your wife.

The front of the store was devoted to fishing: We come from the sea; we return to the sea. Aisles of fishing poles and every conceivable tchotchke for landing a flounder. The names of the rods were poetic: Down-riggers, Inshore, Casting, Muskie, Spinning, Fresh-water. I remembered the bamboo pole I had as a boy, how proud I was of it when we spent our two weeks every summer at the cabin, how it would rest in the corner of my room; how Howard would stick the worm through the hook for me—truthfully, I was squeamish— and how the two of us would wait, oh, how we would wait for a bite, the smallest bite. Once I had caught a fish, I actually caught a fish, a perch, and when we reached home, Pearl reacted as if I had bagged a lion. She gutted and scaled it and we had it for dinner, although secretly I had wished it had been stuffed, mounted, hung over the fireplace mantle.

At the back of the shop, guns and rifles, cases of them, and bullets, all locked in cabinets behind glass. Suddenly, an overwhelming sense of nausea and for a minute, just a minute, I thought I might vomit, right then and there—Gloria always claimed I had a weak gag reflex—and how would I explain that? Oh sorry, I've had a touch of the flu. Picked it up ice-fishing. As if on cue, a clerk appeared, a man in his fifties, wearing a flannel shirt, faded, red; a man with the most implacable expression on his face; a man wearing bifocal glasses; a man who stood there, between me and the guns. What are you looking for? he asked.

No smile, no emotion, a little sinister, actually, and come to think of it, he seemed a little suspicious, as if he was on to me, what I was up to. This wasn't Saks, after all, where you could get by with No thank you, just browsing, free to finger the Missoni sweaters or pick through the ties, or Barnes and Noble where you could walk the aisles, unescorted, take in a few lines of Rilke, pick up the newest Updike and read the first page, without a clerk sizing you up.

What are you interested in? the clerk asked again, not looking like he gave a good goddamn, but with the hint of a smirk, a look suggesting he had bagged an imposter who had no business in this establishment. I couldn't exactly tell him the truth, that my toy gun seemed silly and my reproduction F85 lay in the bottom of the trash can at Stop& Shop and that I was looking for the real thing. But I could be great in a pinch. My, uh, nephew is graduating from medical school and he, uh, likes to hunt, and I wanted to buy him a rifle as a graduation gift.

And then I knew I had blown it. I didn't even want a rifle. Rifles were impossible to conceal. Rifles were for hunting poor defenseless deer, Bambi's mother, for Christ's sakes, or for migrating ducks, lumbering bears, John Fitzgerald Kennedy. I wanted a gun. But how to change the story now? He'd be suspicious. So I decided to take a different route, and play the naïf. Well, uh, to tell you the truth, I've never bought a gun before and am somewhat of a novice about all this. I was hoping you could help me.

The clerk looked at me with contempt. Not allowed back here, he said, as if speaking to the wall.

What do you mean?

You need a license to inspect the merchandise.

Oh, a gun license.

Now all I received was a nod.

Do you have a book or brochure or something that could tell me about how to go about getting one?

Go to your local police station. Fill out an application. They'll finger-print you, give you one. And you got to take a gun safety course.

Oh.

Here. He handed me a card from a stack on the counter and left me alone, as if he couldn't be bothered anymore. JOHN MONTE the card read, printed in a Baskerville Bold font with a revolver pointed in the air, on each side of his name. Underneath his name, it read Firearms Instructor, Mass. Certified #668, Licensed to Carry Courses. There was a business phone and a FAX, and thank God, no web site.

I looked up and then noticed it on the wall, an enormous moose head, forlorn and ancient, staring at me from the furthest recess of the store. I had never imagined a moose so huge, so noble and I felt anger welling up, for all I knew, this son-of-a-bitch clerk could have killed the animal, lumbering through the forest, innocently grazing in Manitoba; this flannelled clerk, this purveyor of death could have been hiding behind some pine tree and blasted him away —yes, it was a him, males had antlers— and then to have the audacity to take him to some taxidermist, to have him stuffed, mounted, a trophy, of a deranged murderous impulse. What had the poor moose done to ever deserve such a thing?

I remembered taping Elizabeth Bishop as she read her poem, The Moose. Bishop was in her fifties then, back from Brazil around '71, '72, living at the Harbor Towers, perhaps the most extraordinary woman I had ever met—I had always had a little crush on her despite her devotion for Rosa.

Here, surrounded by guns and rifles, bullets that would one day tear into flesh, wound and kill, I hear her voice as I had recorded it that snowy day in February. It was for my Spoken Words record project, when I was trying to expand Cavalier Publishing into different mediums. Her otherworldly voice, sure of itself; faint, delicate but oh-so-certain. I remember the poem, a bus traveling through New Brunswick to Boston on a cold winter night. A moose appears. The bus stops. The driver turns off the headlights and the passengers stare at the creature as it looms, yes, looms is the word she used, and then the lines come back to me, the lines describing the moose, Taking her time, she looks the bus over, Why, why do we feel, we all feel, this sweet sensation of joy? It could have been this very moose Elizabeth Bishop had written about, this very moose, blasted away, hanging on the wall, but here at this place, at this moment, there is no joy, only revulsion for this establishment; loathing for the customers who frequent it, and the knowledge that now I have become one of them.

It didn't matter the circumstances; that I would never use a gun to kill. I could not escape from the fact that I was here and if only I had taken the safety course, if only I had the proper certificate in my hand, I could step out behind this threshold and examine the guns and select one for my very own. I could whip out my VISA card and hand it over and then the gun would be mine. All mine. From there, I had no idea, nor did I care to know just exactly where it would lead to, but it would be somewhere, I was certain, somewhere I had never been before.

Two hours later, I took out the card, the one the clerk had given me and call John Monte. It was a tape—somehow I knew it would be—no Hello, just This is John Monte. If you want to talk to me, leave a message. A deep voice and gravelly and he certainly didn't mince words. Then, the ubiquitous beep and I felt on stage: Hello, this is Gabe Freeman. I want to take a gun safety course so I can register and buy a gun. Not exactly eloquent, but sometimes eloquence isn't called for and so I swallowed, left my number and muttered a rather hapless, Goodbye.

But John never called back that day or the next, maybe he had … an accident, and I turned to the yellow pages. So many choices: The Boston Gun Club, which had a certain Paul Revere-ish Sons of Liberty tone, no embellishment, let's get down to business, ready, aim, fire! But it was in Dorchester, an hour away. And then, it seemed that there was something wrong with every possibility. The Gun Owner's Action League, for instance: just what exactly was the action that they were promoting? And The Manchester Firing Line Range LLC: Why the LLC? This wasn't a bank in the Cayman Islands. The most intriguing possibility was the Joe Maffei Integrated Martial Development Center, but when I called there, again, there was only voicemail from a man whom I assumed was Joe, with the slightest touch of a lisp, describing self-defense possibilities from Filipino Martial arts to Korean Ein Kwan Do, as well as No Holds Barred Fighting. There was no chance to leave a message—what were these guys afraid of? Only a website which was not working properly. And if you couldn't manage to keep your website running, how could you be trusted to break a brick in half or fire a 22?

Finally I discovered a name, a name and an address in Waltham and when I called, a plaintive child's voice and for a second, I thought of hanging up. The boy saying, Hello, didn't seem capable of snapping a rubber band across a room, but when I asked for John Lynch, he paused for only a moment, before yelling, Dad, it's for you.

41 / GABE

What if, just what if, strictly out of conjecture here, Al would have had a change of heart and left his wife, Mae, behind? And little Sonny too. A quickie divorce in Rio, then a real marriage to Pearl. Who would've blamed him? Mae was such a bore, hounding him for more quality time with Sonny, dragging him to Sunday Mass, yes, even confession!

If he had only chosen Pearl, we would have been a family, a real family. Gabriel Capone—carries a little more oomph to it than Gabe Freeman. So much easier to get reservations at a restaurant; so much more difficult to imagine what would have become of me.

Because the man I assumed to be my father, Howard Jacob Freeman, was in the publishing, so to speak, business, it was natural that I would have that opportunity, and so I grabbed it, trying to make it a more respectable, to be sure, but always following in his footsteps. University of Michigan, Class of '70, marrying Gloria in '72, then Rachel is born, giving up on my thesis—I should have given Coleridge the cold shoulder and switched to Comp Lit—suddenly Gloria getting breast cancer the week after 9/11.

You'd think Al, of all people, wouldn't have been such a lackey to the Catholic church. If, somehow, he would have defied it; if only he would allowed himself to leave his immigrant past behind him and chosen love over duty, passion over tradition, how much different my world would be. When I sold Cavalier Press after Gloria died, I thought I'd remake myself, so I moved to Cambridge, dug up my thesis, found myself supremely bored by it all, tried a novel. No dice. I was in a rut. All my life, following in my father's footsteps. But that's just it! If I had followed in my real father's footsteps, what would have become of me; who would I have become? Sent off to St. Xavier's or some Catholic mackerel-snapper school, no doubt, no pool halls for me. And then, forget City College, with a proper prep school behind me, I could've gone to Harvard, gotten an MBA, dropped the rather disreputable elements from our family businesses, gone public, issued stock.

I needed to know more about the man, so the day before my tutorial in gun safety—an oxymoron if I had ever heard one—plenty of time to take in a biography of Al. It had been so long since I had taken up a research project, that at first it seemed overwhelming: every detail in Bergren's classic biography, crying out for attention. To my surprise, I found himself underlining, as if I were back in grad school—I couldn't help it, so what if the library charged me for defacing a book—so much seemed important, so many clues, so many revelations, and so fast and furious, no chance to take a breath, for there on page one, second paragraph, information so astonishing, so stunning, so mind-boggling, that as I took in the implications of the simple declarative sentence, I could not believe what I was seeing, and just to make sure, I read it again, slowly this time, taking care with every single word: His mother, a seamstress named Teresina Raiola, and his father, a barber named Gabriele Capone

I froze. This was no simple fluke, no mere coincidence. I felt nauseous. Now there could no longer be even the slightest doubt. Here was the final confirmation I had been seeking: Al Capone was my father. Al Capone was my real father, the father whose blood was coursing through my veins. Pearl might not have been able to marry him, but she had given me my grandfather's name. How like her. The Jewish tradition of using the first letter of a dead ancestor's name for a child, so that his blessed memory, his spirit will live on. But this? Why didn't she run the hell as fast away as possible and come up with any other name: any Tom, Dick or Harry, anything but Gabriel?

I had always had a friendly relationship with my name. It had undergone a sort of renaissance in the late 90's, and seemed to be in fashion again. But still, there just weren't that many Gabes and that lent it a certain luster. Of course, there was the newscaster, Gabe Heater: There's good news tonight! The rock star, Peter Gabriel, Hey, I'm feeling so dirty, you're looking so clean, All you can give is a spin in your washing machine, Gabriel Garcia Marquez and Gabby Hayes, the film and television cowboy clown with the bushy white beard, Hey Wild Bill, Wait for me! and of course, the biblical references. But now I could never feel the same way about it again. For I was named not for a stranger, but someone, who was, after all, not so strange: an Italian immigrant, a barber, a hard-working man, who just happened to be the father of Al Capone.

The following day, an equally propitious name in my path: Arsenal Road, which I headed down on my way to my gun safety lesson. I was pleased with my choice of attire: jeans, a hunter green flannel shirt and J. Crew khaki jacket and just ten minutes away from the parking lot in Medford. John Lynch had told me he would be driving an '85 white Grande Marquis, whatever that was, but now I was recalling our conversation and starting to feel just the slightest bit queasy. For one thing, Lynch's voice: there was something cloying, about it. Oh, a gun license safety course. No problem. Easy as pie. As if he had done this hundreds of times, and for all I knew, he had, but still there was an unctuous tone that was unsettling. But this was silly, he was simply a man doing a job. Of course, Adolph Eichmann had claimed the same argument. That's what I thought at first, before Lynch went on to cement our arrangement. And then there was this lurking sensation after I admitted, I'm not really mechanical and I want to be able to go slowly, that prompted Lynch to reassure me, again employing bakery terms: It's a piece of cake. After which it got even creepier. You'll love it. You're gonna get addicted, he reassured me.

I should have hung up, hung up, hung up right then and there, but Lynch had my number and could have called back, tracked me down, infuriated at the gall of this man who pestered him on the phone, hired him, then hung up. Who knows what he might have done? Road rage, going postal, the possibilities endless. He wanted payment, $125, in cash. And when I asked, innocently enough if we would be meeting at Lynch's home, Lynch all but sneered: I never give clients my address, he replied. So what was he so afraid of?

It was the memory of Lynch's final remark, however, that did it, that made me consider making a U-turn this very moment and speeding home. You'll be a regular Jessie James when we're through, he had said and then the clincher, as if that wasn't bad enough, he added, you'll be an Annie Oakley. Annie Oakley? The quirkiest of last straws, even when cloaked in banter, and it was more than banter, more than sheer repartee; this was madness, this is what it was, and now as I pulled into the parking lot where I was scheduled to meet John Lynch, I wondered if I was being too timid, too gun-shy, and that there was nothing, nothing at all to worry about.

There was his car, the white '85 Grand Marquis, I seemed to remember it was the top of the line Mercury; John Lynch in his enormous white Grand Marquis, a little faded and dented, but still a behemoth to behold; John Lynch, right on time, parked in the corner of the lot, and I pulled in alongside, but before I could turn off my ignition and open the door, Lynch had jumped out, standing there like the Colossus of Rhodes, dressed, head to toe, even his hat, in camouflage, all khaki-olive-green camouflage, which, besides looking ridiculous and a little GI Joe-ish, served to exaggerate his figure, which was hefty to begin with; the guy had to be at least 6'3 and he appeared clumsy. Maybe it was his head, which had a lamentable Howdy Doody-like shape, as if he was a marionette being jerked about by outside forces, dark forces, and then there was the moronic smile plastered on his mug. Suddenly, we were shaking hands, and old John Lynch certainly knew how to shake. He seemed to enjoy the act so much he would never let go. Great to meet you, it's gonna' be great, he boomed. And if all this wasn't bad enough, he was standing to close to me, just inches away, and he suffered from halitosis.

While John Lynch prepared to leave his car, installing some sort of primitive-looking lock on his steering wheel, I felt queasy. This wasn't the way it was supposed to be. I had imagined sitting in a room with Lynch at the blackboard, in front of a diagram of a revolver with little arrows pointing out the trigger, hammer, cylinder, barrel and magazine. I had expected my teacher to be a bit more of a Mr. Chips, patiently helping me load a gun with bullets. I had hoped for a few simple rules: Make the sure the lock is on before loading. Always load the gun with the barrel pointing away from your head. I had pictured actually firing the gun in some indoor shooting range, wearing soundproof earmuffs, and firing at a classic target of concentric circles.

I had pictured Lynch played by a laconic Gary Cooper or maybe Allan Ladd from Shane, but now this psychopath was gesturing towards me and ordering me to Open your trunk and let's get going. Minutes later, we were off, on our way to Bolton, miles away. In fifteen minutes, he was ordering me to take a right down a dirt road through deep woods that were oh so not Robert Frost's. Up ahead, stop, ordered John and just after I braked, he jumped out of the car, ordered me to open the trunk, unzipped his bag and there was the gun,

He held it in the air with a glazed smile on his face. And now he was fidgeting with the barrel, inserting bullets in the cylinder, gesturing for me to come closer, just a little closer, when, truthfully, all I wanted to do was jump in the car and speed away. Instead, I approached him and, finally, he clicked off the safety, and held the gun out to me as if it was some sacred offering. He clasped me on the back. Hold it. Hold it firmly, he instructed me. You wouldn't want to let it fall. Never had I held an object before.

But not too tight, not too tight, he reminded me. Then he put his hand on my forearm and straightened it out, twisting it a bit, so that the barrel was pointed straight ahead. Let's aim it higher, he said. Up, up in the air. I followed his instructions, hoping no errant sparrow was overhead.

Almost forgot, he said, could it be tenderly, and he placed what seemed like earmuffs on me. Then I realized. They would make it quieter for me. John, in his own way, was taking care of me. And nodding at me now. As I stood up straight and pressed ever so lightly, so my finger brushed against the trigger. He was nodding at me and smiling now.

I took a breath and pressed the trigger. Oh, so easy! And the sound, despite the earmuffs, echoing so loud—had I ever heard such a noise before? There was an echo, fainter this time. I lowered my hand, holding the gun tightly.

You never forget the first time, John Lynch whispered and while, of course, I wished he hadn't trod in the sexual waters again, I had to admit he had a point. Want to try again? he asked.

I nodded. So excited I couldn't even talk. I brought the gun up in the air, and with more bravado this time, fired, and then, even though John Lynch hadn't given me permission, fired once more. I couldn't help it. Then I worried, had I done something wrong? Had I incurred his wrath? Oh no, he had the biggest grin on his face, a classic shit-eating grin. We were conspirators now. We were shooters. We were conspirators. Kith and kin, so to speak. Now he was patting me on the back and it, actually, felt rather sweet of him, nothing awkward anymore, more like we were buddies.

It had started to snow, just a dusting, and for a moment, John Lynch, indeed, the whole world seemed frozen in place. No more exuberance; no more me, the hot shot, the pot shot, but more an elegiac tone. An hour later, having delivered John back to his Mercury Marquis and given him a parting fist-bump, I felt mournful and wondered if I'd ever see him again. But then, driving home, I switched on the radio and there was classical music, sounded like Mozart, the Magic Flute, and for a moment, I felt just the slightest bit crazy. What was happening? What was I doing? Why should it matter who my father was. Water under the damn, goddamn murky water. Still, as a kid I had always felt different, an maybe that was because, unconsciously, I realized something was up, that my father was not my father and here I was trying to please my father, reading Sinclair Lewis on an October afternoon when I should have been tossing a football around at the park, trying to understand the conversation at dinner, whether it was necessary to lock up Ezra Pound at St. Elizabeth's after World War II, when I should have been in my room, the lights out, listening to the Shadow letting my imagination reign.

But now, finally, I had been able to do something that had existed only in my imagination, to reach out and touch a gun, to hold it, to know it and the power it contained and SANE and the ACLU and all the rest could all fuck themselves. I was connecting to some DNA that had always been lurking there but never acknowledged. I had always felt different and maybe, probably, no, it seemed fairly certain now, it was because I was different; I was the grandson of Gabrielle Capone and the son of Al.

At home, in the kitchen, I poured a glass of skimmed milk and took three Mallomars cookies from the box in the freezer and plopped myself down on the couch. It had all been so exciting, a little scary to be sure, but still thrilling as I drove to the lesson. Then John Lynch, my own James Fennimore Cooper, my own Davy Crockett. Finally, I had, boldly, stepped up to the plate and smashed the ball out of the park. That echo of the gunshot. How could I ever forget it?

So many missed opportunities in the past. In college I had been crazy about Joan Sturm, but sure she would never go out with me and years later, after marrying Gloria, ran into her on Madison Avenue and confessed my infatuation. At first, I thought I had somehow overstepped my boundaries, but it turned out she had felt the same way about me, married some neurologist instead, and was now divorced. What if I would have asked her out for a drink? But I wouldn't have dared. If Gloria would've found out, it would've crushed her.

When I approached Allan Lomax with an idea for a series of recorded folk tales, and Lomax cancelled the first meeting, I had taken it as a rejection and never approached him again. Three years later Rounder Records produced what I had been dreaming of. And, of course, my thesis, abandoned, and the decision not to move to California. Oh, the list was endless.

When Pearl and I had inherited Howard's, 45% share of Cavalier Publishing, and were assured the rest, when the time came, as Lordly put it, I had no desire to languish life away in the family business. And besides, Cavalier was sputtering out. It was the 60's. The three remaining magazines—and that was using the term loosely— could not compete with Playboy and its slick imitators. Still, I felt compelled to forgo the Peace Corps and to join forces with him when I graduated. It would only be for a while, I told himself, ensuring Pearl would get her fair share and be taken care of—Lordly could not be counted upon in certain respects—and then I would have a windfall of my own and would be free to begin the novel I was destined to write.

Not that my career had been a total bust. No, Gloria had always insisted I was too hard on myself and there was the Spoken Word Collection. I had gotten there first, was referred to, once, in the New York Times as one of the pioneers of Books on Tape. If only I hadn't gotten out of the business so early. If only I had persevered. I'd be, among other things, rich. But after Gloria died, selling out gave me a chance to breath, to be free, to move to Cambridge,

Maybe it was time to put my guns away before I became a true lunatic, yet I couldn't let go of the notion: needing to know how it felt to press a trigger; to find out if, somehow, someway, I would experience a feeling I had never known before, and that feeling would tell me something, not simply about myself and what I was capable of, but about my father and the legacy he had left behind. Would it kindle some long-buried spark or would it put to rest all the ambivalence and anxiety that psychiatry and medication and meditation and proper exercise and nutrition could still not get at: that shred holding me back, or would it be a bust, just one more disappointment to live with, make amends with, gracefully or not-so-gracefully accept?

And so I returned to the Yellow Pages. No tutors for me. No Oxford dons. No John fucking Crazy Man Lynch's, just let your fingers do the walking, leaf through to Gun, to Gun Safety Courses; go back and find that place that had sounded too generic before, too ecumenical, like the UN, bland, vague, neutral, hackneyed, but now it would be just the ticket. and there, there it was and it even had a little ad: BOSTON GUN & RIFLE ASSOCIATION INC. One more step and then I could buy a gun, a real gun.

42 / Pearl

Just like that Gabe calls and changes his visit, only one day later, but so unlike him, especially cause it's on Sunday which means he can't get the special Saturday fare, so something must be up. Maybe a Saturday night date? No, last time I asked he got all hot and puffy under the collar, told me it still was too soon.

You want to know the truth, I always wished he would have been more adventurous. He was, I know this sounds funny, too good. Even flying. I told him after Gloria dies, go somewhere you never been before, Timbuktu, doesn't matter but he fed me some song and dance that he didn't have enough frequent flier miles and, in a year, or two it would make more sense.

43 / GABE

A couple of weeks later, I opened the door to Boston Gun Club. surprised to discover a classroom, an actual classroom, with chalkboard, bookcases and desks, and a lectern at the front, but there the resemblance ended, because on each of the desks, next to a notebook, booklets and a pen, lay a nickel-plated .44 revolver. I sat down, wanting to pick the gun up, but thought that I should wait for the teacher's permission. Cautiously, I patted it. There was a label on the desk reading: HI, MY NAME IS and even though I hated stickers like this one, I had no choice. At charity events Gloria dragged me to, I would balk at filling them out and sticking them on my chest, or worse, pinning then to my suit or sport-coat where they created needless little holes. But it wouldn't do to make waves. I would play their game and so, carefully, I wrote my name on the tag, deciding on Gabe rather than Gabriel—no need for formality. Then, I undid the peeling and read the disclaimer on the back of the sticker: Caution, the adhesive employed may cause damage to certain types of fabrics. I couldn't help but smile. Here, surrounded by guns which could blow your brains out, to smithereens, and the first lesson of the day is to beware of an adhesive backing that might damage your sweater.

Over the next fifteen minutes, I remained in my seat, surreptitiously glancing about as my fellow students trailed in. There were eight of them: a black woman in her twenties;

another in her fifties with peroxided blond hair wearing a pale blue angora sweater; a Hispanic man—well, he looked Hispanic and his nametag read Jose; an older man, maybe sixty, wearing a hunting jacket and thick-lensed glasses and a young man in his late twenties wearing a leather jacket and stylish jeans. Looked Italian. I nodded at them as they entered and gave a little hello. But most of the time I gazed about the room and studied the literature that had been placed on my desk. Inside a pamphlet, published, surprise, by the NRA, I discovered just how conscientious; just how respectable. Why, these were no right-wing lunatics; they simply wanted to be allowed their constitutional God-given rights to offer air gun programs for secondary schools; cooperative programs with 4-H, (here piggy, piggy, piggy, piggy: POW!) and to educate eager Jaycees, Boy Scouts and the American Legion.

Five minutes to eight. Soon the class would begin. I felt restless and glanced about the room. There was a poster next to an American flag. FLAG ETIQUETTE, it read and I wondered if they held other classes in this room, maybe for new citizens. No, this was a gun club. No aliens need apply. This poster was intended for those with guns up their sleeves. I stood up, stretched, walked to it and read it:

RESPECT FOR OUR FLAG

a. The flag should never be displayed with the union down, except as a signal of dire distress. It should never touch anything beneath it, such as the ground, the floor, water, or merchandise.
b. The flag should never be used as wearing apparel, bedding, or drapery.
c. The flag should never be used for advertising purposes in any manner whatsoever.

d. No part of the flag should ever be used as a costume or athletic uniform. The flag represents a living country and is itself considered a living thing.

These people were morons. The entire nation was wrapping itself up in the flag, but the NRA wanted to remind them to take it in from the rain, to refrain from embroidering it on Ralph Lauren sweaters, instead, to regard it as if it were some holy relic, some saint's thigh-bone, The flag is considered a living thing. How can a thing be living? And to be destroyed in a dignified way, preferably by burning. Hullo buddy, got a match?

I remembered flag-lowering at Pine Crest Camp, just before dinner, gathered together circling the flagpole; how peaceful, how bucolic it was: two boys lowering the flag, Bumps Schwartz playing Taps on his bugle, birds singing in the background; the grandeur of dusk, the eloquence of the song: Day is done, gone the sun, From the lake, from the hills, from the sky; All is well, safely rest, God is nigh. One of the two designated boys lowered the flag and then the other would unclip it from the rope. Each camper would then take a side of the flag and they'd pull it taunt, somberly marching together, folding it triangularly as they did, and, solemnly, presenting it to Uncle Mort, the camp director, who would protect it until the next morning when it would be raised before breakfast, while the entire camp recited the Pledge of Allegiance, back in those days when you could make such a pledge and there was no ambivalence, no Abu Grey, no Judge Molita, no shame.

I tried to empty my mind of this constant judgment; I shut my eyes; not caring if anyone was looking, I inhaled and exhaled, slowly, ever so slowly——oh, what if Swami Gurpapu should see me here—what would he make of the situation? He would understand.

And then the lights dimmed and a television sitting by the

lectern, suddenly, turned on. Music filled the air: country music; a cheerful and optimistic ditty, with a zither and guitars, then an Appalachian Springy tune while the symbol of the—surprise!— NRA, that splendid eagle, appeared, followed by some more square dance music, as a scene of a father and a son filled the screen; a father patiently pointing out to his boy the parts of a rifle. An announcer, in a jaunty tone, did what Bob had been unable to do: he set the stage: Whether you're interested in recreational shooting, competition, hunting, gun collecting, historical reenactment, home safety, or personal protection, the basics are where to start! NRA basic firearm training courses teach you the principles of safe handling and shooting which help you develop the attitude, knowledge and skills for the safe and legal use of firearms. Since 1871, the NRA has done just that!

I covered my mouth. Wouldn't do to smile. And for the next half-hour, I exercised discretion, keeping as blank a face as I watched Boy Scouts at target practice, Labrador retrievers, 4-H meets, VFW Conventions; people from all walks of life shooting at unidentified targets, cleaning their guns, posing questions to their teachers, oiling rifles. And they looked so ordinary, so normal, the boy and the girl next door, not one Sirhan Sirhan or John Hinkley or Lee Harvey Oswald lurking among them. In fact, many of the men were a little nebbish, definitely on the pudgy size and the women looked as if they were as likely to be preserving jelly as pressing a trigger. A curious asexuality to the lot and a placid Smoky the Bear appearance as well, but at least the NRA was doing their best for cultural diversity: there were several Asians, a couple of Hispanics and two black Boy Scouts.

This was turning out to be an NRA First Steps Program, FIRST comprising the jazzy acronym: Firearm, Instruction, Responsibility and Safety Training. But first in FIRST was this half-hour movie so sanitized it could have come from Disney: 101 Buck Shots. Lady and the Howitzer. Sleeping Luger. It was tripe, drivel, propaganda. Not a single dead animal, much less person, in the entire production! The only damage inflicted from the guns and rifles was to targets or plates shot into the air, old-fashioned games of skeet; there was more violence in five minutes of Sesame Street than in this production. Skillfully, oh so skillfully edited: families and flags and minutemen marching in 4th of July parades. Not a drop of blood. And then, mercifully, it was over, and just as mercifully, a woman, yes, a woman, approached the lectern and warned us in just four hours there would be a fifty-question test and you had to get a 70% to pass.

But not to worry. Every single question would be addressed. It was easy as pie, yes, pie: that was the actual word she used: as easy as pie, as American as pie, as sweet as pie, and most definitely the applest of pies, and as she lectured, I furiously took notes for suddenly I was anxious: I might be one of those thirty per cent who failed, and if they kept statistics, I was sure more Jews were on the list than, say, Baptists, Catholics or Muslims.

This was not the SAT Verbals. A taste for physical violence was not inscribed in the Semitic DNA and so I had to make up for that with what was there: the desire to perform: academically, theatrically, commercially; no matter; a chance to shoot not with a Lugar, but to shoot up your hand—me, me, me, me— the first one with the right answer so I concentrated on what Bobby was saying and in the process, learned things, all kinds of things I never knew before, listing them in my notebook, putting a number before each new fact, trying, for once, to stop myself from free associating, throwing in allusions to Ezra Pound or the objective correlative.

It wouldn't help for the test; there were to be no essay questions. It didn't matter that a round is not confined to circles, square dances and drinks (hmm, shots of vodka…would have to consult the OED at a later time). No, a round only counted as it referred to guns. And, God forbid, if one got lodged in the gun, STOP FIRING and use a brass or wooden plunger to push it in. (Of course the only plunger I had ever used was of the more traditional kind and something I had never admitted, not even to Gloria was that I always thought I had a certain finesse at the toilet, plunging away, and no one could doubt those were dangerous situations too, for a Jew in the American suburbs, as dangerous, come to think of it, as any, up to now, I had come up against. Perhaps, there was some plunge-correlation. That would be reassuring.

And then, the big news! By the way, our instructor declared after the most pregnant of pauses, These, she pointed to the revolver she was holding up in the air, are NOT weapons. Weapons——she intoned the word as if it were Lucifer himself— are used by criminals, and also, a little less explosive now, in self-defense, by police and soldiers. Fascinating, fascinating, fascinating: she could not include criminals, and police and soldiers in the same breath. These are not weapons, but pistols, revolvers, handguns. They consist of three components: a frame, a barrel and the action. Then, without a wave or goodbye or the least attempt at tying up her lecture, she was gone, and Mike Janus entered the room.

Janus could have been James Dean or Peter Pan at fifty: slim, muscular, on the shortish side, evoking a calm assurance, a sense of good old-fashioned manliness. He wore jeans, not your old Levi's, more stylish, with an ironed crease and he had on a dark green sweater, none of this Paul Bunyanesque plaid flannel for him! And a black leather jacket. Even before he reached the lectern, he held the class in the palm of his hand.

Hello, I'm Mike Janus he said and I'm hoping we can begin to understand each other, Mike continued. To learn the same vocabulary, so that we might have an intelligent conversation together. Finally, someone to relate to; a swain desirous of nothing more than a bit of enlightenment! But then Mike sighed and seemed the slightest peeved for it was not to be so easy: Unfortunately, Hollywood and TV reinforce the public's facile stereotypes of guns and the people who use them.

I couldn't believe what I was hearing: a whole new approach: smooth; articulate, reasoned; but not that of a pipe-smoking poo-bahing, do-nothing intellectual, instead a nimble, frisky man-of-action, one capable of using the word facile, and suddenly, effortlessly, he kicked his foot up in the air and withdrew a revolver from behind his calf. It wasn't like those guns on elegant in its way, even sexy.

Mike Janus paused and gazed fondly at it before announcing a profound truth. A well-cared for handgun will last hundreds of years.

A well-cared for handgun will last hundreds of years. In a throw-away world, in which everything from plastic razors and cameras to pens had fly-away lifespans, guns were different. They were made to last; to endure. For centuries. If only they were well-cared for, and Mike Janus was a man who took care of his guns— I was certain of that; he had his techniques, his methods, his tricks of the trade and I wanted to learn from him, become friends with him, maybe, even go out to a bar with him—-have a beer, certainly not a Cosmopolitan, definitely not a beer—and win not just his respect, but become his friend. Never had I come across anyone quite like this man, and what a man he was, not one of these NRA gibberish yahoo goons, not some steroid-macho brute toting a piece, spot all the better to protect his mascu-lions; Janus was dazzling, brilliant, intensely alive, and oh so certain of himself.

True, there was something theatrical about him —you had the feeling that he had performed all of this before; that some of his lines were just that: lines, but there was no humbuggery about him, no ham; the gun took care of that, effectively rending away all the shmaltz, ones that made me question all that I had

166

taken for granted about guns and the men who shot them and if this was the case with Mike Janus, it could certainly be the case with Al Capone. Perhaps, he was so much more than a simple media creation, and deep, down underneath, there was someone as unexpected as Mike Janus; a character, a presence, a soul: darting about, with a story to tell.

It dawned on me that perhaps my intrigue with Janus was that he didn't seem a simple gunslinger, but that, indeed, there was a curiously feminine quality about him. He was graceful, for one thing; as he bounded, his movements resembled those of a Baryshnikov—whom in some ways he resembled—a certain nimbleness on the feet, that in the old un- PC fifties, might have been called a lightness in the loafers. He was attractive: crew-cut hair: gray hair gray, piercing blue eyes, a face of angles and poetry—and that was unsettling: I did not wish to extend my fantasies to tossing around in bed with Mike—-no, no, no, not at all, but I had to admit I wanted to see more of him.

He was a handsome man, and that was the rub: I had not come to the Boston Gun and Rifle Club in search of beauty. For that, there were museums—I had come to learn to shoot, to see what it might feel like to load a pistol, point it at a target, squeeze the trigger and feel the explosion, to find out what I was capable of; to learn of another world, one that lay beneath all that poetry, all those nights at the theater and symphony and ballet; and while the rest of my class were pretty much what I expected, and a little more dim-witted to boot, Mike was distinctive. There was something, well, no other word would do; there was something beautiful about him, and I found himself attracted to this beauty. No, no, no, I was not about to invite him to dinner, to fawn, to declare my affection over cappuccino, to go all wanton, but for a moment, my defenses collapsed, and I imagined us off in a canvas tent, camping, our sleeping bags close together.

And so I listened to him; I listened as hard as I had as Yo-Yo Ma played the Goldberg Variations at Symphony Hall. I listened to all that he had to say and what was compelling, what was electrifying and in the end, what was so goddamn seductive was that, indeed, Mike seemed to be ad-libbing it as he went along. This wasn't mere propaganda or canned curriculum units from an NRA lesson plan but the words of an original, an American original like Whitman, Emerson, Thoreau; like Kit Carson or Davy Crockett; a man of action, but a man who also knew the value of words.

His resume, for instance, which he alluded to right after his introduction: I sensed Mike took a subtle kind of pride in it, but he recited as in the most oft-hand way: words, phrases, titles rolling off casually as one-two-three. First fired a gun with my granddad. Grandad: a more provincial word than grandfather or grandpa; more regional and unsophisticated, like Jeff in Lassie or John-boy in the Waltons. Then I was in the SEALs. No need to bother to toss in Navy, figured most people would know what he meant, that he wasn't alluding to the arf-arf-arfing marine animal, that these SEALs were nothing to sneeze at, that they were an elite and now, now Mike showed an even more rare modestly: Now I confine myself to teaching the likes of you here at BGRC and putting in my nine to five for the Department of Homeland Security, as a special agent in the Internal Protection Division.

I swooned: here in the same room, a real live breathing Homeland Security Agent, a SPECIAL AGENT, empowered with protecting my grandson from airplanes, anthrax and wily terrorists. Mike Janus, model citizen, Mister U.S. of A., Instructor of Firearms, Homeland Security Special Agent, and deep down, just a guy who seemed regular as they come, decent too, and actually intelligent. No trace of thuggery; more like an Errol Flynn, leaping across a parapet in Robin Hood, swinging on a rope, landing on his horse, protecting the peasants from the Sheriff of Nottingham, with a grace and a charm and a hint of a smile; and not just a smile, but a laugh, a merry laugh — they weren't called the Merry Men of Sherwood Forest for nothing!—for while there was terror lurking round every corner and murder and mayhem round every bend, there was fun to be had and in the end justice would triumph. Mike was off and running, and as he spoke, he walked about the classroom, stopping here and there, to look a student in the eye. Infatuated now, I became obsessed with taking down every word he spoke, or as much as possible and since I could feel myself all atwitter, I decided to go for the bullet approach. After all, given the subject, what made better sense, kept you moving along?

x/ In 1856 Horace Smith and Daniel Wesson introduced the bullet.
x/ Bullets travel 900,000 feet per second. That's supersonic!
x/ rifling which occurs after a bullet is fired is a perfect demonstration of Newton's Law….gyroscopic spin. Screw twist.
x/ The journey of a bullet is in own way elegant: case, primer explodes, powder burns, propellant, now it is a projectile!

As he spoke, Mike used his body to suggest the flight of a bullet: a Ballet de Ballistic: such grace, such charm, and oh so beguiling, he actually ended up with a perfect arabesque—hmm, was there something Mike had neglected to mention in his autobiography, something that didn't quite fit in with the SEALs and the Department of Homeland Security?

He spoke of the projectile as pristine, he alluded to its fingerprints, he explained that the caliber is the diameter of the bullet and the barrel. That in the Wild West decimals were used: .22, .25, .32, 9 mm, .385, .357 and the .44, the .45, the .55. That Magnum is merely a marketing term, and that the bigger the case, the more powder, the greater the rocket ship! These higher numbered bullets have more powder, more oomph, more bang for your buck. Only police can buy them. That nothing beats a rifle, but they have become inconvenient and as morals and customs have developed, concealment entered the picture.

I felt a little dizzy, like I had downed a martini, maybe two: where was this man, this Pied Piper, leading us? And why was he so seductive? But no time for pondering; I felt compelled to take his words down; even if they weren't on the test, they were poetic; they were lyrical; they wouldn't disappear in a puff of smoke.

In the early 20th Century there was a problem in the army with the rifle. John Browning—genius that he was—developed the Colt 45 and for 75 years, 75 years, the army used it till they went with Beretta 9mm in the 70's. The NATO gun of choice!

Then he slid another gun from hidden under his other pants leg and actually twirled it around his finger air like Marshal Dillon in Gunsmoke and held it up. This is a Smith & Wesson. It keeps you honest. You could have heard a pin drop. This was one teacher who didn't have trouble holding his students' attention. It's made of jet aircraft aluminum and titanium. Notice the small barrel. It's close-up and personal. For encounters of the first kind. Ergo, it's double action. This is a supremely clean firearm. Load it from the breach.

I wanted to snatch it from his hand. The $4.95 toy with the orange plug would be humiliating if Mike were to see it.

Now for you, at least now, the 22's the best bet. Cheap, less recoil, accurate, doesn't arc. Of course some parabolic arc. He drew a curve on the blackboard and now, he had lost me, I had no idea what he was talking about—I had barely passed Geometry, but, still I nodded in agreement, like I was Pythagoras Jr., I nodded in agreement—yes, yes, yes, whatever you say, Mike, you're the pro. A parabolic arc, what a splendid feature! And then Mike put the gun down, paused and walked up and down the classroom as if lost if in reverie.

Suddenly, I came to. My classmates were asking questions. There were all sorts of things on their minds and none of them had do with who would be winning this year's Booker Prize: Is it okay to carry an unloaded rifle in your truck? What a stupid question? Who would ever want to do such a thing? Mike patiently explained that for most states guns and rifles had to be in locked containers in your trunk.

What about an SUV? The lady in the back asked. I had difficulty feeling any empathy for her, but Mike went on, and I allowed himself to drift off: Mike's show was over: he was forced to deal with these shmucks in the other seats, to deal with their petty concerns. No more prancing, no more history, philosophy, an end to the Dawn of Inquiry, the Age of Enlightenment. It was only then, that I recalled some of Mike's words, ones I had failed to take down for posterity, one particular phrase for instance: left wing and he wasn't referring to a duck. And now, my head swimming, unsure if I could take anything more in, it was, blessedly, time for lunch.

44 / ADAM

Dear Grandpa,
This is the longest email I ever sent in my life. We've been studying this unit called Ancestry and making family trees and I have to pick one family member and write a letter to them and include five questions I don't know the answers to and say five things you may not know about me. Then I wait to see if you reply which I bet you will and then we staple everything together and I get to make a cover, with a family picture on it, maybe even you!

45 / GABE

It was lunchbreak and I was sitting at a diner waiting for my cheeseburger and fries. So much was happening and I just wanted it all to settle—but suddenly an image of Mike appeared, of Mike and me, the two of us on stage, in a ballet, modern though, like West Side Story; both wearing jeans and white-shirts, but I was ten pounds lighter, forty years younger, a full head of hair, and of all things, sideburns. We were leaping in the air and dancing; and Mike was singing to me, from West Side Story: Boy, boy, crazy boy, get cool boy! Got a rocket in your pocket, keep coolly-cool boy! Pearl and Howard had taken me to see West Side Story when I was what, ten, eleven? My first Broadway musical and of course, we had the album and I could remember playing the record over and over again and in the safety of my room, singing along, snapping my fingers, even dancing to it. And here I'm conjuring up Mike and myself on a stage, the two of us playing the scene, bounding in the air, snapping fingers, challenging each other and Jesus Christ, reaching out, hands outstretched, embracing each other, for a moment, just a moment, before the music takes off again and Mike pirouettes across the stage, stopping, freezing, looking my way, then in the slowest of motion, tossing me a revolver and I see it coming to me, like a ball approaching field and I stand there, frozen, supremely confident that all I have to do is reach out, cup my hands to catch it and it would belong to me.

Was this a crush? He seemed so savvy, so cool, and sure, oh so sure of himself. Mike didn't quibble; he didn't consider both sides of the argument; he knew where he stood; daring, free and buoyant—maybe that was why all the Fred and Ginger fantasies. Really, he was more masculine than Fred, nothing top-hattish about him, more like Gene Kelley, a guy, a regular guy singing, just singing in the rain, but an hour later it was raining bullets and there were no umbrellas to crouch under and, finally, I had made it to the indoor shooting gallery of the Boston Gun and Riffle Club. This was it: the ultimate blue book. Get through this and I would gain the certificate I was longing for.

They had told me on the way in that I had passed the objective test with an 80. Now, all I had to do was to actually shoot a gun at a target. The exercise, itself, was simple enough. I stood in front of a counter with a .44 on it. Twenty-four bullets were lined up; two rows of twelve each. I had to load the gun, aim and hit the target. I put on a pair of plastic glasses and earmuffs. It was loud in the room with ten separate galleries set up.

Then, Mike appeared. Load up, he ordered. Could it be he was winking at me? I so did not want to disappoint him. But this was live ammo. One false step, one itsy-bitsy mishap and I could shoot myself. I didn't want to appear nervous before Mike. I wanted him to like me. Carefully, ever so carefully, I picked up the gun in my left hand. It was heavier than I had imagined. I worried that I might drop it. I took a bullet, then with the greatest of care placed the bullet in the first hole and voila! much to my surprise, it slid right in. I picked up another bullet. Just as easy. Now I had to turn the cylinder to the right to get in the next bullet, but really, this wasn't so hard. Finally, the gun was loaded with six bullets, and I locked the cylinder in place.

But no positive reinforcement from Mike. No Nice job, but

simply on to the next step. There was what appeared to be a clothesline at our side and it stretched down to the end of the shooting gallery. 'This here's your target, he said and I had a moment to inspect it. About eighteen inches by twelve, gray, with a black ellipsis covering it and right in the middle of the ellipsis a white box, maybe two inches square.

I had been expecting a classic bullseye. This target looked like it belonged in an exhibit of conceptual art, not at a shooting range and now I felt like a child at the carnival, aiming at a duck, not knowing the hell what was going on. What in Christ's name were you supposed to do? But Mike, dear Mike, had the answer. Just aim for the center, he told me. The white box. And then he pushed a button and the target, which he had clipped with some kind of clothespin to the line, went tearing down the gallery to the end and it just hung there, fifty feet away, flapping a bit, taunting me, as I picked up my gun and admitted Could you show me how to aim it again? and Mike took the gun, put his right hand this way, resting it on his left that way, and said, That's all there is to it. Easy, he implied, as pie.

He might have been explaining the theory of relativity, but I pretended as if at long last I understood as I took the gun and thanked him. Take a couple of shots, he suggested. I'll be back, and he left me there. Alone.

And so it all comes to this: I try my best to look like I know what the hell I'm about to do as I take my gun in hand and rest it against the arch of my other hand. I point it at a target. I remember Mike: Squeeze, don't push. I take a gulp of air, hold my breath and squeeze the trigger. An explosion. I recoil. The sound of a ricochet and the target I am so carefully hoping to hit goes swinging from side to side and appears…unblemished.

You aimed too high, says Mike. Next time remember to use the notch?

The notch. The notch at the end of the barrel. The notch

which is just a bit above the target. The goddam fucking notch. The one I had forgotten existed.

Not really, I say, knowing it's a lie, figuring he's on to me, just the same. If only he would come forth with something like, Did the same thing myself the first time I shot. Don't let it get you down, son. We all make mistakes, pal. Instead, he replies, This time, use the notch.

And so I pick up the gun, aim at the target and swing the notch into view, just below the white square and fire. No ricochet this time as I hit the target, actually hit it! The bullet went through, leaving a circle, admittedly not in the white box, instead a foot or two below it, but it hit the target. Emboldened, I shoot again and again and again. And once more. Each time I struck the target, the lethal black ellipse; each time the explosion I hear, feel, experience, is less frightening; each time a tiny bit more thrilling. This was actually fun.

Five minutes later, Mike and I inspected the target. True, only one of the rounds had made it to the white square bulls eye and all the others landed up and down the black ellipse in no particular order, but I had fired the gun, I had displayed some sort of proficiency, Mike could assure me, You've earned your certificate, and later that afternoon, safe at home, I could take it out and read it aloud.

Now I could go to the police department, apply for a gun permit, buy a gun, a real gun.

I took off the rubber band from the targets I had thought to buy at the gun club and inspected them. These two were nothing like the one I had been forced to fire at: the gray and black abstract monochromatic blob with the white square, which by the way, now had eighteen holes puncturing it and was carefully rolled up for posterity.

These new targets were identical to one another. One, though, was half as big as the other. No denying it, no abstraction here:

this was a target of a man's body. I imagined it up for auction, listed in a catalogue: Official Competition Target B-34, NRA License No. 1, production and design by the National Target Co. 18 by 12.5. Black silhouette of a man's torso and head on white background. Five oblong circles leading from shoulder area to inner-most circle, bearing the letter X. Circles are numbered 7,8,9, both in horizontal and vertical directions. In upper right-hand corner, chart indicating Number of Hits and Shot Value, as well as Scorer's Initials, Competitors Signature, and Range Officer's Signature A condition.

A couple of hours later, at home with my precious target, I felt the X-ness excess of the targets, as in X marks the spot, square in the middle of the chest, right on the sternum—funny, you'd think they'd go for the heart. And no small coincidence that the circles ended just above the belly button. No points for a stray shot to the groin or scrotum. C'est la vie.

I stood up and unrolled the larger target. It's only difference from the other was that it was labeled B-27 rather than B-34. They must have a whole range of targets and using letters and numbers made it a little easier than ordering say, Charging Lion, or Standing Man And then it struck me: This larger target was...the...exact...size....of...a...human being. I held it up in front of me like I was modeling clothes. No doubt about it. Probably intended for the police, the army, the El Fatah. But why the mention of competitions? Why would they be selling these at the Boston Gun and Rifle Club which touted its roll-out-the-barrel-we'll-have-a-barrel-of-funness, its family days, it's just plain folksy bonhomie.

I poured a glass of Bordeaux, turned on Barber's Adagio for Strings, took out a pair of scissors and meticulously cut the figure away from the target. It really was quite easy—the head didn't even have ears—and then I stood up and gazed at it, eye-level, and for a moment, just a moment, it seemed alive, like my Peter Pan shadow, then I lay it down on the armchair as if it were just sitting there by the fireplace. What if someone should come by now? What would all this look like? I didn't care. In fact, I rather enjoyed having it sitting there in front of me: benign, inert, comical. The fact that it was featureless and frozen made it resemble a mime and lent it an air of the antic. It sat there, not exactly staring at me, for it had no eyes and one needs eyes to stare, but it seemed to be lending me its presence, much as if it were a compatriot, a fellow traveler, a friend.

46 / PEARL

Now or never. Time. To get rid of it. Now. So I called Ruthie. Hello, dear, might you have a couple of hours to help me out? We made a date: for the next morning, for nine o'clock. Wished I still had the old percolator. So I could give her a cup of coffee. The percolator's was stronger, darker, like when I was a kid, when there was always a pot on the stove, when people still dropped by. Oh, let's have another cup of coffee, let's have a cup of Nescafe. But this was the rehab unit and the coffee was back at home, the Maxwell House in the freezer, the percolator somewhere in the cabinet. Chock Full of Nuts is the heavenly coffee, heavenly coffee, heavenly coffee. Chock Full of Nuts is the heavenly coffee. Better coffee millionaire's money cannot buy. What a sweet song, and old-fashioned too, not like TV advertisements now. So dirty. No more jingles. I remembered our kitchen table with Shirley and Gladys, Tessie and Molly and Mom. All gone now. No one to really talk to, like they talked, about everything. Everything. The people here, nice enough, this feeling that they were all used up, like a tube of toothpaste. Brusha-brusha-brusha with the new Ipana.

Yes, call Ruthie and Ruthie would bring the shoebox from the closet. With the packs of matches from the Bahamas, and the little bars of hotel soap, still wrapped up, the ones I could never bear to leave behind, and I'll put it in a paper bag with the hairbrush and give it to Ruthie who'd walk me to the end of the hall to the trash chute. But the trash chute was back by the apartment and it had to go in the trash chute. Because then it would go away. To the incinerator. And never come back. And then I remembered: there was one here too, at the end of the hall. I saw a nurse shlepping a bag there and it looked like just the same kind of chute. It would be okay. Gabe would never know. Ruthie, Ruthie would help. And then it would be over.

But later in the morning, second thoughts. Once it was in the chute it went straight to the incinerator. And then there was nothing you could do about it. This was no hauling away a trash bag with the newspaper and garbage to a can, a can sitting there to be picked up. The incinerator seemed more sinister—sinister incinerator—something evil about it. Like the Nazis. They'd shovel you in and what was left? No proof. The last shred of evidence, the last proof of Ketzel I could put my finger on, touch, bring to my lips: kaput! Forever. But then, but then, but then, what if the old memories faded even more. Away. Like those poor shazitskys in Level 3, the nursing ward, the ones who didn't know what end's up, for God's sake? And the shoe box stimulating the memory cells in the brain so Ketzel could come tumbling back. And those nights too. Not simply what we said to one another, or even what we had done, but what it had felt like. And God knows, there'd never be a chance to feel like that again. Instead, ashes, ashes, all fall down.

The next morning, I crossed the threshold of the Police Department and was dispatched to Room 314, I received my application, an application that had to be notarized, for Christ's sake, and then and only then could it be considered. The application was only two pages and as I started writing, using my best printing, I was surprised at just how easily it went. Name, address, phone number, date of birth, Social Security number, mother's maiden name, father's first name. And then I paused. Of course they were referring to my legal father, Howard. But what if, just what if it, for some cockamamie reason they asked for biological father? Imagine writing out, Alfonse Capone. What would the Cambridge Police Department do with that particular piece of information? How might that upset the old applecart? And then all the rest: height, weight (I shaved off three pounds just to round it off, build (with a shrug, I wrote average), complexion, hair and eye color.

Easy as pie.

Yes, I was a US Citizen.

No, I had never been known by another name.

No, never convicted of a felony.

No, never convicted of sale or possession of narcotic or harmful drugs.

No, never confined to any hospital or institution for mental illness.

No, never under treatment for drug addiction or habitual drunkenness.

No, never the subject of a M.G.L C209A restraining order. Whatever the hell that was.

No, no domestic violence.

Then the topper: the name and addresses of two references. After much consideration, I settled on Sam Berman, who I had known since we had been five years old and Muriel Schuster. She taught English at B. U. and would take it seriously. he and her husband Saul, a judge, had been friends since the '60's. Sure, I would have to notify them both, but they wouldn't be that nosy. I would allude to a novel I was writing. That should do it. As I handed the completed form to the policeman at the desk, I felt a peculiar sensation, a sense of buoyancy. I had pulled it off; he had actually pulled it off. Soon, the license would be in my hands and so would that nickel plated Benelli. But there was a fly in the ointment: the policeman, an Officer Flannery, took the application, but had an announcement to make.

Take a seat in the back office.

I was startled and just a little nervous. I walked to the room and sat down on a folding metal chair besides a desk. On the wall was a poster with WANTED pictures on it. What was the problem? Maybe I had done something wrong. But they'd have to tell me; they'd have to read me my rights; my Miranda.

Something I never would have guessed. Officer Flannery came in, took out a little box. Gotta get your prints, he announced and then one, two, three—how many times had he done this before?—he took my hand in his own and the act, itself, made me feel defenseless, passive, like a little boy as my fingertips were placed on an inked pad and then, starting with the thumb and giving it a little roll, Officer Flannery took each finger and pressed it to the card. When he was done, he handed me a box of tissues. We'll send this to the F.B.I., he explained. Just to make sure they got nothing on you. Another bureaucratic hurdle.

How long will it take? I asked, crestfallen.

Maybe four, five weeks. We'll let ya' know.

Four or five weeks? If I was the commonest of criminals, it wouldn't take any four or five weeks, I'd just fine some fence somewhere, some unscrupulous dealer. Cash on the barrel and the barrel would be mine!

I was pissed, but I continued to play the role of the model citizen as I looked both ways up and down the street before crossing. Four, five more weeks? How much more could they put me through? I felt myself growing angry. At the street corner there was a light and a WALK sign, and this was technically jaywalking, but if they wanted to arrest me, they could just go fuck themselves. After all, jaywalking was hardly a capital offense.

Later, in my bedroom, I glanced at my brush on the dresser. Gingerly, I picked it up and swept my finger against the bristles.

Then, looking in the mirror, I brushed my hair this way and that. I looked different, less the gentleman, more the brute. I removed my own shoebox out of the closet, full of my own memorabilia. And looked through it all: a typewritten document, twenty, thirty pages, on onion-skinned paper browning at the edges, my first novel. Match boxes. The final issue of Buxom Babes, one of Lordly's magazines. How dated and quaint it seemed; how silly so many of the images appeared: lurid, obviously set-up, models air-brushed to within an inch of their lives, leering at the camera in the most provocative of poses, heads up-turned, impossible smiles, glazed expressions, breasts covered discretely or brazenly jutting forth, one absurd shot after another: Eves eating apples, naked genies in bottles, models dressed only in strings of pearls, farm girls pulling petals of a daisy (He loves me, he loves me not); cowgirls baring pistols conveniently hiding their breasts while others dressed as Indians with enormous feather headdresses, crossed their arms, as if they were about to utter How; damsels imitating pythons dancing out of jars while Gunga Din-ish Indians played the flute in the background; bare-breasted women playing football, brandishing machine guns in back alleys, putting golf balls, dangling dog biscuits in front of slobbering poodles; nymphs in front of gas pumps, premium certainly cheaper back then.

The pictures, the ones that captured my attention, were not so contrived, and in black and white, more mundane scenes: a naked secretary at her desk, with the most beguiling expression, and black lace panties, handing her boss a letter she had just typed inspired me to imagine calling her into my own office for some dictation of my own; an exotic Eurasian brunette, naked as the proverbial jay-bird, sitting on a subway, surrounded by male commuters, engrossed in their newspapers, looking out the window; a dental hygienist, wearing a simple nurse's hat and a see-through bib, bending over a patient in a dental chair,

183

cleaning his teeth. These were not perfect women; there was nothing coquettish about them: they seemed intent on doing their job, going about their business, but I imagined myself beside them, surprising them, placing my arm on their back, a sudden electricity in the air.

I picked up Gloria's brush and noticed, laying on top of the bristles, a single strand of what had to be hair. Carefully, I picked up the strand and lay it across my wrist. It was dark, black, glossy. And then I picked up the hairbrush and put my index finger inside, between two rows of bristles. Nothing. I glanced about the bathroom and spotted a nail file, poked it into the brush, as if I were going fishing and pulled. Again, nothing. I tried again. Success! A small piece of hair stuck to it. I put the file and the brush back just where I had found them and then looked up into the mirror in front of the medicine cabinet. A piece of hair, I seemed to remember, a piece of hair could contain genetic matter or DNA. And so it might be possible to retrieve a piece of his hair and to match it up with my own DNA and see if they were related. It might be possible to have proof, to finally determine if this was merely some hair-brained figment of Pearl's incipient dementia or whether it was true, and if it was a lie, I could finally put it to rest for all time, but if it was true, I could know, really know.

I wasn't eager to get all hot under the collar and dash off to the computer to begin my research. Instead, I made a pot of coffee and read the front section of the Times and when I had finished the editorial page and had to decide whether to continue on with the Arts Section or Food, I paused: maybe, just maybe it would be better not to know, because now I had the best of two worlds: it could well be true, but just as well could not, and there was a queer pleasure in having it vague, with both Howard and Al as contenders in the sweepstakes; both in my corner, urging me on, outstretched arms, eager to hug me, slap me on the back, run their hands through my own hair. Hair. One thin strand could spell the difference. Maybe. Maybe not. Maybe the hair had to be more recent. Fresh hair, so to speak. But hadn't there been articles about DNA-ing mummies and wooly mammoths? Only one way to really know. And so begrudgingly, with a sigh, I approached the iMac and turned to Google, imagining myself in a play, not a comedy, nor a tragedy, instead, a great Shakespearean historical play, Gabriel the First.

Three thousand years ago, King Solomon, faced with a similar question, held an infant in the air, threatening to cut it in half but then rulers could still rely on wisdom to prevail. I typed out DNA paternity hair, three little words: DNA paternity hair, then pressed return. Seventy-four thousand answers. Of course, they didn't arrive majestically like Solomon, and they certainly weren't heralded by language from the Old Testament but they did make their points.

FIND OUT YOUR HERITAGE WITHOUT LEAVING HOME! PUT THOSE QUESTIONS TO REST FOREVER. IS HE, OR ISN'T SHE? WE'LL GIVE YOU THE ANSWER NOW. ALL WE NEED IS ONE OF THE FOLLOWING: Sweaty t-shirts, undergarments, semen stains, vaginal stains, paper or plastic cup, glass, ear wax, fingernail clippings, socks, urine, licked stamps, cheek swabs, dried blood, chewed gum, dental floss, cigarette butts, used tissue, dried skin, used razor, hair with roots.

So it comes to this; this is who we are, this is who they were, the they who conceived us; the they who raised us up. This is how we should search them out, come to know them, repay them, bring them down: as ear wax on a Q-tip, as a toe-nail clipping, as a stubbed-out cigarette butt, a wad of dried-up Juicy Fruit gum; Kleenex used to contain a sudden sneeze, or hair with roots.

Throngs of satisfied customers: sobbing mothers embracing daughters, fathers carrying babies on backpacks, a black man, the spitting image of Kofi Annan, looking down with pride at a five-year old even though the boy looked just like Louie Armstrong. And there were Asians and Hispanics and Asian-Hispanics too; oh, what a melting pot of DNA lay before me, even though they were probably models. No, these people had to be the real thing. How else to explain their desecration of the English language, their passion for getting a good deal, and their complete and utter bathos? Who could make this up? Who could be their target audience? All these endorsements were sincere and genuine. And it wasn't just these yokels who were weighing in, it was also the marketers of the test:

If the child knows the identity of their biological father, they may gain a sense of 'identity'; for most people, it is important to know who their father is and what sort of person they are. This may set their mind at ease and answer questions about themselves, such as what characteristics they have inherited from their father. It can be argued that a fundamental right of a child is to know who both their parents are, however, although this knowledge may benefit the child, it is not necessarily beneficial to the other parties involved. And it can be yours for only $199!!!

Time to visit Pearl, while she was still at Level II, before she returned to her apartment, while it was still possible to get the brush and see what genealogical treasures it contained. Then it would be simple: mail in a strand or two of hair, a swab of my own sputum, maybe a little spunk on the side, and BINGO, there'd be the answer I've been waiting for.

47 / ADAM

I waited till Sunday night to talk to Grandpa and he asked me what he usually does, How's tricks? I don't exactly know what that means because I've never been big on magic but I got it, sort of.

Nothing much, I say. I never like saying Nothing much, but sometimes it's all I can think of. Grandpa, though, is very good at getting me to talk.

Anything wild and crazy happening in school? he asks.

I bring up the Doomsday Clock even though I think, maybe, I shouldn't because my mom and dad don't seem to enjoy talking about it very much. I actually think it's starting to annoy them. He seems interested, though, and asks me some pretty good questions which I've never thought of before like how can scientists really know what time is Doomsday and then he points out something extremely interesting, that there are trillions and trillions of other planets and at least a billion of them probably have life. So we're not the only ones. And maybe it won't be midnight for thousands of years and other life forms will help us figure out what to do to prevent Doomsday.

Look, he says just 200 years ago there were no cars or radios or televisions or cell phones or computers.

You got a point, I said.

Maybe you could even help, he says. Become an environmentalist.

I'm only a kid.

Still, he says, You could take a stand.

Then he gets all excited. You know there was a book maybe fifty years ago, about atom bombs and the end of the world, he said and that was half-a-century ago,

People have been predicting doom for a long time.

What's it called?

On the Beach. Come to think about it, it may be a little too grown up for you. Then he laughs.

What's so funny? I ask.

Because when people said that to me when I was your age, I resented it, and cause that made me want to read the book more.

So what do you think we would do with Jasper if it turned Doomsday? I ask.

Adam, boychick.

He calls me boychick sometimes. Yes.

We'll cross that bridge when we get to it. Know what your grandma would tell me to do when I was worried about something?

No, what?

Go outside. Get yourself a breath of fresh air.

Did it help?

I can't remember, he said. But it didn't hurt.

48 / GABE

Back at Heritage, visiting Pearl. I ask, So how's the arm, Ma? She held it up and looked at it, disinterestedly. It's a goddamn nuisance.

Does it still hurt?

Not as much as before. But I'm getting nudgy. Can't you talk to them? I want to go home.

The nurse said a few weeks more, till you can handle it.

Why should they me telling me what to do? There was an edge to her voice, a flash of anger.

Because they make the rules. They've seen lots of patients in your position.

She shook her head in disgust. Well, this patient ain't so patient.

Remember what you used to tell me; a watched pot never boils.

That, at least, got a smile out of her. You were such a little pisher.

What do you mean?

I couldn't say anything, you'd want to know why. Always with the questions. Even when you were three, you were very perceptive.

I was taken aback. It was the first time I could remember her ever using the word perceptive. I never would have guessed that she would have been that psychological, especially when

I was a child. I wanted to hear more. So, you thought I was smart?

Of course you were smart. What with the questions and the books.

When did I learn to read?

Who remembers? But it was early on. And then there was no stopping you.

It was in my genes, I said, feeling rather chipper to hear her talk this way, and then I realized, well, perhaps, it wasn't in the genes after all, and as long as she was in such a good mood, wondered whether this would be a time to push her a little, but now she was rubbing her forearm. Does it hurt, Ma? I asked.

Just a little ache.

Do you put the cold pack on it, like the doctor suggested?

Sometimes.

I'm going to get it for you.

It's in the freezer.

I retrieved it and settled it on her arm, and she curled up with it, holding it down with her other hand. Oh, oh, oh, she sighed. That feels good. Funny, most of the alder cockers I eat with swear by their heat packs, but for me, nothing beats this.

'Some say fire and some say ice.'

Whaddayamean?

It's from one of dad's records, the poets. Robert Frost.

You still have the albums, right?

Yeah, in the basement, in Boston.

What are you gonna do with them?

Good question. When I move, I suppose, maybe I could give them away, to libraries or something. But who listens to records anymore?

She moved the ice pack in circles on her arm. Your Dad was so happy back then, so happy.

Why you think that was?

He was doing something on his own, at last. Free from Lordly. And it was respectable. Plus, it would bring people pleasure. A different kind of pleasure than their magazines.

Pleasure's a funny word, Ma.

What's so funny about it?

I was baiting her—I knew it, but| couldn't help myself. Because isn't that what everyone wants? When you performed, isn't that what you were offering?

I just thought of it as getting a paycheck.

Yeah, but besides that, when the audience applauded.

She seemed to zone off for a moment. A far-away smile. Oh, you knew when you had a good audience. When they wanted you back and wouldn't let up. It felt good. And then we'd milk 'em for a while and give 'em an encore.

Did you always do the same one or did you just decide, right on the spot?

She paused. I can remember a couple. I'll Be Back, Fish Gotta Swim,' and just a minute, just a minute, I'll be Seeing You.

Suddenly, I imagined the world without her, sooner rather than later, and how I would miss her. Couldn't help it, started to cry. Not wanting her to see me, I tried to distract her. Sing it Ma.... And then she did, in the way she used to when I was a boy, casual, off-handedly, so it didn't even seem like singing at first, as much as if she were reciting a line or two from a dictionary. And then, now that she had my attention, now that she caught me staring at her, transfixed, she started to sing, slowly, matter-of-factly, exquisitely in tune, and with just a trace of sadness to her voice, the most tender of touches:

I'll be seeing you
In all the old familiar places
That this heart of mine embraces
All day through.

191

And now she was gesturing with her hands. Even the cast could not stop her from pointing out the children's carousel, the chestnut trees, the wishing well. And a smile crossed her lips, a trace of a smile as she continued. If she saw me crying, that was just too bad. Old Pearly, she still had it in her, she still could knock you out with a song. She could purr/. She could belt it out. And then for a moment I caught her pausing, looking around the room and I wondered what was happening, but, no, it was all part of the song, part of her act:

I'll find you
In the morning sun
And when the night is new.
I'll be looking at the moon,
But I'll be seeing you.

I struggled to speak, to find the right words, but all I could say was Ma, and then she broke the spell, she bowed and smiled. I played along and clapped. Then, I decided, what better time? I tried to modulate my voice, to speak casually, as if the words were just coming to me. You know, Dad with his books on tape and his poetry and you dancing and singing, isn't it funny, you both wanted to do the same thing, entertain people. Not the most elegant of segues, perhaps, but it worked. She nodded, as if she were pondering just what I had said.

Emboldened, I continued. I read something the other day, oh, I don't know where I found it, some magazine, maybe the newspaper, this quote that really got to me. It was about prohibition. Goes something like this: 'When I sell liquor, it's called bootlegging. When my patrons serve it on silver trays on Lake Shore Drive, it's called hospitality. I simply give people pleasure.'

Nothing, nothing at all. Her face remained implacable. So what's that got to do with entertainment? she asked.

And she had me there. It was a leap. How to make it and reel her in.? Oh, I don't know. Having a drink or two. You still like your scotch and Frescas. I like my wine. A couple of glasses for me and I feel looser and everything seems more fun, more entertaining.

She seemed to consider the logic of what I was saying. You got a point, she acknowledged.

Back to task. That quote, oh yes, now I remember who said it. Who?

Al Capone. I uttered the two words carefully, impassively, so the full weight of them might better register. Silence, and then a flicker, a flicker of emotion on her face and she turned away, casually, as if there was nothing to it, but I knew then, I was certain then; she could not look me in the face. I thought, finally, I had got her.

Ma, did you ever see him?

Who?

Oh, this was rich. I was tempted to be sarcastic, to reply Herbert Hoover, but, no, that might make her more defensive. Better to play it casually. Capone. You played his club sometimes, didn't you?

When we were in Chicago, we occasionally played Colosimo's. I might've seen him there once or twice, but he was always surrounded by bodyguards. And then she asked a question of her own. So why you want to know?

Oh, I don't know. Pause. Just curious, that's all.

She inspected a fingernail, then put her hand to her mouth, as if she was stifling a yawn. I'm feeling a little tired, she said. Maybe I'll take a little nap.

This wasn't going to go anywhere, and I was angry. Once again, oh so evasive. Still, I felt nervous. What if she should be suspicious of me? There'd be no more chances to get through to her, to learn the truth. Okay, I'll get to my hotel, take a shower, come back for dinner. I stood up and approached her. Can I give you a kiss? I asked.

She smiled, almost coquettishly. Since when can't a son give his mother a kiss? she asked and I leaned down and kissed her on the cheek, then, surprisingly, she placed the cold pack on the table next to her chair and placed her hands on my shoulder, kissing me him on both cheeks. Now don't be late for supper, she said.

In the hallway, I was furious with myself. If only I had been more emphatic, maybe she would have talked more. Something in me, however, had held back from confronting her. It wasn't just being cagy, either. The idea of her with Capone, carnally, disturbed me. The motel could wait.

In her apartment, I searched the top of her closet for the shoebox. But it wasn't there. I brought in the stepladder, climbed up, looked at the top shelf, but all that remained were plastic storage compartments with sweaters, winter clothes, shoes. I felt frantic, as if I was capable of ran-sacking the apartment but managed to constrain myself and deliberately searched through every drawer, under the bed, the vanity in the bathroom, through each shelf in the kitchen. She had simply moved it somewhere else and it was just a matter of finding where. She couldn't get on the stepladder, so she must have moved it somewhere convenient.

But it was nowhere and suddenly, I wondered, if for some crazy reason she had given it away, thrown it out accidentally,— but no, she would never do that. Maybe the cleaning woman, yes, the cleaning woman, with Pearl at Level II, maybe the cleaning woman took it—but that didn't make sense—what would a cleaning woman want with a box full of old papers, pictures, a tarnished hairbrush?

I wanted to call Pearl, to wake her from her nap, when her defenses were down, to demand her to tell where it was, but that would be too dramatic. But I waited until dinner, just after we ordered. Ma, I stopped by your apartment, to check up on things.

And?'

And, well everything looked okay. They stopped the paper, finally. And I got your mail from the desk. But you know, the shoe box?

The salad came and she pretended to be eating it.

I have lots of shoe boxes.

The one you keep your treasures in.

Oh, that shoebox. She spoke the words casually, as if we were discussing a slice of bread.

Well, it wasn't where it usually is.

She blew on her soup and took a sip. That's because it's not.

Now I was pissed. It was if she was playing a game with me. She knew exactly what she was doing. Still, I cautioned myself to keep calm, to refrain from taking the bait. Oh, I replied, So where did you put it?

It's with Ruthie.

Ruthie?

Ruthie.

And why, if I may ask, did you do that?

A pause while she picked up a roll from the basket and took a small bite. She promised to take care of it for me.

Safe from what.

She shrugged. Look, you stopped by yourself, you said it yourself, you wanted to check up on things. So you certainly can't blame me from worrying.

If it was jewelry, I'd understand.

My jewelry's in the vault at the bank.

I know that. I'm just trying to understand what would make you do such a thing. Who would be interested in your shoebox?

You never know. Esther Bluestein's cuckoo clock it was an antique, was taken when she was visiting her kids.

But your shoe box?

You never know. And I figured what it could hurt? If someone wanted to steal a pot or pan, I wouldn't care, but what's in that box is priceless to me. My most precious memories.

In the car, I found it in my wallet, Ruthie's phone number, and in less than an hour she had confessed she hadn't had a chance to throw the shoebox out yet, but then we met up and she gave me the box, a little suspiciously, I thought. Then back to my motel to pour through it. For a moment, as I eased the car out of Ruthie's driveway, I felt squeamish, as if what I was doing, what I was imagining was just a little bit out of bounds, but bounds locked you in; bounds restricted you and this feeling was so different, so exquisitely unlike all those I had been bound up by in the past. Giddy, free, boundless.

Back in my room, I opened it and took the brush in my hands, stroked the bristles and absently minded brought it to my scalp. I wanted to stroke my hair with it and, indeed, began to, catching myself only just at the moment the bristles were about to touch my scalp. Later. Now there was more important work to be done, work that couldn't be contaminated.

I set up a little lab on the desk, sweeping it clear, removing a pillowcase from the bed, spreading it out, smoothing it down. Then I took the brush by the handle and shook it. Nothing. I tapped on the handle. Still nothing. No need to get nervous. It had been sitting in this shoebox for who knows how long. I went into the bathroom. Thank God for amenities! A tiny Nail Care kit lay on the counter, complete with emery board and one of those pointed wooden sticks to push up your cuticles. I took it back to the desk and sat down, trying to remain calm, even though I was sure this was the decisive moment. Holding the brush in my left hand and with my right pushing the pointed wooden stick between two lines of bristles, I jostled it. Nothing. Then, trying to keep myself from the frenzy I felt approaching, I moved up and down another row of bristles, applying more pressure, up and down, back and forth, up and down, and then, slowly, delicately, as if this were the most critical of neurosurgery, I removed the stick and touched the end of it to the pillowcase.

And there it was, maybe only a quarter of an inch long, but unmistakable, there it was, all that I really needed: a hair, a single hair, black, oh so black, unlike any Pearl had ever harbored on her head. It had to be from him, and there had to be more. Up and down, up and down the rows of bristles, and one, two, three more hairs, joined their brothers. There were four of them now, a quartet.

No more need for questioning now; or begging Pearl, who could not be trusted anyway. Now the truth could be known.

Four strands of hair: one, straight, maybe a half-inch long; another just the barest hint of a curl—he was Italian and Italians were known for their curly, kinky hair—the third a good inch, solid, unmistakable; the last strand not quite a semi-circle, like a smile or an ark, a regular Noah's Ark, emerging not from just forty days, but years, sixty some years. The euphoria, the joy, the bliss, but only for a moment for suddenly I remembered: a root, a root; the hair had to have a root.

A quick call to the motel desk clerk for a magnifying glass. No dice. A frenzied drive to the local CVS and $7.89 later, I had one, not quite the classic Sherlock Holmes version, but rectangular, more like the one I used when I collected stamps as a kid, and then $5.95 for tweezers—it couldn't hurt—but when I arrived back in my room and inspected the hair under the glass, all hope was gone. Each strand was a mere line, straight, curled, it didn't matter, a line with no root at the end, no bulb, nothing you could go on. Frantic, I took the brush, jabbed it with the tweezers, hunting for more hair. A few strands, straightest of strands. I banged the brush on the side of the table. Nothing. After all this time, nothing. Trembling, taking hold of the brush, the brush that I had been certain belonged to my father, my real father, I held it to my cheek. Now I would never know who I truly belonged to. It would all be the merest of conjecture. I felt a deep longing, a profound yearning, not simply to have my curiosity satisfied, one way or the other, but to have confirmation, from some authority.

Then it struck me: there were, indeed, other possibilities all listed on the website: Sweaty t-shirts, undergarments, semen stains, vaginal stains, paper or plastic cup, glass, ear wax, fingernail clippings, socks, urine, licked stamps, cheek swabs, dried blood, chewed gum, dental floss, cigarette butts, used tissue, dried skin, used razor, hair with roots. But one seemed more unlikely than the other. And yet, yet, yet, if I could pluck a hair from him, it would more likely have the root emerge with it. And then there were fingernail clippings.

And hair and fingernails continue to grow…after you are dead! Yes, perhaps a little unorthodox, just a tad on the macabre side, but if somehow I could get to the graveyard, unearth the coffin, open it up. Of course, it seemed impossible, ludicrous, some might say mad, but still it could be done and then in just a minute: pluck, pluck, pluck, a locket of hair here; clip, clip, clip, a few fingernails there, all safely deposited in a nice zip-lock plastic bag. A speedy Yartzheit prayer. Yisgadeel, yisgadesh. a stone on the grave, a quick exit. It could be done.

Of course, it was difficult to imagine doing it myself. There must be people, however, who did this sort of thing. Specialists. Perhaps these DNA shyster firms faced with similar dilemmas had a kind of SWAT team: ex-Navy Seals, down-on-their heels veterans of the Iraq War who'd move in fast, use those infra-red glasses that could see in the middle of the night, have just the right tools to pry off the coffin lid—voila!—then minutes later, be helicoptered out. Not necessarily a likely scenario. But somewhere there was someone who would do it. There was always someone. Who would do anything. It would be expensive: ten, twenty thousand dollars. Who knows? It's not exactly like they're listed in Craigslist.

But there must be an easier way, a saner way. Then it struck me. Sonny, Al's son, still alive in Florida. He was walking around, maybe this very moment, just full of his father's DNA. So, somehow, get to Sonny, talk him out of some or make him an offer he can't refuse! I called 1-888-576-GENE, the number for GENETREE where the ad promised from 9:00 AM to 6 PM Mountain Time our courteous staff of technicians and counselors are waiting to assist you. They'd know. They'd have to know. And three rings later. Hello, you've reached Gene Tree. We'll be with you in a moment. Your call may be tape-recorded for training purposes.

And then the music. Oh, what idiots. Who needed to hear Hello Dolly now? Finally, a human voice and tongue-tied and desperate, I managed to get out the $64,000 question. Uhh, is it possible to find out, to determine if you have a sibling, well, really a half-sibling, with a DNA test??

The Gene Tree techie reacted as if he heard this request every day, as if there was nothing in the least peculiar about talking to a stranger with such a burning, haunting question.

Of course.

Oh God, did quality control train them to reply in such a manner? Breezy, two syllables, authoritative. Of course!

Oh, I replied, a little surprised this was all going along so swimmingly. That's great.

Now let's just make sure we mean the same thing, said the tech. Half-siblingship exists if two or more individuals have one common biological parent. That's what you're interested in determining?

Exactly.

We can do a more complete reading if we can also have a sample from the parent in question. Is that possible?

Well that might be difficult. Extremely difficult.

Not to worry. Of course, then you won't be able to use the results in court.

Who said I was going to court? Al had spent enough time there. No need to drag his DNA back in. I was growing annoyed. Look, all I want to know is are you sure this will work?

If there's a fifteen per cent correlation, then we'll say, it's unlikely. Anything over ninety and we'll say likely.

That was good enough for me. This might be a little tricky. Sonny, Al's only child, and most probably, my own half-brother, was not known for showboating his connections to his dad. He led a solitary existence. Who could blame him?

Oh, the poetry! The only child of Capone, a florist: inspecting roses and carnations at the wholesale flower market; creating bouquets for weddings and funerals. Valentines would never be associated with massacres, only with the busiest day of the year; red as in roses, not blood. The fragrant smell of lilies, gardenias and Sonny's favorite, magnolias. It was unfair of his father's rivals to poke fun at him, to imply that he was somehow less a man because he dealt in hot and not whore houses; that the only funerals he attended were ones in which he dropped off elaborate arrangements; that being a florist was a profession for the effeminate, the pansy among the pansies, but that never stopped Sonny.

Yes, I had become Sonny's Boswell. Whatever there was to know, I was determined to know it. Each detail of his life, even the most mundane, captivated me. Google was our lifeline, bringing us closer and closer together. As a child, an only child, I had wished for a brother, a sister, some sib to deflect some of Pearl's attention away from me. When, later, I had asked her why she and dad had no more children, she skirted the question: Que sera, que sera; whatever will be will be.

Sonny, who had managed to create a life for himself and his family that was simpler, and yes, less lucrative, that that of the man who just might be our father, but it was full, for a while of that most elusive of qualities: joy. At five o'clock, he would close up shop, make up a small bouquet of yellow tea roses or tulips, his wife Diane's favorite, and arrive home, to his doting (if increasingly tipsy) spouse and to their girls. No entourages, no retinues, no bodyguards: a home full of flowers and daughters, all doting on him. Daddy's home! Daddy's home! Who could ask for anything more?

And after Pearl Harbor, Sonny, always the good boy, felt he should do something for the war effort. He gave up the store and volunteered. Now every day he arrived at the Miami Air Depot training to be a mechanic's apprentice. A lowly job, some might say, but with a name like his, he never would be called grease monkey; he never would be abused. No more lilies and pachysandra, instead, engines and turbines, time to get your hands dirty, not with potted petunias, but with oil, and with grease. He learned how to wield a welder's torch and ended up on an aircraft assembly line. All for the war effort; all to defeat the Krauts. After the war, he became a used car salesman, but quit after the owner of the lot ordered him to roll back odometers. Alas, this was just the beginning of the end for him, and after Al died, there was no will, no money, nothing. A small cashier's check from Chicago every month, just enough to get by.

Now you don't have to be Sigmund Freud to realize the consequences of a name: Sonny, always the boy-child, the son; Sonny, as in son of, and in this case the son, the progeny, the off-spring of you-know-who, and while the apple may not fall far from the tree, this particular apple was always urged in the other direction. He would have everything his father had been denied: education, respectability, privilege. Yet it didn't exactly work out that way. Ten years later, mother and son opened a restaurant, Ted's Grotto, with Sonny as the maitre'd, but despite the excellence of the veal marinara, it never broke even and Sonny ended up working in the warehouse for a tire company in North Miami. By this time, his wife, Diane, had called it quits. She began drinking after the girls left for school and continued throughout the day. Eventually she packed her daughters up and moved to California. Sonny worked up to sixteen hours a day to send them checks.

At least he had a hobby: marksmanship. He was one of the best rifle and handgun shots in the country and while he was shlepping tires from trucks to the warehouse to earn a measly paycheck, was offered $25,000 from the Springfield Firearms Company to tour the country, showing off their line. One requirement, though. Drop the name, Capone. People might get the wrong idea.

And then it happened: Sonny's fifteen minutes of fame. On a sweltering Friday afternoon in August 1965, he purchased three bags of groceries at the Kwik-Check Grocery in Miami Beach. But he also stuffed two bottles of aspirin and a package of double AA Ever-Ready flashlight batteries into his pockets. Just his luck, two undercovers from the sheriff's shoplifting detail were on the prowl and arrested him just outside the store. The manager of Kwik Check said, He's a real good customer. All I can say is I hope he comes back. And as he was escorted into the police car, Sonny remarked to the policeman who had just handcuffed him, I guess everyone has a little larceny in them.

Two years' probation and newspaper headlines around the country. Sonny was humiliated. Nine months later he petitioned to change his name. I should have done this years ago, he told the judge. And the judge couldn't resist a little lecture, exhorting him to give up his shoplifting ways so that nothing will be visited upon the heads of your children. Later, in the 1980's, Sonny moved to California, to be near his daughters and then back to Florida again where he remarried and retired.

There was nothing, however, despite all my fervid Googling, about him dying. Sonny was, most likely, alive and kicking. But how to find him? Then I remembered, he had changed his name to Brown, that was it, Al Brown. A quick Google search for Al Brown Al Capone, proved the deadest of ends. Then, I Google Albert Francis Capone name change and there it was, from the Gettysburg, Pennsylvania Times, May 11, 1966, People in the News—Albert Francis Capone Jr. Has Changed His Name. To Albert Francis. Didn't exactly require a lot of imagination. Still, you had to admire him for wanting to retain some of his previous nomenclature. Albert Francis. Al Francis. Tame enough, no connotations; bland, inoffensive: Hi, Al Francis here. Want to offer you an insurance policy I think you'll be interested in. And to think that the great news came from Gettysburg, the four score-and-seven-years-ago Gettysburg we have come to revere, that-these-dead-shall-not-have-died –in-vain Gettysburg, where the Capone chick has come to roost.

I call 411 and ask for Miami, Florida. There are four listings for Albert Francis. One must be him. But which? I Google Miami Florida Private Detectives. 495,000 listings: 211 Private Investigators and 318 Investigation Services, including some fly-by-night looking agency, THE SEARCHERS, offering a FREE TRIAL. I send them my email address, my phone and answer the question: Who are you searching for? My long-lost half-brother, Albert Francis, last known in Miami. Must be in his 90's. Had a floral store and restaurant in Miami, Ted's Grotto. Arrested once in August 1965 for shoplifting. (Went under another name then. Legally changed name in '66.)

Give them time, time to come up with something. Or nothing. But somehow this wasn't reassuring. I looked at other similar businesses, Fortress Investigations, Nu-Line (could be a carpet cleaner) Alpha Group (ho-hum), Nanny Surveillance (too esoteric and hinting of a porno flick)) Naked City (same problem, but definitely poetic if ultimately ridiculous), Dante Investigators, (the reference to the Inferno was intriguing) Gold Shield (too hackneyed), Florida Apprehension Team (sounded like a bunch of beagles),

Mr. Mike (how could anyone trust a gumshoe who went by Mr. Mike?) and my favorite for the corn sweepstakes, Sherlock Investigations.

They all sounded too generic and dumb. And why would a detective need to hide behind a corporate moniker? What was he trying to conceal? What was good enough for Sam Spade should be good enough for me. I refined my search, hunting now for a name, a name that would look just right printed in black letters on a door with frosted white pebbly glass, a door that would open up to an office with a desk, an old-fashioned one, no computer station in sight, and in the drawer of the desk, a bottle of rye whiskey, a gun, a Rolodex on the desk and a phone, an old-fashioned black dial phone. Tripe. Sentimental tripe. A private detective needed to be computer literate, probably have an ergonomic chair, a cell phone, of course, and would more likely have a joint in the desk as a pint of Jack Daniels.

I scrolled through the Miami Yellow pages. Finally I settled on one, Mark Landsman, Private Investigator. 3561 Collins Avenue. Dialed him up and surprise, a voice, a human voice answered, a voice inspiring trust: deep, basso profundo, a little weary. No hype, no blather. Just a voice saying, Hello.

I told Landsman the whole story. Agreed to wire his bank a $1000 retainer Then, after I hung up, it struck me, oh, the coincidence of it all. At the end of the month, it was my grandson, Adam's, Bar Mitzvah and he and his family lived In Jupiter, outside of Miami. Why did it not strike me till now? Time to slow down, get it together. Change the dates of my flight. Fly in early. Meet with Landsman, maybe even get an address. Introduce myself to Sonny. And then a day or two later, show up for the Bar Mitzvah. Be embraced by my family members, the ones I could be sure of.

49 / RACHEL

It must run in our genes, this tendency to search and investigate, to dig deeper; to ruminate. Maybe if I had been analyzed, I could have figured it out, where it all comes from. But look where it got me. It got me Law Review, it got me clerkship. And partnership. If we would've stayed in DC, who knows what I'd be doing now. Dad always claims I could be Attorney General. I think, though, uh-un. I cast my net and fell for filthy lucre.

Brian and I had just gotten married when the offer came and the thought of all that loot—even Dad was surprisingly taken with the idea of his daughter making six figures—and the matching offer Elliot got, well, we couldn't resist.

It wasn't as if there was a family business waiting for me. I learned all about Cavalier when I was sweet sixteen and snooping around the closet in the basement. A collection of magazines that made my head spin. Plus, I hated snow, and sleet for that matter. Had been on the swimming team in high school. Third in the state, free style. Always dreamed of my own pool. Fresh water not chlorinated. We could buy a house, a house with a pool, spread our wings, have a good time. And we did. We never had to worry. Private school? Sure, why not? Italy in July? Just make the reservations.

50 / GABE

Right in the middle of everything, a phone-call from my neighbor, Sam Berman. Well, not my neighbor anymore— he moved to Wellfleet after Marge, his wife, died four, five years earlier. We'd see each other a couple times a year when he was in Boston, go out to dinner, always a steak house, have a drink or two, schmooze about the kids, the old days, politics. Sam had been connected to the Democratic Party in the 70's, a big Dukakis man. Come to think of it, his father had been blacklisted by McCarthy. That's why it was so ironic, the news he was so anxious to deliver.

Remember the house next to us? he asked.

The one you tried to get me to buy? With the stone fireplace?

Yeah, the Swicky place.

Well, this couple from D.C. bought it. Lawyers. They rent it out in August.

What can a place like that go for? I asked.

In August, height of season, sixty-five hundred, maybe seven thousand a week.

No shit, I replied.

And I just found out who will be renting this August. Might surprise you.

I bite.

A certain Chief Justice of the United States Supreme Court.

No.

Yes.

Jesus fucking Christ, you going to be neighbors with Harold Molita?

Just spent an hour with his detail.

You mean?

The Secret Service.

What was it like?

All very palsy-walsy. Did I stay up late, get up early, let a pet run, have parties?

What'd you tell them?

The truth.

Did they ask about your politics?

Uh-un. Steered clear of that. Wanted to alert me there'd always be a car by the entrance to our road and sometimes personnel—they called 'em personnel—around. Warned me he'll be walking on the beach, sometimes early, but not to worry, he liked to be alone.

Sam asked about me, the kids, what was new, tried to fix me up with his sister-in-law again, invited me to visit this summer. Had to give him credit, he was always generous even though he knew I didn't much care for the Cape. Come for a couple of days, he urged me. Maybe we could talk some sense into the judge.

Sense, of course, was something we'd never be able to talk Molita into. The man was a viper: duplicitous, a wolf in sheep's clothing who was spearheading the drive to turn us into the most corrupt of Rome's. It wasn't merely handing over the election in the first place, which led to the phony wars and the corporations unleashed to buy even more elections. It wasn't his assault on abortion or African Americans being denied their rights to vote. It wasn't the disenfranchisement of everyone except for big business and banks. And the attacks on the Environmental Protections Act. The Climate going to hell. It was that he was only sixty and there was no end to the man. He could be wreaking his particular kind of havoc on the planet for decades to come. If anyone deserved to die, it was Molita and now my old pal, Sam Berg would be right next door to him and I could be too.

Out of the blue, I think of Adam, of his Doomsday Clock. Then it hits me, for the first time as Sam is rattling on about Molita. I, of course, cannot pay any attention to him; I cannot even pretend. My idea, so stunning in itself—I had never really thought of myself as an assassin before—that I have to, somehow, put my hands around it, it is just so preposterous, so ludicrous, so absurd that it just might float away, and I am afraid to let it go, determined to capture it, but like some butterfly, it is fluttering off into the distance. I must, I order myself, reach out in the air and seize it in all its monstrousness; its ambition; it's grandeur. It is mine. All mine.

I need to settle myself down. A drink and some peace and quiet. A chance to think. Then, Sam changes the subject. Gabe, my man, he says. Just remembered, the gun.

I whimpered. I actually whimpered. How could he have read my mind? The gun? I repeat, feigning ignorance.

The gun. The letter I got from the police. Wanting a recommendation for your permit. What in the world you, of all people, wanting with a gun?

I'm writing a novel, I said, pleased with myself, my duplicity. And, a pause, It's a mystery. Yes, a mystery! And I need the protagonist to shoot a gun.

He swallowed it, hook, line and sinker.

51 / PEARL

Head bursting. Bursting at the seams. Nothing works. Nurse, nurse. Can't talk.

Pearl, will you smile for me? Can you give me a smile? Pearl, can you move your finger. Your pinky. Her voice. Fading away. My arms don't work. Nothing. Works. Nurse, nurse. My mouth won't work. No sound. Dizzy oh so dizzy.

52 / GABE

The much dreaded, long anticipated phone call: Mr. Freeman, I'm afraid I have bad news. Your mother's had a stroke. That night, holding her hand, I could scarcely believe that she should come to this: still, silent, so obviously somewhere else. The doctor had explained it matter-of-factly: A massive ischemic stroke. The unfamiliar word ischemic.

Then, forty-eight hours pass, and somehow it becomes clearer, the odds grimmer as the stroke guy, the specialist delivers the news, the tempered news: This doesn't look good, but they're doing remarkable things in rehab these days.

What's the best we can expect? I ask.

She might regain some of her functioning. You can never tell.

And if she doesn't?

It's tricky to predict. You need to be prepared.

For what? I sense he's stalling, this doctor who could be all of thirty. I want to shake him. Enough hedging, enough dilly-dallying. Just answer the question. Just answer the goddamn question.

That she'll remain in this condition, mute, completely paralyzed except for what we've noticed with her left eyelid.

And how long…might she go on like this?

It could be…years.

The full weight of the doctor's words overwhelms me. Pearl is condemned, but there is to be no end in sight. Pearl will never be who she was. So what to do? How long can I sit here, holding her hand? What to say beyond the obvious? All the phrases tumbling out, the one I say over and over —I love you Ma—-eventually, enough's enough. How many times can you repeat the obvious? And I was not about to go all Dylan on her. Do not go gentle into that good night. Uh-un. Not in a million years. Do go gentle, Pearl, gently, in your sleep, maybe a nap.

Blessedly, she appears asleep. This is what the doctor suggests will be permanent, until, who knows, her heart or another stroke strikes. When I ask him, ever so gingerly, Is there any way we can, perhaps, help her along? Wink-wink. He gives me his hospice spiel, how I should contact hospice, how hospice is experienced in such matters. Hospice, hospice, hospice. All I really wanted was for him to turn to his black leather doctor's bag, as if doctors still carried bags anymore, then to take out a needle, and for it all to be over. Instead, hospice, hospice, hospice.

But what about my question; my ultimate question? Not about how she could die, but how she had lived, back in Chicago. How she had lived, and whom she had lived with; who was it, anyhow, who gave her me. Pearl held the key and now I would never have it; I'd never know who my father was.

Of course I felt guilty. Feeling sorry for myself at such a time. Then it all came back; her pleas— not really pleas, always came off as mere rational requests—that if the time ever comes, I'd take the ultimate care of her just like we took care of Shmowie and Impy and Nipper and Magoo, all our dogs. We put them to sleep. Not hospice or doctors or some kindly nurse.

Surely, that's what she'd ask me now, if she could talk. If only she could talk. Then it hit me. I could. I could help her, help her as I had never helped her before, and it needn't be such a big deal, as it seemed to be for so many others, so many other sons and daughters. This wasn't stooping to that old chestnut, matricide. The trick, and it seemed to me in what was feeling like a wave of enlightenment lifting me up, was to be quick, quick and gentle, and, of course, not to be caught. No, no, no, that wouldn't do: SON OF SCARFACE MURDERS MOTHER! Not exactly my kind of headline.

We needed another opinion, I tell my daughter, Rachel, on the phone, and, suddenly, I sound like Howard: Let's discuss it, put it off, give it a day, sleep on it. But she wouldn't want to live another day, another hour. How do I know? She's my mother. And who can blame her? Still, what it could hurt to see her granddaughter, her great-grandson one more time. Wouldn't that make going, somewhat easier?

What about for them? It would be easier not having to see her like this, but to remember her as she was, in her prime. And Pearl was always vain, never left the house without her makeup on, wouldn't wear a bathing suit the last twenty years, still a blond. Pearl would hate being remembered as she is now. Others would cling pathetically on to some form of life, afraid to let go, but not Pearl. The show's over, take your bow.

How to do it? How to help her? But of course. The pillow. The spare pillow I discovered in her dresser drawer. Just press it over her face. And what if someone should walk in? Too big a chance. Too great a risk. Maybe though, at night, close to change of shift, how long would it take?

An hour later, back at the motel, with my computer plugged into the Internet, unlike all my previous homework, however, my previous voyages through the internet that, often, seemed to have lives of their own, I proceeded with caution and with stealth, can't forget my PRIVATE BROWSING. No cookies, no memory, no search history, no trails or evidence to be left behind. One night of internet abandon. The ultimate question: How do you humanely smother and then the possibilities appear: a dog, a fish, a bird. A bird?

Keep typing: your mother. But even reading about it makes

me sick. There is no such thing as a bad question. Guess again. There are all sorts of them, like the one no one on the internet, other than me, seemed to entertain: Is a feather pillow quicker than a foam rubber? You'd think so. What I did, learn, however, was how to do it, and that it would take longer than it did in the movies. Three minutes, just to make sure.

The next morning, sitting by her bed, contemplating such an act, rehearsing it in my head, I mull it over. Maybe it would be wise to talk it over, talk to Rachel. But that would complicate it. She'd need to see her like this to make the right decision, a true mercy killing. Any delay is cruel, inhuman. Prolonging the inevitable. Still, I have to protect myself. When Anthony Genna was gunned down in Chicago, Al was in Cicero. On Valentine's Day, when Bugs Moran's gang was slaughtered, he was in Florida. The list was long, but always Al had an alibi. This was trickier. Couldn't exactly order a hit man.

During change-of-shift, when the three to eleven nurse meets with the eleven to sevens, there was thirty minutes you could count on to be undisturbed. That might be it. The perfect time; the perfect crime.

And so, the next night, when the nurse, pauses by the door at 10:30 and bids me good night, I reply, Have a good weekend.

You get yourself some sleep.

I will in a while. Like to watch the news with mom, then I'll head out afterwards.

Wish more of our patients had children like you, she replies, closing the door. Two hours later, I moseyed over to the nurse's station, and chance of a lifetime she was asleep, softly snoring in her chain.

I walked briskly to Mom's room, positioned my chair next to her bed and held her hand, ready. Everything that I had to say had already been said. I turned down the volume of the TV. Animal Planet was on, a program about kangaroos.

Pearl seemed to come to a little when I slid the pillow from under her head, then when I gripped it in my hands, I steeled myself. It wouldn't do to waste any more time. And as I was doing it, a little voice in the back of my brain whispered, you are a murderer, but it went away, just like that, and never came back.

I took a deep breath and then and only then, looked at Pearl as she lay there facing death. It was then, before I could dwell on it a moment longer, that I opened her mouth the best I could with my right hand, whispering, One, two, three, like I was going to jump into the ocean. I thrust the pillow down upon her face. I could hear her gasping and pressed a little harder, but gently. It wouldn't do to leave any redness, any mark. Three to five minutes, that's what it took, three to five minutes. I glanced at my watch and continued to press.

I shut my eyes, took another deep breath, then a faint rattle, the death rattle. I could smell urine—this often happens right after death—but there was no way of really knowing until I could remove the pillow, calm myself down a bit, observe her face, hunt for her pulse, and, suddenly, a release of emotion—I had been working so hard to remain resolute—and I calmed myself down. It's over, almost over.

Finally, I remove the pillow, put it back in the dresser, kneel by her bed, search for a pulse. Nothing. I sit back down in my chair, holding her hand, as I search for her pulse. It still may be there. Nothing. I remove my hand, curl up in the chair, shut my eyes, even fake a little snore—how good I am at this—and it must have been convincing because when the nurse arrives, twenty, thirty minutes later, she tends to Pearl, then shakes my shoulder. Mr. Freeman, Mr. Freeman, wake up!

Rubbing my eyes, maintaining my Oscar performance of Dutiful Son By Mother's Bedside, yawning—God, how easy this was—I pretend to wake up and muster a little yawn. Oh, I must've dozed off, I mutter.

215

Mr. Freeman, she replied, her voice gentle, sweet. Your mother has passed away. Passed away in her sleep.

'Oh no! I cry.

She wasn't alone, the nurse says. Bless her. Had her son by her side

53 / RACHEL

When dad called to tell us grandma had died, I didn't recognize his voice. I had never heard him sound so sad before, so flat and affectless, with this little, unfamiliar, stammer, which got to me as much of the news of her death—I had been prepared for that—but his voice, it was that of a different man. After I hung up, I felt ashamed, because, suddenly, I resented having to take time off from work, even for Grandma. Dykstra vs. Comcast: three years of my life. With a little luck, if we won, the biggest case of my career.

I wondered how it would look if we only spent one night. Or if I flew in just for the day. Then it struck me: could this to be to our advantage? How would a jury respond to an attorney in black, in mourning her beloved grandmother?

I knew what grandma would have said, Milk it for all it's worth. Always leave them clapping, the show must go on. She was so the consummate performer. Brought me taps when I was five. How thrilled I felt as we went to the shoemaker, he was Greek and had a funny accent. I can remember him hammering the taps into my shoes. Pearl insisted I put them on, right there in his shop and, suddenly, I was playing the Palace. She sang some song—When the red, red robin comes bob, bob, bobbin' along.—and I couldn't stop myself from breaking out into a little number.

And here I was, just an hour after she had died, wondering

how to use her death to my advantage. Whatever was best for dad, and within reason, I would do. Grandma trumped Comcast. Whatever I decided, I'd be okay, but I wondered about Dad. On the phone just after, that was one thing, but later when it sank in? They were always so close, and, lately, he had been acting a bit peculiar.

54 / GABE

Rabbi Saunders, who used to visit Pearl, was such an asshole, but, still, he was a whiz at funerals, and no, it was not so much a funeral, he informed us, aa a celebration, a journey, a journey of a beloved matriarch, who will live forever in our stories and our memories—yisgadal, yisgadash—and whilc hc was blathering on, I realized that mother rhymes with smother, and then I actually sympathized with Saunders, who was only trying, in his feeble way to comfort us with whatever pablum was at hand. I, however, found most comfort sitting by my grandson on one side and my daughter on the right. There, in the synagogue, the organ playing one of Pearl's favorite tunes, It Was Just One of Those things, I do a quick tally of who's there—maybe sixty mourners. So many of Pearl's friends already dead. She would have wanted to have a decent audience for her, as she would have put it, swan song. I wondered how many would be there at my own funeral and how I would die and just who, if the occasion presented itself, would be with me at my particular end, to help me, if I needed it, along? Adam and Rachel at my side? I glanced at them. Suddenly, I felt very old.

I thought of Scalia. Then I decided I would do the deed. By hook or by crook. I would spend the night at Sam's cottage at the Cape and bring a gun. And then I would shoot him. Somehow I would do it.

55 / ADAM

We were at the synagogue in this special room, one just for mourners, and there was this rabbi who seemed in a good mood for a funeral, and he took out a knife and made a little tear in my shirt. Right on the pocket. Nothing will be the same anymore, he says. Some tradition from Moses. Seemed weird, a rabbi with a knife.

While everyone was crying and the rabbi cutting people's clothes, I had this memory flash. Great-grandma once asked me what I wanted for Chanukah and I told her a pocketknife—I was going to camp that summer and it would've been cool to have one—and she got mad at me. She got truly pissed off. Don't play with knifes, she yells. You can cut yourself bad. And they leave scars.

Mom had asked me if I wanted to say something at the funeral but I was afraid I'd cry in front of everybody. Great grandma was a little strange at times, but she was fun. And she always made me feel good. She would do this little tap dance when I was a kid and sing this crazy song, On The Good Ship Lollypop. It would crack me up. And she made me rugelach. There were these funny stories she'd tell, about Mr. and Mrs. Mallard and their six ducklings.

56 / GABE

Back in Cambridge, I was a wreck, not because of Pearl, but because of Molita. Couldn't stop thinking of him, of all that he was responsible for. Molina: Samuel C. Molina, the single most dangerous man on the planet, and speaking of the planet, it was his vote (5-4 Citizen's Rights vs. EPA), which stopped the agency in its tracks and rendered the Climate Change act null and void. It was his vote (5-4 in support of the President) which allowed for the invasion of Syria and the deaths of hundreds of thousands of men, women and children. It was his vote, 5-4, 5-4, 5-4, which gutted the Health Care Act.

If I had my druthers I'd take Chief Justice out, one clean shot. No need for senseless cruelty. But in order to stop him, to do the deed, I needed a gun, a gun that couldn't be tracked back to me. Then, from out of the blue, I remembered John Lynch, good old John Lynch, the camouflaged gun safety instructor who I had paid off and fled from; the guy who was just a little too familiar, but who seemed oh so happy when I handed him the money.

There he was listed in the phone book and when I called, his son answered, just like before, Dad, it's for you, and then when I was about to confess who I was, in a moment of inspiration, I decided to lie. Hi, this is Matthew Spofford, I began. Somehow the name came to me, from out of the blue. I'm hoping to have some gun safety lessons. For a. target pistol. Suddenly I was not so sure of myself. What if he was taping the call? What if he already had my phone, and my name?

No need to worry. He jumped at the bait and promised to meet me in the morning, back at the scene of the crime, by the Arsenal Mall. And he was there, right at 10:00, a man of his word, but when he recognized me, he seemed peeved. Are you gonna run away again? he asked. Like a little baby.

How dare he speak to me like that? But rather than indulge in repartee, I played supplicant, reached into my pocket, took out a wad of bills, peeled off a fresh one hundred—somehow I thought he's appreciate new ones, cold hard cash—then handed it to him. For your travel time and gas, I said. A little smile on John Lynch's face, a tiny squirrely smile.

I was nervous. What I was about to suggest was a crime. What I'm interested in, I continued, before he could pocket the bill, Is, well, I want to buy a gun.

'Gainst the law, he replied, the flattest of tones, no more Mr. Nice Guy.

I counted out five one-hundreds. What would it take? I asked.

Then that creepy smile. What's to keep you from getting a license, getting it legal? He stepped up closer. You want to be some Annie Oakley? he asked and then, I remembered, he had called me that before and there was something sexual in it. I didn't like it then; I didn't like it now. Still, this was my chance. I couldn't blow it. I want it. Today, I said matter-of-factly.

That'll cost you, he said, locking eyes with me.

How much? I asked.

He seemed to consider it, but only for a moment. A thousand bucks.

Well, that has a nice ring to it. Must admit, I was a little shocked at the words as they came out of my mouth, and a little proud. I decided a bold move was called for and took out my wallet and counted out ten one-hundred bills.

In a moment he had opened his truck and handed me a leather case with a revolver inside, and a dozen bullets too. Minutes later, after handing him the cash, and with the gun safe in my glove compartment, I drove away.

Back home, I made a little nest for the gun, in my middle dresser drawer, underneath my socks. It seemed nice enough, cozy in its own way, and over the next few days, I'd return to it, to retrieve the gun, to hold it in my hand and point with it, at nothing in particular: a lamp, my toothbrush, a carton of Tropicana. I was, innocently, watching the news one night when there was a piece about Molita—he had just given an interview to some right-wing rag—-and, inspired, I jumped up, ran to my bedroom, grabbed the gun while he was blathering on, made it back just in time and aimed at him as he sat there all smug and supercilious; aimed right at his forehead—-and, surprise, it was easier that you'd think—if he had really been there and I had thought of to load a bullet or two, I could have nailed him. It was only a month till the Supreme Court recessed for the summer and he'd be next door to Sam, when I'd have my chance. But would I dare? I wanted him dead, of course; who in their right mind wouldn't? But what would it do to Rachel and her family? How would it affect Adam?

It would. It would have to. For the rest of his life. Still, other things would affect him, monstrous things that Molita was responsible for. Immigrants denied citizenship, Pakistanis waterboarded, abortions outlawed, minorities denied voting rights, corporations funneling billions to control elections. And, ultimately, the environment. Molita attempting to make the EPA unconstitutional, get us out of the environmental bills with China and India. It wasn't like there was much time left. All the climate scientists, well most of them, said there was ten, maybe fifteen years while we could still do something. By the time Adam was thirty, half the animal species would be extinct, fierce costal storms would wreck the planet. Bats, butterflies, bees all dead. Sayonara elephants. Global starvation.

Sure, it would be traumatic for Adam to see my picture on the front page, to have his beloved Gaga an assassin. But think if the long haul, his long haul; he's forty, fifty, sixty, with kids of his own. Think of them then, the planet collapsing.

Not such a far-fetched scenario. And even if, despite Molita's departure and a new Supreme Court Chief Justice who was less rabid, the planet still goes to hell, at least we would have given it the old college try.

57 / ADAM

Grandpa.
Yep.
Has mom talked to you about vacation?
You mean, the three of us getting together?
Yeah.
We're talking about it.
Wherever we go, can we go fishing?
Why not?
But we'll throw them back, right?
Throw them back?
 Because fish are being depleted. Cods are gonna be extinct.
No problem.
Mom found this cool house. It's got a ping-pong table.
Where is it?
On Cape Cod.
 Oh, my.
Grandpa are you there?
Oh, yes. I'm still here.
Can we bring Jasper?
Some places won't allow dogs. But I'll find a place. Leave
it to me.
How could we not include Jasper?

58 / GABE

An hour later, another call, from the detective, and the words, the words I was dreaming of: I think I have your man.

Really?

Still goes by the name of Albert Francis.

Immediately, I think of Sinatra.

Got a pencil? Landsman asks. 5628 Bay View Boulevard. In South Miami Beach.

That night, no matter how desperately I sought it, sleep wouldn't come, so I took an Ambien and lay in bed, imagining Sonny, Sonny who I wouldn't even be able to call by his proper name, instead, Albert. How ridiculous, how sad that it had come to this and, yet, how understandable. What he must have been through. Couldn't even go to college and have a fresh start. Trying so hard to do the right thing, the decent thing, and at every corner, the whispers and smirks, the slurs and innuendo. Still, how strange it was all going to be: showing up at the door, the guy was probably stone deaf by now—you couldn't just knock, how'd he hear you? Imagine trying to get the point across in sign language!—maybe he had some kind of blinking light. Okay, so then he shows up. How to get started? Hello, Mr. Francis? You don't know me, but I'm your long-lost half -brother. No, no, no, please just a minute of your time. Please! And then I imagine myself in black face, like Jolson, falling to the ground, kneeling down, belting out a tune. I remembered when Jolson first fell to his knees. Because he had a terribly infected toenail and he was on stage and couldn't take the pain anymore and wanted to relieve the pressure!

Desperate to stop Sonny from slamming the door in my face; I could hear myself singing—sometimes the Ambien made me feel just a little giddy before finally knocking me out— in the voice of Al Jolson, how strange. Then it hit me Al, Al. Two Al's, after all. And, of course, the Pearl connection. Pearl had played with Jolson, before him, actually, warming the audience up. She had met him once, liked him, confided, He always behaved himself, just like a perfect gentleman, which she might not have said about the other Al. I felt the Ambien now, as if I was being rocked to sleep, but this was no lullaby, no Rock-a-bye Baby, this was Jolson with his over-the-top, schmaltzier-than-thou histrionics; the crooning, the whistling, the hammering-yammer and yodel, the minstrel love song not from some genuine African-American who was entitled to belt it out, but, instead, the lament of Asa Yoelson, the rabbi's son from Lithuania, AKA Al Jolson of Broadway. Slather that blackface on Asa, pucker up those lips, paint 'em red, bug out your eyes, ah the grotesquery of it all, but, ah, what Al could still inspire:

I've been away from you a long time
I never thought I'd miss 'ya so
Somehow I feel, your love is real
Near you I wanna be.
Swanee, how I love ya, how I love ya
My dear old Swanee.

Then Jolson whistling, like a bird, a bluebird drunk on moonshine, and off in the distance, the band is playing, so many banjoes, it really is most amazing, and, no, I am not asleep—I actually blink to make certain—I loathe any art, any epiphany that relies on contrived dream scenes to liven things up—and imagine Sonny's face after he has hears the story of our, yes, our father; after he realizes he has a new brother, I imagine him starting to weep, stepping up to me, and finally, after sixty years, finally we embrace.

The next morning, sipping my coffee, reading the New York Times, I feel not quite so giddy, but chastened, the feat I am contemplating is a difficult, perhaps, impossible one, and the fact, that, now, I have not simply one, but two reasons to be in Miami seems not mere coincidence, but cosmic, beshert, astonishing, and just a little scary. That Sonny—he would always be Sonny, no matter what he did to his name—and Adam, my own grandson, should have paths crossing like this, no mere coincidence, no happenstance, nothing of the kind: there has to be some cosmic connection. To reunite with my brother and a few days later attend my grandson's Bar Mitzvah, it didn't make sense, or made the most of sense, depending on how you looked at it.

Best to change the reservations immediately. Simply fudge it with Rachel, tell her I'll be there on Friday, yes, Friday morning before the service and actually fly in Thursday and if they run into me, say, at the airport while they were picking up god-knows-who, act like it was a surprise. Decided at the last minute to come in early but knew how busy you'd be and didn't want to bother you. Rent a car, drive out to see Sonny. Leave Friday open, in case I needed to up the ante.

But maybe, just maybe it would all go so well, so swimmingly, that Sonny would invite me to lunch, and we'd drive to a wonderful Italian restaurant where my long-lost sib would suggest exactly what to order: The veal piccata and polenta and grilled vegetables. Me, I gotta go easy on the pasta these days. And we'd compare cholesterol and reminisce about our childhood and discover all sorts of extraordinary coincidences: we both got a D in Geometry, played right field, have cowlicks (at least when we had more hair) on the left, and Worcester Sauce made us gag. Hesitantly, the conversation might drift to politics. What if, God forbid, after all this brotherly love, that Sonny was a Republican? But no, no son of Al Capone would ever fall for a Republican. No offspring of the man called Robin Hood could stomach a king who stole from the poor to give to the rich; no Capote bambino would be blind to the lies, the smug morality and venality of the preacher lining his flock up for the slaughterhouse while inventing tales of wolves at the door.

And finally, finally, just before dessert, we'd swap stories of our father. Of course, it might be difficult for Sonny. He had helped to nurse him after he had been released from Alcatraz, when the ravages of syphilis were wracking his body and shutting down his brain. That couldn't have been any picnic and now, two cups of coffee in me, I finally felt able to explore the implications of that moment two months ago, as I made the great discovery. Until then, all I knew of the disease was that you caught it while fucking, that a Wasserman test detected it, and that before AIDs, and before penicillin proved a cure, syphilis had been the sexual scourge of all time. And then I realized the truth, the truth that none of those actors who played him, Wallace Berry, Paul Muni, Rod Steiger Jason Robards, Ben Gazzara, Robert DeNiro, Neville Brand and John Jones, could ever know, what did anybody know, anybody but Sonny and myself, and perhaps a few scholars and historians? Everyone thought they were so fucking smart: watch a movie, read your goddamn textbook in American history, surf the History Channel, think it's for real, but all of it malarkey, hokum, pablum cooked up for the masses. Black and white footage, the more the merrier, photos of the Saint Valentine's Day Massacre, and of DeNiro wielding a baseball bat, finishing off a stoolie at a conference table: all of it lies, or if not lies, not quite the whole unvarnished truth either, for there were reasons for Al's occasional lapses: clear, justifiable, legitimate reasons: Al Capone was a victim; an innocent victim, of a merciless affliction. He was a wonderful son, a devoted family man, a beneficent benefactor, a friend to the poor, so all right, he did get mixed up in a business which was illegal was involved with certain unsavory associates. He was not perfect. But who of us is? And who of us has suffered syphilis?

All those two-bit, know-it-all, Mr. Method actors played him, tough, low and menacing, with that silly ersatz Italian accent thrown in for effect, but to hear him as he actually would have sounded if I could known him, been bandied on his knee, even the most clichéd keechy-keechy-koo would have been a blessing, or, maybe a story, something simple, no strings or morals attached, a story like the three bears and Goldilocks. So many voices in the world, each one different, such a range, from the pip-squeakiest to the dulcet baritone of Caruso, and who knew what Capone sounded like? Who really knew? It wasn't like he had a radio show or made speeches recorded for posterity. No, there was nothing at all. If only Spoken Word had been around back then: Dante's Inferno as read by Al Capone. What a hit!

I fond Pinsky's new translation—-it had been a present—and unread. Where could it be? So many books. From so long ago. So many, lined up, expectantly, pleadingly, as if they'd ever be read again; what a waste; what folly. Bertrand Russell, Spinoza, Primo Levy—where is the goddamn Inferno? Finally, after scanning hundreds of titles, some I would just as happily grab and throw in a heap, I never wanted to see them again, and some, ones I still loved: Sinclair Lewis and Melville, Twain and Roth. Finally, up on a top shelf, there it is. I reach for the book, feel my back tense. Got 'ya. A hardback: The Inferno of Dante.

Funny cover. Fiery red: a slap-dash sketch of a black body with a pitchfork piercing it. Nothing exactly left to the imagination. I retreat to the couch, sit down, open it, the paper fresh, so white, the thrill of opening a new book. A glance at the translator's note: Dante invented terza rima (the interlocking rhyme pattern aba, bcb, cdc, etc.) for the Commedia, and its effect—combining onward movement with a feeling of conclusiveness in each step—seems integral to the poem, something well worth trying to approximate.

I am intoxicated, as if I've just downed a couple glasses of champagne. The world is topsy-turvy, and, oh so suddenly, more interesting, more alive, oh so much more fun. This guy has hit the nail on the head. He's got it! ONWARD MOVEMENT: exactly the way I have been feeling lately, off and on, though more on lately, ever since the discovery of the initials on the hairbrush and the most compelling natural rhyme scheme in the world, AC, AC, AC, AC, not simple alternating current, but the most powerful force of nature: energy, energy I never knew I possessed, driving me on. I reread the line again for this is positively, exactly what I am feeling at this instant: onward movement with a feeling of conclusiveness in each step. I remember Dr. Jackson reading The Inferno aloud to an auditorium full of sleepy freshmen and feel the vague flutter of enchantment now as I did then: Midway on our life's journey, I found myself in dark woods, the right road lost. Suddenly, images of Florida, of all that lies in front of me: Miami, Sonny, Adam and Molita. I realize that I have become a blunderer, so out of touch from my daughter, my grandson, the family, my own family; not the meshuggeneh Capones who haven't exactly been there for me through thick and thin, Sonny, Al, all the rest, consuming so much of my time, my life, while my own flesh and blood drift off, forgotten, abandoned by the side of the road. Adam, for instance: the soon to be thirteen-year-old

Bar Mitzvah boy, today-I-am-a-man, grandson. How long, until Pearl died, had it been since we've spoken? Maybe two weeks.

It had been so much easier when he was younger, when the two of us would go off together for hours: playing Crazy Eights, Sorry, Monopoly, at the movies seeing some God-knows-what epic. And then those trips together for ice cream. Who did I have to eat ice cream, much less frozen yogurt with, anymore? An afternoon spent with Adam and no need for klonopin or guns or meditation or ludicrous chases after a mobster father. An afternoon with Adam was all I could ever need. Was there any greater nakhes than Adam calling out as he first had when he was only a one-year-old, not grandpa or grandfather, but Gaga? Somehow the little monkey, from out of the blue, had made me into Gaga: the loveliest, most sublime word in the world; one expressing precisely how I, myself, felt about the boy, for I was gaga over him: infatuated, crazy, wild! The child could do no wrong. He was brilliant, witty, profound; a marvelous athlete, a bon vivant, a raconteur.

I was distraught. Of course, once he turned ten, eleven, he didn't have as much time for his Gaga. Of course, he was even embarrassed calling him by that name when his friends were around and when he would have to refer to me, he would slip into Grandpa, which, of course, I understood, even if I could never quite forgive him. There was not as much time for Grandpa anymore. Adam always surrounded by a bevy of friends—at least, the boy was popular—their tee-shirts emblazoned with sports teams I had never heard of and floppy shorts and iPods and cellphones ringing with the most ludicrous of digital melodies. Such noise; such commotion; such poignancy as Gaga fades into Grandpa, not quite a fogy yet, but still gray-haired and antique, complaining of the noise level at restaurants and weddings, wondering if it had always been like this, but for Christ's sake, why does the band have to play so loud?

But still, would it have hurt to have called more often? Once, considering it, I had decided not to; didn't want the boy to think I was badgering him, still what would be the harm of emailing him, just letting him know I was thinking of him, then not to make it too maudlin, which was anathema to the pre-teen; maybe making a little joke: Thinking of your present. What do you say: socks or pajamas? But what if he thought it wasn't funny? It had been so easy when he was younger. Puns, riddles, plays on words, that marvelous morning when he was five and got his first Waiter there's a fly in my soup joke? Why did the chicken cross the road? Knock knock, who's there? So many jokes. So many punch-lines. So much giggling and laughter, that time he couldn't stop and wet his pants; oh, how easy it had all been. So what if now, if his hormones are kicking in and he cherishes his independence and wants to be surrounded by his friends, texting and cell-phoning and always on the way to here and coming back from there?

Still, I should have called. Gloria certainly would have; she would have picked up the phone, knowing full well the answering machine would most probably pick it up, but that wouldn't have stopped her: Hello, Adam, she would say. It's Grandma calling, just to send love to you and letting you know I'm baking your favorite chocolate chip meringues for your big day!

And then a little mini funk. At times like this, I especially missed her. How good she was with Rachel and Adam, never for a moment doubting herself, perhaps, even when she might have, but in there, so sure of herself, her role, her mission in life. So much different than our daughter, Rachel, who, often, seemed torn between the law firm and Adam. Wanting to go for partner, suffering because she'd have to miss the Halloween play at school. Of course it was different with Gloria, she came from a different generation. It was easier for her. What if she were still alive? I considered the question

233

and again, a wave of shame, as I realized life would be more complicated, perhaps, not as simple. Her reaction to the news about Al: shock, incredulity, a shake of the head; no, no, it can't be; pleas to forget all about it, to let sleeping dogs lay, to not cry over spilled milk, although the spunk that Al had spilled that fateful night was certainly frothier than anything that came from a bottle! Yes, that had been the problem, the one that would never disappear, despite the therapist she had dragged me to when she accused me of holding in my feelings; when, sobbing, she had begged me to reach out to her and confess what was haunting me. I can feel it weighing you down, sweetie, let me in! Is it something I'm doing? Just tell me. But I knew there was no point in talking: it would only depress her; there was nothing she could do to change. It was her character, her personality, her disposition: nothing could make a dent in that. She was more conventional than me, as simple as that, and in a funny way, it was reassuring, allowing me to reach for the wild cards, to lurch this way and that, knowing she'd be there, on the tried-and-true path, to steady me; to always be there, with a cup of soup along with the occasional grating platitude. A plate of chocolate meringues (she always kept a Tupperware box of them in the freezer) and a look at the brighter side, just like, surprise, Pearl. I retreated to the kitchen, opened a package of Almondine biscotti, each one only thirty-five calories, one gram of fat, three of carbohydrates, then took the package into the den, along with a glass of skimmed milk.

Suddenly, an image, of the cookie jar, the cookie jar in the kitchen on the shelf in front of the window. Pearl's cookie jar. It was always filled: Fig Newtons, Oreos, Mallomars. A round red jar with COOKIES spelled out in white, and some flowers painted below. I wished she had kept it. Now I would never know what had become of it. I wished I could call her. I could always count on her being so happy to hear my voice. She would pick up the phone, her tone tentative, even suspicious. Mom, it's me. Then you could almost hear her voice melt. What's cookin'? With Rachel and Adam, you never knew if they'd even pick up the phone or just leave it on voicemail, they had such busy lives, whether you were, God forbid, intruding. Can I call back, Dad? Just leaving for an appointment. In the middle of dinner. On my way out the door. With Pearl, she had all the time in the world, and, of course, who in the world would she rather talk with than me? How I missed her, her banter, her jokes, her philosophy, and now she was gone, forever. Why had it not struck me before? Why had I not cried before, as I was crying now? Why had I not felt the loss before as I was feeling it now? And would it ever, one day, go away?

I picked up The Inferno and held it to my chest, sinking back into the couch as I closed my eyes, conjuring up the studio after Lordly died. Chanticleer Recording. How amazing the unconscious, how, like lightening, the fantasy springs forth as the door opens and Al arrives. Dad, I cry out and the visitor flashes a smile, a million-dollar smile. He is dressed in a natty navy cashmere topcoat and wearing a matching fedora; he looks only thirty and we greet each other. Dad, dad, here I am! An enormous hug, a bear hug as I collapse in my father's embrace. Mi piccolo bambino, mi magnifico figulo, Gabrielle! And Louise, our secretary, runs to the corner and returns with coffee and we sip it with the cannoli he brought from the North End and my father is pleased, clearly pleased with all the attention, though one would assume that he is a man somewhat used to attention, but that doesn't matter, because this is his son, his boy, named after his own father, and such a good boy, furbo, fastoso, a vate.

Here dad, let me help you with your coat. Over here, dad, over here. Sit down, dad, in front of the microphone.

He lights a cigar, then taps his index finger on the microphone: One-two-three, he says, and then I refuse to testify on the grounds that it may incriminate me, and I start to laugh and he reaches his hand up in the air for silence and suddenly it is still, perfectly still as he sits before the microphone and opens the Inferno, studies it, smiles and for just a moment shuts his eyes, as if to better savor the words before him; he brings the fingers of his left hand together, raises them up to his mouth and kisses them, lets his hand drop, opens his eyes and looks at me, his son, smiles deeply at me and then clears his throat.

Lo giorno se n'andava, e l'aere bruno
toglieva li anima che sono in terra
da le fatiche loro; e io sol uno

He speaks slowly, easily, and with leisure: each word distinct, yet each blending into the ones that come before and after. The effect: rich, lyrical and deep, as if a spring is bubbling, water from deep within the earth, cold fresh water, with a trace of mineral. And then he translates in English, just as the script tells him to:

Day was departing, and the darkening air
Called all earth's creatures to their evening quiet
While I alone was preparing as though for war

I bring the palm of my hand to my mouth, as if to keep myself from crying out—although of course I never would, never would interrupt my father in mid-sentence—for it had not occurred to me just why I had chosen this particular poem. It was as if Dante had written the lines expressly for my father. Day was departing, and the darkening air called all earth's creatures to their evening quiet. Lo giorno se n'andava, e l'aere brunotoglieva li anima che sono in terra. I tear up as I realize

236

just what I have accomplished, bringing my father here, making such a request. So many people wanted so much from him. So many never leave him alone. Who had ever thought to ask him to sit down with coffee and cannoli, to read a poem? For posterity.

M'appareccjiava a sostener la Guerra
di del cammino e si de la pietate,
che ritarra la mente che non erra.
....

And he continues to read as if the words are his own; as if he has just delivered them, just christened them, just spoken them aloud for the first time; as if he, Alfonse Capone, is Dante.

Startled, I awaken from my fantasy, turn to the Table of Contents of the Inferno. Even it seems lyrical! Canto upon Canto: all is there: Dark Woods, Entrance, Fore-Hell; 1st Circle, 2nd Circle, 3rd Circle...the Pit of Hell...across Acheron to Limbo. Oh, those Incontinent Sins, the Plain of Fire. Yes, yes, The Violent Sins: Violence toward Others, toward Self, toward God and Nature and Art, Blasphemy, Usury, Thieves and Falsifiers! And now, as I reach for another Almondine cookie, I wonder if I am nothing but a falsifier, if all of this is merely the most ludicrous of fantasies, if I have finally become unsprung. No, I decide, a little close to the deep end, perhaps, but that's the price to pay if you're through treading water, if that was all in the past, and finally I am swimming, powerfully if not gracefully, towards some beach, some shore, in Florida. Time to call US Air, to change the reservations. Who cares if there are penalty charges. Here's my VISA number and my expiration date. My expiration date.

The following week, on Thursday morning, Flight 5254 for Miami, my gun safely wrapped in my boxer shorts in my suitcase—I'd like to check it if I may—I tell the clerk issuing my ticket at the airport.

An hour later, I gaze out at the sky, remember Pearl singing Cole Porter's The Heaven Hop, and feel light as a proverbial cloud, even as I go through my carry-on bag to make sure I have it, the gift I have created for Sonny. It's a book, or rather booklet, only seven pages long. The front cover—beige cardboard, I chose it after great deliberation, reads simply, Our Father's Words. Inside, the words of Al Capone, what he has said to reporters, courts, friends like little Anthony; the unvarnished truth about the man, at least as he chose to present it. While certainly Al was a showman, like Pearl, and while he certainly played to his audience, when left with his words, it seemed possible to have a sense of just who he really was.

You want respect, you keep up your appearance. I told the boys that. You show them on the take that know how to dress. The creeps and the bankers with their pinstripe suits and their silk hats. You show them you know how to keep up with em. Nah. You stay ahead of em.

You know where I learned that. In my old Five Points neighborhood in New York. The successful guys. They dressed it. I watched em watch me. And I always surprised em. They'd expect some grease ball with spaghetti on his tie. They always wanted to talk about the scar. I made em talk about my clothes instead.

When I came to Chicago I had only forty bucks in my pocket. I went into a business that was open and didn't do anybody any harm. Hey, don't forget, Prohibition began one minute past midnight, January 17, 1920. Just happened to be my 21st birthday, Some coincidence, huh.

I'm bighearted Al, all right. They say I organized Chicago. How could one man organize a city of three million? They blamed everything but the Chicago Fire on me.

There's enough business for all of us without killing each other in the street like animals. I don't want to end up in the gutter.

I ain't trying to tell ya people are dumb, but I ain't trying to tell ya they're smart either. You want to hear what they don't know?—-it's how to think fast. They don't know how to get there first. There's guy that say I was lucky. I wasn't lucky. I thought fast. I got there first before some other guy. And I learned from boxers that when you gotta hit a guy, hit him hard, hit him so he doesn't get back up.

They call Al Capone a bootlegger. Yes, it's bootleg while it's on the trucks, but when your host at the club, in the locker rooms or on the Gold Coast hands it to you on a silver salver, it's hospitality. All I've ever done is supply a public demand. You can't cure a thirst by law.

If people did not want beer and wouldn't drink it, a fellow would be crazy for going around and trying to sell it. I've seen gambling houses, too, in my travels, you understand, and I never saw anyone point a gun at a man and make him go in. I never heard of anyone being forced to go to a place to have some fun.

Now get me right—I'm no angel. I'm not posing as a model for youth. I've had to do a lot of things I don't like to do. But I'm not as black as I'm painted. I'm human. I've got a heart in me. I'll go as deep in my pocket as any man to help any guy that needs help. I can't stand to see anybody go hungry or cold or helpless.

Ask my wife about my private life. I live like any other businessman. Home every evening for dinner. Then smoking jacket, slippers, an easy chair, and a good cigar. Not much of a drinker. Nuts about music. Music makes me forget I'm Al Capone. With me, grand opera is the berries. It lifts me up until I think I'm only a block or two from heaven.

Maybe Sonny would throw this booklet away or maybe this would touch him, soften him up a bit, encourage him to keep his hackles down and contribute a bit of his DNA to his long-last sib. I held the book on my lap, close my eyes, think of Sonny, Sonny who was with Al at the end. Al's end, Pearl's end: each so different. Al, obsessing about some imaginary factory he owned in Florida, one that employed twenty-five thousand workers; Al, gazing out the window at the sky; Al, mumbling to his fox terrier, Nipper. Then one afternoon, just a few days after his forty-eighth birthday, a stroke— like Pearl.

Suddenly, that feeling I had been experiencing lately, the relief. Pearl was no longer in pain. Pearl was no longer my responsibility. She'd never know about Molita. I was free, free as I had ever been, to do what I wanted in life.

59 /GABE

Gabe sounded distraught when we spoke, but his mother had died, and a man's entitled. I was a little surprised that he wanted to visit—he never seemed crazy about the Cape— and I thought something funny might be up, but no, he says he just wants a walk on the beach, a nice quiet walk on the beach and I felt for the guy. So I invite him up, to spend the night.

In the morning, I'm toasting some bagels—he had brought a pound of nova along with a beautiful bottle of pinot noir— and he's looking out the window. The trees are still pretty bare and we had a fair view of the Swicky's back deck. All of a sudden, he grabs the binoculars—-I'm a birder, usually have a pair out—and he looks out toward the deck.

What's to see? I ask.

He seemed lost in thought.

What you looking at?

Oh, looks like, no, just gulls. Over at the deck of—what's their name?

The Swicky's, I reply. Soon to be Molita's. |

Is that their bedroom window?

Yeah, the master.

What a world, he says.

You know, I'll be gone for a week when they're here, I tell him. I'll make you the same offer I make every year. Stay here a few days. Relax, walk on the beach. Enjoy yourself.

He puts the binoculars down, gets up, pats me on the back. Maybe I will, Gabe says. Maybe I just will.

60 / Gabe

Finally, Sonny's house, the glimpse of it, the shock, that it should come to this, to a place so perfectly ordinary: a tiny one-story white stucco ranch with two-car garage, screened-in porch. A palm tree in front. Stripped green awnings. A house that would never make you think twice. Over the front door, the numbers 2280. Yes, this was it, X marks the spot and suddenly I felt flustered, anxious, as if I might be making an enormous mistake. I repeated my lines, the ones I've so carefully rehearsed, taking Pearl's homily to heart: 99% of the act is in the rehearsal. Present in hand, the book of our father's words, I advanced up the sidewalk to the front door, swallowed hard, knocked.

No answer. Tentatively, I pressed the buzzer. Waited. From inside, a muffled noise: steps, perhaps, and then it happened so fast, I could feel the breath knocked out of me as the door opened and a tiny, wizened bald man appeared, staring me in the face, quiet as a mouse. He was thin and feeble, wearing a short-sleeved blue crew shirt and madras shorts, but it is his face I sought out, for anything, anything at all just the least bit familiar, but no, no shock of recognition, nothing at all. The hearing aids, big and bulky, perched in each ear.

He seemed a stranger, a stranger you'd see on the street or at Walmart. What-do-ya-want? he asked, slurring his words together, suspiciously, perhaps, but nothing, yet, hostile about him.

243

Mr. Francis? I ask.

He nods.

Mr. Albert Francis?

That's my name. Don't wear it out.

I am surprised by the words, by the expression, alarmed by the implicit threat. I apologize for bothering you. I tried to call first, but your phone was unlisted.

If you're selling something, then you're wasting your time—

Oh no, I'm not a salesman.

So I've won a million bucks in the fucking Publisher's Sweepstakes, he says.

Sonny has a sense of humor, just like his father. Might be best to engage him for a moment. I smile and replied, No, wish I could say you had.

So what do you want? If you're a reporter—-

Bingo. This was the guy! No, no, no. I think…I may…be… related to you. I was wondering if you could spare just a few moments—

But Sonny was shaking his head. Never stops, he said. Every few years, something like this, some crackpot scheme, some crazy hunch, but this is a beaut, a real beaut.

Quick, before he can slam the door, I make my pitch. Just listen to me, just for a minute. My mother worked at Colosimo's.

Sonny stops in his tracks. So did they all.

She was a chorus girl, a singer. A Colosimo Cutie.

And?

And she was….with…your father.

So were they all.

And then before he went to prison— prison had a nicer ring to it than jail—they split up.

He looked bored, supremely bored.

And then I was born.

Nothing personal pal, but there were a lot of other fish in the sea, if you catch my drift, who might've done the deed, why ain't you at their kid's house now? What right you got pinning it on my old man? As he spoke, I noticed the hearing aids in his ears and how he seemed to be cocking his head at me, maybe all the better to read my lips.

Because my mother just told me. Told me the whole story. For the first time. Confessed she married my father because she was pregnant, scared, didn't know what to do. Not entirely true, of course, but it sounded good.

How'd I know you're just not making this whole thing up, to get a story out of me, like the son-of-a-bitch reporter from Vanity, Vanity, Vanity-what-the-fuck, Fair. Pal, I think it's time for you to excuse yourself and go back it is to where you came from—

I have something.

I have something too. My fucking fist and I may be eighty-one, but unless you leave me alone—

Look! I took it out of my pocket, the hairbrush with the initials. That got Sonny's attention. He inspected it, then whispered, A C.

He gave this to my mother. And she has stories, stories you couldn't make up, wonderful stories about him.

Like what?

That he sort of took care of her family. Her father had cancer. Pretended to rent their basement for his furniture business. Gave them money.

With that, Sonny sighed, slumped, appeared to give in. It's goddamn hot out here, he said. You might as well come inside. He ushered me into a small living room. A recliner sat in a corner, opposite a large television tuned to a soap opera, the volume off. A pale gold French provincial couch against another wall and a breakfront full of bisque figurines, statues, pictures. All around the room were plants, flowering oranges, hydrangeas. Sit down, Sonny said and I complied, then glimpsed on the wall a picture of Al and Mae on their wedding day. I could feel myself reeling.

Look, Mister, didn't catch your name.

Freeman, Gabriel Freeman.

He blanched, as if that bit of information had pulled the rug out from under him. His own grandfather's name. But he didn't let on.

Look, Mr. Freeman, so what if your father was my father. Lot of water under the dam, what does it mean to me?

I understand. I understand, after what you've been through—

Pal, and now there was an edge of malice to his tone, Don't need to hear from you about what I've been through.

I'm sorry. It's just that since I've found this out, you might imagine, it's all been rather surprising. I've done a lot of research. Here. I handed Sonny the book.

But maybe I was overplaying my hand because, now, he seemed even angrier. What the hell is this? He reached for a pair of glasses, paged through it, silently, and at one point, smiled. I am beside myself. It all seems to be working. Thanks, Sonny said as he closed the book. Appreciate the effort. But now if you'll excuse me.

I have a favor to ask.

So finally.

This may seem a bit odd. But I'm trying to make sure of what my mother has told me. I want to know. For sure. It means a lot to me.

Sonny seemed to consider what I said and nodded.

But in order to test for paternity, I need something from your father, and that seems out of the question. But it would also work if it was from you.

Sonny gets to his feet. Sorry, Mister, what was it, Freeman, this ain't no Red fucking Cross blood drive. Appreciate you driving up, this little family reunion, but I think it's time for you to go.

No, no. No blood. Much simpler. Here, see, I dive into my pocket, bring out the swab in its plastic container. If you'd just put this in your mouth for a second. Even a drop of your sputum would work!

And then the phone rings and Sonny reached for it and I can't tell what's going on, but Sonny has lightened up, he's chatting away, and I get this idea and whisper to him, Can I use your bathroom? Sonny frowns but points to a door off the hallway and I trot in, close the door, scout around, looking everywhere: A dirty Q-tip, a toothbrush, an old piece of Kleenex, maybe a disposable razor or strand of hair, hair with a bulb at the tip. After a minute, I flush the toilet, to make it sound like I've actually used it.

Then I spot an old toothbrush and just as I reach for it, Sonny barges in. Doesn't even bother to knock. What the holy fuck you doing? he screams.

I'm sorry, so sorry, I answer. Just thought there might be something that could be helpful. Anything at all. You see I've been a little obsessed about this lately and I figured a piece of dirty Kleenex or a—

You sick fuck! screams Sonny. You come into my house. I invite you into my home and then you try to steal my toothbrush? You fucking thief. Get the fuck outta here!

A vein seemed to be throbbing on Sonny's temple. Whatever you say, Mr. Francis, whatever you say. I pocketed the toothbrush, but Sonny was so agitated he didn't notice.

Get out! Get out! he yelled and I raced outside, hopped into the car, jammed the key in the ignition, burning rubber, driving away and, incredibly, Sonny is in the middle of the street chasing the car, actually running after it, but he is not exactly a sprinter anymore, and I took a right and lost him, not pausing to catch my breath till I reached Sunrise Boulevard. After another mile or two, I slowed down, pulled over to the side of the road, threw the car in park, thrust my hand to my heart—oh, how it is beating—and took a deep breath. I reached for the toothbrush, considered it for a moment. It read Colgate—no Oral B for Sonny who seems a more meat-and-potatoes kind of guy—still, it was blue and white and rather jaunty with, most importantly, four rows of alternating blue and white bristles. Must be a little DNA there. Maybe a long shot, but then here was the Kleenex, which I removed from my pocket, studying it as it rested, innocently, inside the Ziploc bag. I brought it up, just inches from my eye, and yes, it really was there, a dark area, sort of oblong, toward the middle of the tissue. It was a tiny bit puffy. Perhaps, just perhaps Sonny sneezed and this was ground zero! But it would work even if he had only had a runny nose and used this for some mopping up action. Then it hit me, it had all been so dramatic, so compelling: I had forgotten to make the offer, the money!

Maybe turn around now, park the car discretely down the street, have ten one-hundred dollar bills ready to hand over, but no, now was not the time. Sonny was furious. No telling what he would do. Better to wait: Send the Kleenex and the toothbrush in, see what turns up. And then, if necessary, go back, or maybe write a letter, and make the offer. There was something rather matter of fact about Sonny. The chance for a thousand or five thousand in cash—tax-free, how Al would appreciate it—if that was what it would take, for putting a cotton swab in his mouth for a minute, Sonny didn't seem like the kind of fellow to pass that one up. I glanced at my watch. There was still time to UPS the evidence to Gene Tree.

61 / SONNY

Used to reporters with their own particular axe to grind, their own questions, but begging for my toothbrush, my dirty Kleenex, my, God-forbid, toilet paper, this guy takes the cake. Wanted to wring his fucking neck—that would teach him a thing or two about family—instead, poured myself a scotch, calmed down, thought it over. No, I didn't really care who the hell he was. Just never wanted to see his ugly face again.

Times like this used to lose myself in work. Drove past the store last week, some spic Taqueria or whatever they call it now. It was the war that closed us down, the fucking Japs. So I became a welder. We needed the money. After Pop dies, Diane ups and splits with the girls. You can take my college degree and shit on it for all the good it did me and flush my life down the toilet as long as you're at it. And now this nut shows up at my door, wanting to play kissy face. I could tell if he was related and he wasn't. I'm the last of the Mohicans, the last of the Capones. My girls, they're girls. They carry my blood but blood doesn't matter without the name. Besides, they're in California, thousands of miles between us. It's me, Sonny, the last of the Capones, for all the fucking good it does me.

62 / ADAM

Rabbi Feldman, Mom and Dad, Grandpa Gabe, aunts and uncles, cousins and teachers, friends and members of the congregation. My Torah portion today is one that you may recognize from Passover. It's the story of four sons. The second of the four children is the wicked child. Rabbi Isaac Luria, a great mystic, noticed something truly unusual about him. Although he is condemned, he is not placed last among the children. Is the wicked child really so wicked? Could there even be something positive about his wickedness

Listen to his question. What is this service to you? By saying to you, he's not including himself. And he should. But, at the same time, I think we have to give him credit for even asking the question at all. It's an interesting one and thinking about it has caused me to think a lot about questions in general.

Today, when we have a question we can't answer, we usually don't turn to God or rabbis, but to—Google. And it never fails us. Google's quick and it's easy. Just type in your question. There are billions and billions of questions, all with answers. Knowing they're all there makes us feel good. But does this mean that we should turn away from God?

The Wicked Son, by asking a question to his elders, is a much different kind of guy than the one who doesn't even bother. So, is he so wicked anyway? I know some might think it's a stretch, but I think he deserves a closer inspection.

63 / GABE

The kid was a fucking genius. As he finished his speech, standing before the rabbi, receiving some kind of private blessing, I sat there, all but trembling, for not only was Adam profound, but he had a way with words; a lovely conversational style. What really got to me, though, was the portion itself. Could it be mere coincidence? The wicked son? What he has to teach us? To tell you the truth, and what should we be dealing with, at last, but truth, I was a little spooked. Was the big guy in the sky, the grand and most exultant of poohbahs, Yahweh, sending a message to little ol' me?

No time for such questions for suddenly I was called to the ark, and stood at attention there, gazing out at the congregation. Who'd guess what I had, oh so recently, been up to? Prostrating myself on a bathroom floor; kneeling before a false god, a rattled octogenarian, no less, beseeching him for some snotty tissue of Kleenex, stealing his toothbrush, just three days later, beaming by the bimah, reaching out toward a rabbi, embracing the Torah. As the congregation chanted blessings and songs of joy, I gazed out at Adam, my grandson and, blissfully, felt myself in the now-est of nows, all thoughts of certain possible family members, like great-uncle Sonny, who hadn't been invited, blessedly absent from my mind. I offered the Torah back to the rabbi and reached for my handkerchief, the one I discovered in Pearl's shoebox, Howard's hanky, and dabbed a tear from my eye. Alas, the handkerchief reminded me of the sheet of Kleenex—surprisingly pink, definitely used—which, perhaps, even now, is being whisked across the country to a lab, along with the cotton swab which I had inserted in my own mouth. Ashes to ashes, dust to dust, mucous to sputum, blood sweat and tears, DNA spiraling back to basics, the most basic of basics, while standing here in the House of God, under the Eternal Light, let there be light, Dr. Dover's laser, which got this whole ball of wax rolling in the first place, not that it really matters anymore.

It is then I decide, I cannot do it. Kill Molita. I am no Booth, no Oswald, no Hinkley. Oh, how I wished I could, but I simply didn't have it in me, no matter who my father was. Or wasn't. I wouldn't be able to live with myself afterwards, not because I had assassinated Molita, but because what it would do to Adam and Rachel. Well, maybe I could. Just maybe, time to look into silencers. Or lobster rolls with arsenic. Something more discrete. Without my name attached to it.

Minutes later, seated, I listened as Adam began to chant in Hebrew, what a lovely voice the boy has, puberty has barely struck, there are still cracks in his voice as he chants: Mignova shabu bareet sheet, aiyim. Erez morar shivyat halom. Berea pre mahart, mayitzka. Ancient words, over five thousand years, sung by a boy just approaching manhood and now, it seems Adam is more sure of himself—a smile escapes his lips, he lets himself go and he falls into the classic davening motion, moving his body up and down as he sings. But now he pauses for a moment and my heart stops—it's okay, Addy, everyone makes a mistake, just don't let it throw you off—but the rabbi whispers into his ear and he repeats Lo'yo aloyhim, and he is back on track, nothing to worry about.

Half-an-hour later as the rabbi is using my grandson's Bar Mitzvah as a chance to deliver an impassioned speech about a fundraising drive for the latest building fund. I beat a hasty retreat to the men's room—never been quite sure about what to do with a tallis when I'm using a urinal—then I put my hand in my suit pocket and take out the harmonica, the one from Pearl's shoebox.

Where could it ever have come from? For some reason, I have resolved to give it to Adam today. Impulsively, I put it to my lips, then just like that, as if it has a life of its own, I play the first opening of Camp Town Races Come to Town, and manage to get it, Do-dah, do-dah. How to explain this?

Suddenly, I remember playing a harmonica at camp, and just how easily it came to me, the only instrument I had any talent at, as if I could play by ear. And how it delighted Pearl. She told me a story about a friend of hers in vaudeville who became famous and rich playing the harmonica.

An hour later, at the Kiddush, I hug Adam, never want to let him go, then he asks, Could you tell I got stuck?

I reassure him, No one gets it perfect. I can still remember the word that stopped me, bereshees.

Really?

Really. Not true. I just made it up. But he seems to feel better. You were great, Adam, really great. You were awesome.

Then he shows me a poster, sitting on a table with other pictures of family on it. It's of Pearl, all lined up with the Colosimo Cuties and there are a couple men standing to the side, one with a big cigar. I feel myself swoon, but hold on tightly to the table, for the dearest of life, unable to take my eyes away from the picture. It is Capone. A smiling, sinister Capone, staring at the camera, looking as pleased as any man can be.

Fortunately, Adam is called to the front of the ballroom and I return to my table and glance up at the stage. Candles surround an enormous, braided challah which sits on a table covered by an embroidered white cloth which had been Pearl's.

In just a minute or two, the candle-lighting will begin. This ceremony will be somewhat different from the one an hour ago as Adam read from the Torah. This ceremony will not be found in Deuteronomy or Leviticus or David. This ceremony is, what, maybe a dozen years old at best, and the only scholars interested in it might be a few anthropologists from Brandeis studying assimilation.

Certainly simple enough. The Bar Mitzvah boy stands before a group of candles and invites people to light them, one a time. So far, so good. But it is what he says as each candle is cringe-worthy. He recites a poem in honor of a relative, a friend, a group of friends who are important to him. They trot on up to a round of applause and light their very special candle. Certain candidates automatically make the cut: great-grandparents, grandparents, brothers and sisters, parents, aunts and uncles and cousins.

The poems themselves: cursed abominations of the a-b rhyme scheme; poems devoted to the cutesy, to the funny, to the obvious. treacle. Now it is happening and there is nothing I can do to stop it:

They live in Goshen, New York, Upstate,
A place we all travel to celebrate,
For Passover, then Hanukah with presents galore,
All set in a pile from ceiling to floor.
Their house is a showcase of artwork you can see,
From travels to Israel, Indonesia, Tahiti.
Now they've traveled to celebrate in Miami.
Please light this candle,
Aunt Laura, Uncle Jack, cousins Mark and Lee.

Why this? Why couldn't he leave us with his eloquent speech at the altar? How could this marvelous, precocious, wisest of children turn into such an absurd toady? Of course, of course, of course: now he is an adolescent, only doing what all of his friends are doing, but why didn't his parents argue him out of it or at least have edited this doggerel. Then, even worse, the thought that they might have helped him compose it. That this should come from the lips of the great-grandson of Howard Freeman, who has never lived to hear this; Howard who recorded Dylan Thomas and William Carlos Williams and Marianne Moore as they read their own words so that future generations, including Adam's, should more truly understand their art.

And what of Al? What if Adam should light a candle for his long-lost great-grandpa and throw in a poem on the side:

And from Chicago, our patriarch, Great Grandpa Al

Who took me fishing, taught me pool, my greatest pal

You made red sauce and called me bambino

And made me happy when I was low

You performed mitzvahs for the poor during the Great Depression

You taught me many an important lesson.

Uh-oh, now Adam was summoning me. Well, it could be worse, and it certainly wouldn't do to run away, to shirk my obligations. I strode up the stairs of the stage, Sydney Carton, A Tale of Two Cities, it is a far, far better thing that I do.

Grandpa Gabe is quite a guy

And now to him I slap a high five

He loves books and musicals and all kinds of poems

All over the world he has roamed

He makes me laugh, he makes me think

With a basketball, he taught me to sink

Once with him I climbed a tree

Come on Gaga, light candle three.

I acquit myself well, smiling, waving to the crowd, remembering Pearl, playing to my audience I light a candle, think to hold out my hand, and Adam slaps me five and that gets a laugh. Then I step off the stage, walking to the back of the ballroom as Adam lights a candle for:

Great-Grandma Pearl,
She danced and pranced across our great nation
And was a huge sensation
If she were alive, I just know she'd want to be here
To Pearl, the sweetest, the funniest, and most dear.

At every Bar Mitzvah there's a candle like this, for someone dead, and always, always the sage observation that if he or she were alive, he or she would want to be here. Not exactly a revelation, better to be at a grandchild's Bar Mitzvah than moldering in your grave; not what you'd call breaking news. Still, this poem isn't quite as bad as the others. It was true, she did dance and prance; she was a sensation.

I arrive at a table with a chocolate, yes, chocolate fountain on it. Surrounding it, platters of strawberries, cookies, dried apricots, pineapple. From a golden calf in the Sinai to a fountain of chocolate in Miami. How can you resist? I dip in a slice of dried apricot and take a bite. Now it seems the candle-lighting ceremony is over and from all over the ballroom guests are clapping and shouting, thronging Adam, pushing him in a chair, lifting him in the air, higher, higher. The DJ plays a hora. If only Pearl was here. How she could dance! But she is gone. And how easy it had been to kill her. Yes, that was what I had done. Killed her. And like all of this, a blessing, a real blessing.

Howard and Al, Pearl and me, and Rachel and Adam: all mixed up. Will I ever know? Maybe Sonny's Kleenex will shed light, maybe not, and ultimately, what does it matter? The

DJ is playing Hava Nagila, the ballroom is full of singing and dancing, Adam has a ferocious grin on his face. Where does it come from? Who cares? I rush to the chair to join the mob, to lift him higher, higher in the air.